'Let me go!'

She tried to get up, but his hands lightly restrained her.

'All right. How much?'

'I . . . I beg your pardon?'

'I said, how much? I'm sorry, I must have misread the signals or something. I thought we'd agreed . . . that you wanted . . .' Lachlan shook his head angrily, his voice harsh. 'Look, whatever your price is, I'll pay it. Just let's get on with it.'

'My . . . price? Good grief!' Melissa hissed at him. 'Just what do you think I am?'

He stared at her in frank surprise. 'Lady, we both know what you are. That's not the issue here.'

'Oh, but it is! How dare you insinuate that I am to be bought!'

'Aren't you?' he said quietly. 'And how else were you intending to pay for your transport to the Arrow but on your back?'

Victoria Aldridge is a fifth-generation New Zealander and quite addicted to the country of her birth. She married young and very happily and spent some years travelling widely before settling down to have three children (now aged seven, five and four). Victoria Aldridge's husband has a design and build company in Wellington and due to his unfailing support, she has been able, over the past few years, to involve herself deeply in her children's Montessori education, complete her BA and to begin writing. *Melissa's Claim* is Victoria Aldridge's first Masquerade Historical Romance.

MELISSA'S CLAIM

Victoria Aldridge

MILLS & BOON LIMITED
ETON HOUSE   18-24 PARADISE ROAD
RICHMOND   SURREY   TW9 1SR

First published in Great Britain 1989
by Mills & Boon Limited

© Victoria Aldridge 1989

Australian copyright 1989
Philippine copyright 1989
This edition 1989

ISBN 0 263 76386 2

Set in Times Roman 10 on 10¼ pt.
04-8904-91406 C

Made and printed in Great Britain

PROLOGUE

THE SAILS of the clipper *Persephone* gave a sudden loud snapping sound as they billowed with the strong westerly wind which habitually came sweeping across the Tasman Sea each evening as the light began to leave the sky. As she picked up speed, the clipper began to wallow in the choppy seas, salt-spray flying into the eyes of the passengers crowding the decks for one last look at the coast of Victoria. The dinner bell rang in the dining-room and the passengers began a retreat to the cosy lamp-lit warmth of below decks from which wafted the enticing aromas of broiled fish, lamb chops in gravy and egg custard with fruit. Women holding tightly to their bonnets accepted the arms of their male companions, exclaiming at the slippery state of the water-drenched decks. Excited children were at last rounded up by their exasperated nannies and mothers and herded below to their dinners.

Finally, only one passenger was left to stand alone at the railing, staring fixedly at the continent he had just left, the last rays of the setting sun burnishing his fair features the same ochre shade as the flattened contours of the land. The *Persephone* pitched sharply downwards over a particularly large wave, eliciting a few shrieks and exclamations of dismay from the diners seated below as their plates, cutlery and glasses all slid to the restraining lip of the secured dining-tables. But the man at the railing did not move even then; his long, solid legs in the worn moleskin trousers needed to brace only slightly to absorb the shift in the ship's equilibrium.

David Frampton, who was watching the lone figure from behind the shelter of a lifeboat, was a man of considerably lighter build and was forced to grab at a rope hanging from the side of the lifeboat to keep himself

from falling. A passing sailor looked at him curiously,
and so, as nonchalantly as he could manage, he moved
to another position, almost directly behind the man he
had been shadowing for the past twenty-four hours. He
was debating with himself as to how and when he should
make his presence known to the man at the railing, or
even if he should do so at all. His friend's large, callused
hands were clenched tightly round the wooden
rail, the knuckles showing white through the tanned skin,
despite the deceptively relaxed stance of the rest of his
body. His clean-shaven, strong-featured face was devoid
of emotion save for the hard, bitter lines newly set at
the corners of his mouth. He was a man grieving in a
kind of private hell, and David was far too tactful, and
too much of a good friend, to intrude upon his solitude.
He had already turned to go below decks when the ship
lurched violently again, and this time David was quite
unable to save himself. Slipping helplessly over the wet
deck he collided with the broad hard back of the other
man who spun round with an oath.

'Easy now, Mack, easy!' David gasped nervously,
seeing the blind fury in his friend's eyes and the clenched
fist on the rail. 'It's only me!'

The man named Mack sighed, and helped David to
stand steadily again. 'What a damned fool you are,
Davey,' he muttered, although the harsh words were
muted by his soft Highland inflection. 'Wanting to get
yourself laid out, were you?'

David eyed him cautiously, still unsure of his welcome.
'I did tell you that I'd be going with you, wherever you
were headed.'

'Ay, so you did, and I've been trying to give you the
slip ever since. I thought I'd succeeded, too.' He shook
his head in exasperation. 'Can't you take a hint? As clear
as day I told you I didn't want you with me. None of
what has happened is your affair, and it's getting far too
dangerous now. Stick with me, lad, and I can literally
guarantee you'll end up with a bullet in that thick skull
of yours!'

'I don't remember your turning aside from a dangerous situation when you helped me to get away from that lynching-party at Ballarat!' Mack gave a short dismissive laugh, but David continued doggedly, 'You could have been killed, then...'

'That was different, then, and you know it! You didn't have anything like a fighting chance—anyone would have done the same as me.'

'I don't see any difference—and no one else wanted to get involved. You were the only one. You didn't know me from Adam in those days, and yet you cared enough about simple justice...'

'Oh Lord, Davey, spare us! You make me sound like a saint, lad, and both of us know very well where I'm headed when I die,' the big man mocked gently.

'But...we're partners as well, Mack, don't forget. We've worked side by side in that mine back at Ballarat for the past half year. We've seen each other through all the good times and the bad. Don't you think I owe you something?'

'Owe me? Hell, no, you don't owe me a thing—no one does!' The grey eyes were abruptly cold. 'And that's the way it should be, lad.'

Undeterred, David stood his ground. 'I thought we were friends. And to me that means loyalty—from both sides.'

There was a long silence before the tension left Mack's shoulders and his face relaxed into the expression of good humour that was so much more natural to him. 'You mad wee Sassenach! All right then, come with me and be damned—I can do with some company!' He shook his head in despair at the look of relieved delight that crossed David's face at his words, and added pensively, 'Life is just one big adventure to you, isn't it, lad? I hope to blazes that it never stops being that.'

'So do I, Mack! So do I!'

Mack turned back to the railing, and David watched his friend's hard profile in concern. It was so good to see him smile again after what had happened in Melbourne. For a time there he had thought his friend to be completely destroyed, his mind and reason gone, along with his pride. David would have personally liked to have strangled Phyllida Blakely with his bare hands for what she had done to this big, easygoing man whom he had come to care for as deeply as he would a brother. For the first time in many years Mack had given his heart and his trust to one woman—and had been extraordinarily fortunate to have escaped with his life.

'Er...Mack,' David ventured at last, 'where is this ship headed?'

Mack looked at him incredulously. 'Do you mean to tell me you didn't bother to ask when you bought your ticket? What if I said China?'

'Well, I've always wanted to go to China.'

'Then you'll be heartbroken to learn we're Auckland-bound.'

'And what's in Auckland?'

'Lord knows—I guess we'll find out when we get there.'

David waited for a moment before saying casually, 'What about trying the new Otago goldfields? The word is that there's about to be a big rush there, with even more gold than there was at Ballarat. With a rush that size there will be thousands of men there, with more coming every day; and it will be a safe bet that hundreds of them are on the run, like you. All you'd have to do is to change your name, take a new identity...'

'For the hundredth time these past seven years! I'd do that anyway, Davey—I can't remember when I last gave my true name to anyone. But mining again? No.' He shook his head. 'I've just about had a gutsful of that. It's a game for fools and dreamers—always the next bend down the river, the next shovel of dirt, the next day...I was thinking of finding work on a farm again; it was what I was raised to do, after all.'

'But mightn't it be better to lie low for a while? On a farm, in a small community, where everyone knows everyone else's business, you could be pretty easy to find.'

'Ay, maybe you're right at that,' Mack said slowly. 'Later, perhaps. But I've heard you talk of Otago before—you've got an uncle there, haven't you?'

'Yes, in Arrowtown—it's a mining camp in Central Otago. He runs a hotel.'

'A hotel in a mining camp?' Mack looked at him quizzically, possessing as he did a thorough and intimate knowledge of the drinking habits of gold-diggers.

David laughed. 'Well—he calls it a hotel! But, yes, it will be a grog-shanty, if I know my dear old Uncle Tobias. At any rate, he's my father's brother, and apart from a very sweet and highly respectable little cousin in London, Uncle Tobias is just about all the family I've got left in the world. I'd rather like to see him if we're going to New Zealand—that was one reason why I suggested going to Otago.'

'And it's a fair enough reason too. Otago it is, then.' Mack looked across the dark sea to where the Australian coast had long since disappeared, and for an instant he looked so defeated that David impulsively sought to re-assure him.

'It will be a new start, Mack. A new life.'

'A new life? Ay, and I've had plenty of those in my time. Will I ever be able to stop running, I wonder?'

'I'm with you now,' David said stoutly, and was a little hurt when Mack burst out laughing.

'Fighting words, lad!' His face sobered as he realised David's sincerity. 'I'm sorry to sound so ungrateful. You're a damn fool, but you're a good friend, Davey. Thank you.'

A steward made his way down the deck towards them, sure-footedly carrying a large tray of glasses covered with a snow-white napkin. 'Last sitting for dinner, gentlemen,' he informed them as he passed on his way to the cabins below.

'Shall we have something to eat?' David enquired.

'You go ahead. I'm not hungry.' Mack made his way up the deck to sit astride one of the wooden passenger benches facing the stern, turning up the collar of his thick woollen jacket against the chill wind. David de-

bated with his empty stomach for a moment and then
went to sit beside him.

'I'd rather be alone, Davey,' Mack said gently.

'I don't know that you should be just now!' David
burst out, unable to restrain himself any longer. 'I can't
just let you sit and brood over that stupid bitch!'

'Don't call her that.'

'I can't think of a better name. And here you are,
acting like a gentleman over her!'

'Ah. If I'd acted like a gentleman, I wouldn't have
been caught in such a vulnerable situation with the lady,
would I? Now just shut up about her, will you—I don't
want to talk about it.'

He felt in his jacket pocket and brought out a small
flask. 'Here,' he said, proffering it to David. 'Keep
yourself warm.'

Accepting it as a peace-offering, David took a deep
draught of the neat whisky and handed it back. Mack
took it almost absent-mindedly and screwed the top back
on without having a drink himself. David was surprised—his friend was a hard drinker, and if ever a man
had deserved a shot of Dutch courage, it was now. He
began to speak, but cut off his words as he realised the
other man could not hear him. His eyes were staring
unseeingly out to sea, and only a tiny muscle working
in his jaw betrayed his inner turmoil.

For that moment, Mack was back in a hotel bedroom
in Melbourne, lying on cool white sheets, his body dark
against the ivory softness of the woman he held. The
moonlight filtering through the lace curtains at the
window lit upon the diamonds in her midnight black
hair as it lay across the pillow. Her arms were clinging
to his back, her voice gasping and husky with passion
in the darkness, her perfume surrounding him like a mist,
befuddling him, taking him out of his senses...and then
she had recoiled sharply from him as the door burst open
and Slater's men had come in with guns in their hands,
knowing just where to find him, this time.

'Damn!' he groaned suddenly, his face and heart tight
with anger and humiliation. 'Damn, damn, damn!' He

sprang to his feet and strode to the side of the ship, throwing his head back to take great gulps of the sharp wind, like a drowning man. This time, David left him alone.

From below decks came the sound of the other passengers gradually leaving the dining-room and going to the saloon or retiring to their cabins. One by one the lights went out over the ship to leave only the navigational lamps on deck, and still the two men remained above, watching the stars of the southern sky glittering in the clear black canopy overhead. After a time the only sound was that of the wind in the sails and the hissing of the waves as the hull sliced endlessly through them.

Finally David spoke. 'If they should find us in Otago, what do we do then?'

'Then it's the finish,' replied the other man calmly, his face blank in the starlight. 'I'm not going to run any more.'

CHAPTER ONE

THE BOOKING CLERK at the office of Cobb & Co. looked up in irritation from his desk at the young woman waiting patiently for his attention at the counter. 'Yes?' he snapped rudely. The figures in his ledger were refusing to balance, no matter how he added them and in whatever combination. The very last thing he needed this morning was a customer interrupting him, and this rain-soaked, bedraggled young person looked like the worst kind of time-waster.

Admittedly she was an attractive-looking young woman, somewhere in her early twenties, tall and slim with the sort of regular, self-assured good looks often found in young ladies of what the clerk termed 'good breeding'. But even down here in Dunedin, the most far-flung outpost of Her Majesty's Empire, he could tell that her crumpled and muddied dress was at least five years out of date. Her fingers, as she struggled with the wet ribbons of her plain bonnet, were devoid of any jewellery, let alone a wedding ring. 'Yes?' the clerk repeated, impatient at her silence.

She managed at last to remove her saturated bonnet and held it away from her side slightly as it dripped miserably on to the wooden floor of the office—another mark against her in the clerk's eyes.

'I'd like to know the cost of the stage-coach to Arrowtown, please.'

Her clear, slightly clipped voice matched her cool green stare, challenging him for his lack of manners. Who does she think she is? he thought disgustedly. Pretending to be what she so obviously was not! Genteel young ladies of means rarely bought their own tickets—and they most certainly never bought tickets to places as iniquitous as the Arrow! Someone needed to show this young person

12

her place. He looked her up and down as chillingly as he could, but she seemed quite impervious to it, and after a long silence, he was forced to say curtly, 'Five guineas.'

'I would like a ticket, then, please. I am Miss Melissa Edwards. When does the next coach leave?'

'Tomorrow at dawn; that's four o'clock.' He did not bother to ask whether she wanted to book her return ticket—he knew what the answer would be. Watching her open her reticule and take out her purse, he mentally shook his head in disapproval at her and the world in general.

This latest gold-rush was not a good thing for Dunedin, he had decided some time ago. The strikes at Gabriel's Gully in 1861, they had been for the committed miners. Thousands had come from Australia and California to try their luck, and most had gone away disappointed. But this one, just two years on, was shaping up to be much bigger, and every hustler in the Pacific seemed to have crawled out of the woodwork to try to make his fortune. The once quiet, Scots-settled, town of Dunedin had been transformed almost overnight by the thousands of new arrivals. Those men who did not actually pan for gold themselves catered for the needs and vices of those who did, and as for the women—here he peered down at the silver-blonde chignoned head of the young woman who was by now riffling in agitation through her carpet-bag on the floor— well, it was perfectly obvious what this one was going to be selling, out in the goldfields!

The clerk realised that he was not the only one scrutinising the female at the desk; the tall, dapper gentleman leaning idly against the mail counter opposite was eyeing the young person's form with evident appreciation. Oh, yes, thought the clerk to himself, she'll do all right for herself, I dare say!

Now the young woman was raising a shocked, ashen face to him. 'It's all gone!' she said in a desperate whisper. 'My money—it's all gone!'

He shrugged dismissively and turned back at last to the ledger on his desk. He had better things to do than become involved with some silly female who had not had the wit to look after her money properly. Besides, with her type of expensive good looks, he gave her not more than a day before she made herself more than enough to take her wherever she wanted to go. The gentleman studying her admiringly from across the room would be a fair start, he supposed, sniffing disparagingly to himself.

On the wooden veranda outside the coach company's offices, Melissa felt like being violently sick. All the money she had left in the world, all ten guineas of it, gone! From where she stood, slightly elevated above the harbour, she could see the forest of masts of ships from all over the world that had come to this town. Among them she could make out the *Spirit of Liverpool* looking slightly spectral in the still mist remaining after this morning's heavy downpour. She had just endured four months of cramped monotony on her, and how she had looked forward all those months to standing where she stood now! How she had cheered along with the other passengers at the first sighting of the North Cape of New Zealand and days later as they had entered the mist-enshrouded hilly enclosure of Dunedin harbour. She wondered bitterly which of her fellow-passengers had gone through her personal possessions and taken her money. It had been in her purse last night when she had checked it and returned it to its hiding-place under her mattress, and the only time she had ever been parted from it had been when she was on deck early this morning to experience the arrival at their long-awaited destination. Everybody on board would by now have passed through customs and immigration and dispersed to any number of destinations, impossible to track down, even if she went to the police. And it was only ten guineas—not much to some people, but everything she had in the world! She felt tears start to trickle down her cheeks, and violently wiped them away with her fingers. Tears would accomplish absolutely nothing—she had come to learn that hard fact of life through all the lonely grey years in a London boarding-house. She needed to take a direct course of action—but what was she to do?

She eyed the brown oozing mud of the grandly-named Princes Street below her with distaste; her sensible leather boots and the hem of her serge dress were already caked to a depth of inches, so she supposed it was finickity of her to be averse to another immersion in the stuff. But still she hesitated. At a discreet cough behind her, she turned to find the tall gentleman she had noticed staring at her in the coach office.

'May I be of any assistance to you, madam? You appear, if I may be so bold as to observe, to be a little distressed.' His voice was soft, pleasant and well bred. He was immaculately attired in an expensive-looking suit, and as he politely removed his bowler hat, his thick dark hair gleamed. While tall, he was not a big man, and his features were finely chiselled, almost delicate. His handsome face bore an expression of the utmost concern and civility, and she instinctively found herself distrusting him.

'Thank you sir, but I think not,' she said firmly, and began to move away.

To her consternation, he followed, moving subtly against her so that she was forced to stop after a couple of yards. 'But didn't I hear you say that you required transport to Arrowtown, madam?' he persisted.

She hesitated, every instinct telling her to gather her skirts and run, while common sense and good manners bade her be civil to someone who might only be trying to be helpful. As she wavered, the gentleman made a graceful motion to draw her attention to where a closed coach stood at the steps to the coach-office veranda. Two men were loading boxes on the top, and the four harnessed horses stood shaking their heads impatiently, their wet coats steaming slightly in the warmth of the new sunshine. The driver was already at the reins, casually chewing on a wad of tobacco.

'My coach will be leaving for Arrowtown in just a few minutes. I would be honoured indeed if you would

consent to accompany me on the journey. You need have
no fears for your safety, and I can assure you of every
comfort.'

She bit her lip in an agony of indecision. In the normal
course of events she would never, of course, have
dreamed of accepting his offer, but this was not a normal
event. And what if he was simply the kind gentleman
he seemed to be? What if this turned out to be the only
way she could get to Arrowtown without any money?

As if divining the decision at which she was about to
arrive, the gentleman reached over and unlatched the
coach door. The vehicle was obviously near-new and
looked very well sprung. The seats inside looked invit-
ingly near... Taking a deep breath, she accepted his extended hand and climbed up into the coach. She sat on
the far side, holding her carpet-bag tightly on her lap as
if for protection, still very unsure if she had made the
right decision.

The gentleman climbed lightly into the coach after her,
seating himself on the seat opposite, on the far side, just
as a gentleman should. 'There, that wasn't so bad, was
it?'

She smiled at him nervously. Was there more than just
a hint of amusement in his voice?

'Shall I have your bag put on the roof?'

'No, thank you. I might ... need something from it.'

Now he was clearly laughing at her, and the finely-
cut mouth turned up briefly at the corners at her lame
reply. His eyes, steel-grey, regarded her in a manner she
could not call anything but calculating, and she tensed,
carefully sliding her hand along the seat, searching for
the door handle under cover of her voluminous dress.
The sunlit street outside was crowded with passers-by
and other vehicles—it would take just a second to jump
out and be safely away.

Her distress must have shown on her face, because he
abruptly turned away to draw a package of mail out of
his breast pocket, obviously letters brought in on a recent
ship and collected from the Cobb & Co. office. He
crossed his long, elegant legs and began to sort through

the pile. He stopped at one particular envelope and stared at it for a long moment before opening it. She tried hard not to stare at him, but the slow spreading smile on his face as he read through the contents was impossible to ignore.

'Good news, I take it, sir?' she asked, determined now to make the effort to be civil.

'Yes. Very.' He looked up at her, but she felt that he was not speaking to her so much as to himself. He threw himself back into his seat with a short laugh of pure pleasure. 'Very, very good news. My mother's just died.'

She stared at him, her eyes widening with horror. Her instincts had been right: he was not to be trusted, but not for the reasons she had so feared—he was obviously a madman! She did not hesitate, but thrust the coach door open and leaped down to the road, aware even as she jumped that he had moved to stop her, that his hand was stretched out to detain her. She slipped, and almost fell in the mud, but regained her balance quickly and ran across the wide quagmire of the street, her carpet-bag bumping against her legs. A dray pulled by two horses was coming up from the direction of the docks, and the nearside horse reared up slightly in alarm as she almost collided with it.

It took the man at the reins a few seconds to calm the animal down, and Melissa sent him a look of apology when their eyes connected. She met a glare of such blazing ferocity that she automatically took a couple of steps backwards in shock. The driver's eyes slid over her head to where the strange man was still watching from the window of his coach. She turned, despite herself, and saw the driver's hard white look of hatred mirrored on the other man's face, and it took her breath away. Then the dray was past, and she was able to squelch quickly through the mud to the verandas of the shops on the other side of the street.

Anxious only to get away from the stranger and his carriage, she turned up a less crowded side-street, making her steps purposeful despite the confusion of her thoughts. There must be a way of getting to Arrowtown, there must! If only she could think of it. Her footsteps slowed as she realised that, whatever the direction she was heading, it could not possibly be the right one. The street she was in seemed to peter out somewhere at the base of the hills enfolding Dunedin. It was lined with shops and a goodly number of hotels built of wood or stone, or a mixture of both, generally garnished with corrugated iron. The style betrayed the Scottish origins of the earliest settlers in this part of the country. The façades varied between the highly ornate to the painfully unadorned, presumably according to the degree of success the owner enjoyed in business: those hotels containing public bars were by far the most prosperous looking of the commercial buildings. On the outskirts of the commercial district, she stopped outside an emporium that had thoughtfully provided public seating outside, and she thankfully sank down on the hard bench, dropping the carpet-bag, which seemed to be becoming increasingly heavy, beside her.

The sun had by now chased the last reluctant vestiges of mist away from the hilltops, and the sky was a brilliant clear blue. Beyond the shops opposite her, houses meandered charmingly up the hillsides, some very modest and others decidedly grand, with towers and bay windows, set in beautiful gardens. At the end of the street, by contrast, was a hillside covered in unkempt lush grass and the shapes of dozens of sodden, grey, army-issue tents. For a moment she wondered what they were, until she remembered hearing about the miners' camps while she was travelling out on the *Spirit of Liverpool*. The camps had been set up to provide housing for those men who had come to Dunedin lured by the promise of gold. Many of them were financially unprepared for the costs of setting themselves up in a claim, or they proved unable to withstand the rigours of mining life. While they worked in Dunedin to pay for a passage back to England or Australia, or to another part of the Colony, the New Zealand Government had been forced to provide them with shelter.

But such shelter was not offered to a woman in her position, she thought miserably, averting her gaze from the sad little camp. The only way she could get a roof over her head would be to take a position as a maid or waitress in a hotel. She had no references, no experience, and it would no doubt take her months to earn enough to pay the coach fare to Arrowtown. It had already taken her months to get this far, and she was determined not to be defeated so close to her goal! No, there had to be another way to get there, a much faster way.

The sound of the storekeeper coming outside made her start, and he gave her a cheery grin before setting about sweeping the dirt from the boards of his veranda and back on to the street. 'Good morning to you, madam,' he greeted her in a rich Welsh baritone.

'Good morning,' she replied, wondering if she was expected to go within the cool dimness of his emporium, with its dusty smells of oats and new rope, to make a purchase.

But he seemed quite happy simply to have someone to talk at, and, after propping his broom up against the doorway, stood beside her regaling her with tales of the extremes of the Otago climate and the problems he had trying to keep his floors clean with a dirt road outside where there should have been a nice cobbledstone one like the one in his home town...

Melissa tucked her filthy boots out of sight beneath her skirts, and made agreeable noises while waiting politely for him to draw breath, when she could ask him about alternative ways of getting to the goldfields.

The Welshman only desisted, however, to shade his eyes from the now-glaring sunshine, and exclaim, 'Well I never! If it isn't Mr MacGregor again!' He stepped forward to wave to a man on a dray coming up the street.

The driver turned to draw up beside the emporium's hitching-post, and Melissa saw with a hot flush of embarrassment that it was the same man whose horses had nearly ridden over her in Princes Street just a short time before.

'You're not back already for another load are you, Mack?' the storekeeper was greeting him. 'They must be finding a mighty lot of gold out there!'

'Ay, they're doing that, all right,' replied the driver with a grin, his teeth very white in his darkly-tanned face. 'It's bedlam out there these days—puts Bendigo and Ballarat to shame!' His voice was deep and resonant, softened by a Scots lilt and a slight twang that Melissa guessed must be American.

She could not see his entire face as his battered, broad-brimmed hat was pulled low, and she was reluctant to meet that cold forbidding stare again. Pretending to busy herself in her reticule, she kept her eyes lowered as he passed by, following the storekeeper into the emporium. If he remembered her, or noticed her at all, he gave no sign, much to her relief. His workman's boots left a trail of mud that the tidy Welshman would no doubt have to hurry out to clean up later; it would not do for her still to be sitting here looking like a vagrant woman when he came back out. Wearily picking up her carpet-bag, she had taken but one step before she froze at the store-keeper's next words from inside the emporium. 'You're back off to Arrowtown now, are you?'

Arrowtown! What a marvellous coincidence! She turned to go inside to ask for a ride, when the sound of Mr MacGregor's voice agreeing stopped her in her tracks. No, there was no way in the world that she could ask him—she was absolutely positive that he would turn her down after that fearful glare he had turned on her when she had presumed to bump into one of his horses. Besides, the distressing memory of the unpleasant stranger outside the Cobb & Co. offices was still very fresh in her mind. If she were driven to it, she could possibly have defended herself against the slighter gentleman, but this Mr MacGregor was a huge, rough-looking man, and not one she would have dared to cross. On the other hand, he appeared to be the solution to her problem.

As she stood looking at Mr MacGregor's dray, one of his horses at the hitching-post whinnied softly, catching her eye as if it knew what she was thinking.

How long did it take to get from Arrowtown to Dunedin?
No one on the ship coming out had been certain, with
estimates varying from anywhere between a month to a
couple of minutes' stroll to the nearest unclaimed nugget
of gold. It could not be too far, though, she reasoned—
even if she went in the dray for just a few hours, she
could no doubt walk the rest of the way. She had heard
that most miners did walk out to the goldfields...

Melissa looked up and down the street. There were
very few people around this far from the bustling commercial centre surrounding the docks. Further down the
street some children were playing with an old can, and
a couple of miners laden with packs—the inevitable pans,
pick and spade strapped on top—were making their way
past her, but just now no one was looking in her
direction. She went down the steps and walked casually
to the back of the dray. Through the gold-painted letters
on the shop window she could make out the storekeeper
and Mr MacGregor with their backs to her, busy looking
at something before them on the counter. The heavy wet
canvas covering the crates on the dray was not fixed at
the end, and, as quickly as she could, she pushed her
carpet-bag through a gap between the boxes and clam-
bered up after it.

Inside the emporium, the storekeeper looked up from
the list of provisions that MacGregor had given him and
gently nudged his customer. 'Will you look at that?' he
said in surprise, nodding his head towards the dray. The
two men stood in silence as they watched the young
woman struggle for a foothold on the wooden side with
her slippery boots. Then with creditable agility for
someone wearing such heavy skirts, she wriggled her way
under the canvas covering the load on the back. The
storekeeper sighed as the black-stockinged legs slid from
view, and turned to MacGregor with an envious grin.
'An' she's such a pretty lass, too, Mack. 'Tis a pleasant
ride you'll be having back to Arrow, and no mistake!'

His customer was silent for a long moment, staring at
the dray thoughtfully. Then, becoming aware that the
Welshman was waiting for his reaction, he shrugged

lightly. 'Let's hope so,' he said with a small smile. 'Now, where were we? Yes—two sacks of flour...'

Melissa had managed to wedge herself into a narrow space at last, and was struggling to drag the heavy canvas over her head when there hoved into view, only inches from her face, a pair of shining blue eyes and a wide, muddy grin.

''Ullo, lady,' said the small boy conversationally. 'Wotcher doin'?'

'Nothing!' she hissed at him in exasperation. 'Oh, go away, do!'

His grin widened. 'Giz a penny, then.'

'I haven't *got* a penny, honestly I haven't! Now will you please *go away*!' Desperate now, she ignored his outstretched hand and pulled the canvas over her, praying that the horrid little boy would tire of his game and go away before the fearsome Mr MacGregor came out again.

Almost immediately there came the sound of heavy boots on the veranda approaching the dray. 'Hey, mister!' piped the little boy. 'You got a lady in your dray!'

Resolving to box the little brat's ears the moment she got out, Melissa tried to compose her features into an expression of dignity as appropriate to the occasion as she could make it—or would tearful remorse go down better? she wondered. And yet, unbelievably, she could hear Mr MacGregor's voice saying easily, 'Have I now? Then aren't I the lucky one!'

Scarcely daring to hope, she held her breath as the insistent little voice rose with indignation, but all that happened was that Mr MacGregor unconcernedly threw a number of heavy objects up on the clapboard end of the dray and then climbed up himself. There was a sharp slap of the reins, and they were away. She would have dearly loved to have pushed back the canvas to pull a parting rude face at her juvenile blackmailer, but decided against it—the storekeeper might well be watching their departure as well. Instead, she lay still, wondering just how tolerable her journey was going to be, after all.

The wooden crates surrounding her all tinkled slightly with the movement of the dray, and on one of them she could make out the stamp, 'Produce of Scotland'. There were also a number of kegs and several assorted sacks, but it was difficult to see very much under the canvas.

Melissa thought wryly that hiding in a dusty dray loaded with bottles of liquor was hardly the way she had envisioned herself arriving in Arrowtown to take over her inheritance, but perhaps she should not be so surprised: nothing since her nineteenth year had gone as it should. Charles Edwards, her charming, handsome father, had never had any visible means of support, despite the delightful lifestyle he had provided for herself and her mother. When he and his wife died in a coaching accident five years before, Melissa as their only child had inherited nothing but a mountain of overdue bills that her father had skilfully been evading for years. She discovered that the smart house in London and the beloved country retreat in Hampshire had only been rented to her father. The carriages, her father's racehorses, their personal jewellery, were all sold, and yet she had only just managed to meet all their creditors' claims. She had no other relatives in the country, and her parents' old friends all seemed to vanish suddenly, or be out of town when she came to call. But the hardest part had been saying goodbye to the family servants, all of whom were owed back pay and several of whom had cared for her since she was a baby. Neither was it easy to learn to live alone in a small room in the attic of a run-down boarding house in an insalubrious part of London after living all her young life in a large, sunlit house filled with love and laughter and constant visitors. Yet she had come at least half-way to accepting that this lonely impoverished existence would be the only one she would be likely to know for the rest of he life. She made a very little money by setting paste diamonds on to combs in her room for a small shop in Bond Street, and by giving music lessons to a number of young pupils in their homes.

There was no room for a piano in her tiny room, nor would the sound of music have been welcome in the

boarding house, presided over as it was by a ferociously
surly old couple in indifferent health. So there was always
some pleasure to be gained from touching a keyboard
again, even if it had to be someone else's piano in
someone else's home. But all too often her small pupils
would be wriggling impatiently upon the music stool,
plainly longing to be upstairs in the nursery playing with
their latest doll, or else outside in the private garden,
playing under the watchful eyes of their nanny. It was
at times far too evocative of her own childhood and the
family home she had lost, and many times she would
take the long way home, walking steadily for hours,
hardening herself for the greyness and emptiness of the
cold room at the top of the stairs that was her home
now.

And then, after five long years, the letter from the
old family solicitor came, asking her to call upon him.
He had to inform her that her mother's brother, Tobias
Frampton, had recently died in the goldfields of Central
Otago, in New Zealand. Only two beneficiaries were
named in his will: Melissa's mother, Charlotte, and his
nephew, David Frampton. As her mother's sole heir,
therefore, Melissa had inherited half her uncle's estate,
which proved to consist of an establishment called the
Regency Hotel in a place named Arrowtown. She had
not seen her cousin David for many years—the last that
anyone in the family had heard was that he was in the
Ballarat goldfields in Australia, following in the footsteps of his itinerant uncle Tobias. Desperate for a new
direction to her life, Melissa had insisted on travelling
to New Zealand as soon as possible, although the family
solicitor had been positively aghast at the prospect. She
could clearly recall his horrified expression as he had
stared at her over the top of his pince-nez.

'Miss Edwards,' he had wheezed, 'have you taken
complete leave of your senses?' He had harangued her
for an hour on the perils of the journey, the dangers of
places like the New Zealand goldfields for an unpro-
tected young woman, the eminent sense of allowing her
cousin to buy her out, and the sound advantages of a

nest-egg for a spinster in her precarious position. She had listened politely, but the more he argued, the more resolute she became. Any life, no matter how fraught with peril, had to be better than the half-life that the solicitor planned for her. At length, realising that she would not be moved from this reckless course of action, he had advanced her enough money to pay for her fare and to get her as far as Arrowtown. He was able to console himself for his failure in part by assuring her that her cousin David would no doubt have been contacted by the time she arrived in Arrowtown, and the chances were high that he would be there to meet her. Melissa, however, was not in the least deterred by the prospect of running the hotel on her own, at least for a while, and almost hoped that she would be the first one there.

The Regency Hotel—how grand it sounded! But she was realistic enough to be prepared for it to be much more modest than its name suggested, and of course quite different from the small hotels she knew in the English countryside. She could not help envisaging, however, a smallish brick or stone building, whitewashed, with a little flower garden in the front. There would be stables, naturally—all country hotels had stables—and perhaps she could keep a pony again, just as she had when she was a child.

The hours passed as she lay lost in rosy contemplation of her future that was growing ever closer. At times, the jolting of the dray became severe, but she was so tightly wedged in between the crates that movement was kept to a minimum, although the hard boards she lay on were bruising her rib-cage and arms. It was not unbearable, however, and she was almost asleep when there was a sudden loud cracking noise, and the dray slid violently to one side.

'Jesus!' The man at the reins cursed.

The heavy crates abruptly slid down to the edge of the dray, following the sharp incline of the wagon. The edge of the canvas flew up, caught by a strong gust of wind, and outside, directly below her, Melissa saw the sickening drop of a seemingly bottomless ravine. As the dray swayed gently up and down, she realised that the back wheel on her side must be suspended in mid-air, over the cliff.

'Help! Oh, please, somebody help me!' she screamed, abandoning any further ideas of concealment in her terror. She started to claw her way backwards, when the dray swung wildly down again. The red perpendicular cliff-face topped with scrubby bush on the other side of the ravine swung crazily in her vision. A small sack which had been placed on top of one of the crates slid out from under the canvas and spun down out of sight. I'm next, Melissa told herself. I'm next ...

Somehow MacGregor's voice broke through her panic. 'Don't move. Just stay exactly where you are!'

Melissa did as he said, closing her eyes tightly so as not to see the lurching drop below. There was the sound of a rope being hurriedly secured to the front of the dray and then MacGregor's voice, cajoling, calming, urging his horses on. After an eternity, the wagon steadied, moved forward a little, and then, with one almighty heave, the rear wheel hit the ground again. She scrabbled at the canvas prison over her head, desperate to get her feet on firm ground again.

'Stay down. Stay *down*!'

MacGregor's voice was closer now, and quieter. She hesitated, fighting her natural urge to free herself, but then she heard again the same sharp cracking noise. Gunfire?

There was a silence before she heard MacGregor's voice, calm and even slightly sardonic. 'Whoever you are—it's quite safe to come out. I'm completely unarmed.'

Peering out from underneath the upturned edge of the canvas, Melissa saw the branches part in the clump of trees just above the track they were on, and three men stepped forward cautiously. One was the strange man in the carriage in Dunedin! She ducked her head instinctively in fear, but then reasoned that he could not possibly see her under the dark shadow of the canvas cover. Cautiously, she dared to raise her head again.

The man from Dunedin had a revolver pushed conspicuously in his belt; the two men behind him had revolvers in their hands, aimed directly at MacGregor, who was standing quietly at his horses' heads. Somehow they looked rather unlikely highwaymen to Melissa, and her suspicions were confirmed as soon as MacGregor spoke.

'Hello, William. Couldn't you have chosen a better place to stop for a chat? I came close to going over the side.'

'That *was* the general idea, MacGregor.' How calm the two men sounded! Melissa marvelled. Almost as if they had met on some busy street corner.

'I see.' MacGregor rubbed his chin thoughtfully. 'What's brought this on, then? It seems a bit extreme, even for you.'

The man he had called William gave a short laugh. 'I don't think so. Let's just say I've finally decided to get rid of you for good. You're scum, MacGregor, and your time's run out at last!'

MacGregor raised his eyebrows in surprise. 'You've taken long enough about it. So this is where it ends, is it? You haven't even got the guts to face me man to man, have you, Willie? Why not? Not so sure you'd win?'

From where she lay, Melissa could see only the back of William's head, but she saw his neck flush crimson under MacGregor's taunting.

'I don't have to prove anything to filth like you. You're too far beneath my contempt for that!'

'A pity. I've a rifle in the back of my dray, and it might have been only fair if you'd given me half a chance to defend myself against the three of you.'

A rifle? Melissa did not hear William's reply to that. Her hands were silently moving around under the canvas, feeling under the fallen sacks and between the crates. It must be here, she told herself firmly—MacGregor obviously meant her to find it. But it took just one stomach-churning, frantic minute to confirm that it wasn't there.

She could feel the blood pounding in her ears. This simply could not be happening! Perhaps, if she were simply to make her presence known, it would all turn out to be some terrible warped joke—after all, the two men seemed to know each other well, and William certainly did not *look* like the sort of highwayman who would commit cold-blooded murder on a deserted road. On the other hand . . . he had appeared to be positively unbalanced from the little she had seen of him in Dunedin, and perhaps, for him, anything could be possible. If she were to show herself now, she might get a bullet in her heart for her pains, or maybe they would... She dismissed that last possibility. She would leap over the cliff herself before she would let that man put a hand on her, but at least she would die out in the open air and not trapped under this suffocating canvas!

Moving silently so as not to startle the men standing just a few yards away, Melissa began to extricate herself from the tangle of boxes and bags that had fallen over her legs. As she did so, her fingers slid under a crate and touched something hard and smooth and wooden. Holding her breath, she carefully eased the rifle out from underneath the heavy box. There was a slight rattle of glass from the crate as the end of the barrel slipped out, and she waited for one long moment, her teeth clenched in terror. But no one seemed to have heard. All the times she had tramped through the dewy Hampshire fields behind her father, loading his guns for him in the shooting season, paid dividends now. Silently and expertly she opened the rifle to check that it was loaded, cocked it, and, with the end of the barrel, raised the canvas slightly to see what was happening.

'Well, let me at least unhitch the horses,' MacGregor was saying, for the first time beginning to look tense. 'Why should they go over, as well?'

'They'll have to, I'm afraid,' William said smoothly. 'Or it won't look like an accident. But don't worry—we'll relieve you of some of your load before it goes over the side, and ensure that you have a good wake.'

MacGregor's eyes flickered over to where she lay, and she knew that he was about to tell them that she was there. Hoping that he alone would see it, she moved the barrel of the rifle slightly and he at once looked away, back to William. 'Are you going to shoot me first, or just push me over?'

'I want to see you jump, MacGregor.' Melissa even then was shocked by the naked venom in his voice. 'I've waited years for this, and I'm going to make sure I enjoy every second of it!'

Taking a deep breath, Melissa pushed the canvas away from her shoulders and rose to her knees, levelling the gun on William's back as she did so. There was not a flicker on MacGregor's face to give her away.

'Put—Put down your guns! All of you!' Far from sounding assured and in control, her voice was almost non-existent from a combination of fright and too many hours without water. It sounded, even to her, like an agitated gnat.

First one of the men turned to face her, then the others, shock dawning on their faces. For one absurd moment she thought they all resembled nothing so much as one of those strange medieval morality pageants she had once seen performed at a fair, where the personae of virtue and vice meet frozen in a morally uplifting tableau for public edification. Except that this was horrendously real.

William was the first one to move. 'Well, well, so we meet again,' he said quickly, a pink sliver of tongue flicking nervously over his lips. 'How pleasant. Now you just give that to me, my dear, and . . .' He began to move towards her.

'Stop where you are!' She found her voice. Loathing and resentment took over from fear as she looked at him squarely and steadied the rifle. 'Drop your guns, and . . . go away!'

William shook his head gently from side to side, his eyes narrowed. 'You're being very rash, my dear girl. Do think about it—there are three of us, and you'll have time for only one shot.'

'Then I'll have to make it count.' She lowered the rifle to his chest, and tightened her finger fractionally on the trigger. It was enough: William's mouth tightened in anger and defeat.

'Drop them!' he snarled to his men. 'I've no wish to be shot in the foot by some half-witted slut!' He pulled his revolver from his belt and slowly, holding it between thumb and forefinger, threw it over the cliff behind Melissa.

'Mr Price...' began one of the other men, obviously more reluctant to part with his weapon.

'Throw it over, lad. I'm sure Mr Price will soon buy you another one,' MacGregor said soothingly. The men obeyed, their faces sour.

'Now go.' Melissa motioned with the rifle in the direction the men had come from.

The other two men retreated, but William stayed a moment longer, glaring at MacGregor. 'I mean to finish this, MacGregor. There'll be a next time—when you won't have some female's skirts to hide behind.'

MacGregor's face was impassive. 'Get out of here, William.'

'I hope you can trust this one more than the last...'

'I said, get out of here!' There was more heat in the Scotsman's voice this time.

William turned away from him to nod with ironic courtesy to Melissa. 'I owe you for this, my dear.' He spoke so civilly that at first she misunderstood his message. Then he strode up the mountain road and was out of sight round the bend in a few seconds. They heard a carriage door slam, the crack of a whip, and then the sound of a coach wheeling away into the distance.

'Bastard,' MacGregor muttered into the silence, and then turned to look at Melissa standing like a Valkyrie on the back of the dray. 'Do you really know how to use that?' he asked, motioning towards the rifle.

'Yes, of course! Not that I *could* have, really. Shot someone, I mean.'

'Just as well, then.' He grinned suddenly. 'If you'd startled the horses, you're mighty close to that cliff-edge.'

Looking behind her, she saw what he meant—in all the excitement she had forgotten about the dizzying drop just a few feet away. Her stomach abruptly turned to water and she closed her eyes in panic. 'Oh, my goodness!'

He took the rifle from her nerveless fingers and effortlessly swung her down to sit on a small boulder at the side of the track. 'You'll be aching all over by now, I expect.' When she nodded, he patted her shoulder as consolingly as if she were a small child. 'I think a drink is what we need.' He moved the horses forward, fastening the reins, and then pulled a full bottle of whisky out of one of the crates at the back. 'Here, take a good swig of this.'

She stared at it uneasily. Her experience with alcohol had been limited to an occasional glass of champagne given to her by her parents as a special treat at Christmas or on a birthday. 'Don't you have a glass, or even a mug to put it in?' she asked, unable to keep the disgusted edge out of her voice.

The corners of MacGregor's mouth quirked in amusement. 'Listen, lass, out here the most a lady can expect is to get first gulp at the bottle—so drink up; I've need of a drink myself.'

She did as she was told, holding a measure in her mouth and swallowing in such small amounts as her protesting throat would allow. Since she had not eaten or drunk anything since early that morning, at first her empty stomach contracted unpleasantly, but within a few minutes she could feel a growing warm glow inside her, and her tense limbs began to relax. She passed the bottle back to MacGregor. She was longing to ask him about what had just occurred, and also expected him to have a few questions of his own about what she had been doing in the dray. But he seemed to be in no hurry to resume the conversation and simply sat silently beside her, swigging with an alarming expertise from the bottle of whisky.

The dray was stopped on a very steep and heavily rutted mountain pass. As far as the eye could see, there were nothing but burnished hills rising steeply to distant mountain ranges capped with snow even now, in February, towards the end of the New Zealand summer. Below, where the track fell away, she could see the bottom of the bluff that she had very nearly gone over to where there was a glimpse of a slate-grey, foam-rippled river. At a sudden image of her broken body far down there, being quickly swept away with the wreckage of the dray amid the foam and the rocks, she gave an involuntary shudder. It would have been a horrible way to die.

At last MacGregor corked the bottle and laid it beside him on the grass. She steeled herself for the inevitable interrogation. He turned to look at her directly for the first time, and she caught her breath. For one shocking moment it was William Price's eyes she was looking into, but then the illusion passed and she wondered why she had even thought for that second that the two men looked alike. MacGregor had a hard, lived-in sort of face, the clear grey eyes startling in his dark, weathered tan, but the lines round his mouth and eyes seemed much more made for laughter than severity. He had taken off his hat to reveal thick, unruly, light brown hair bleached almost white on top by the sun. He looks like a fallen angel, she found herself thinking... and quickly pulled herself up by the mental bootlaces. Angelic he might look, but there was unmistakably devilment shining in his eyes, and she very much doubted that he was a man to be trusted too far.

'Shall we talk about it now?'

'About...what, Mr MacGregor?' she asked guardedly.

He did not answer immediately, but instead studied her face as intently as she had his, his eyes tracing each line of cheek, chin, mouth, seemingly pleased with what he saw there. 'I've completely forgotten,' he said at last, and leaned forward and kissed her. It was a soft, fleeting kiss, a mere promise, but she had never been kissed on the mouth by any man before, and drew back indignantly. Then he smiled at her, and she was completely lost. This time, when he kissed her, her lips opened under his and she wound her arms round his neck, unable to stifle a tiny moan of disappointment when at last he pulled away. He chuckled, and helped her to her feet, holding her close for a moment. Standing beside him like this brought her back to her senses abruptly. What a huge man he was! The top of her head came only to his shoulder, although she was tall for a woman, and while he was lean, he was at the same time heavily muscled. Her arm as it rested on his looked so frail by comparison... What on earth was she doing, playing the wanton with this big, dangerous stranger who could break her as easily with his strong hands as she might thoughtlessly snap a twig?

He reached out to take a strand of the hair which had escaped from her chignon to tumble loosely down her neck. 'What a remarkable colour,' he murmured, studying the sheen of pale silver on his palm. He looked up at her with something like regret on his face. 'You'll cause quite a sensation out here—but I guess you already know that, don't you?'

He slowly replaced the strand behind her head, and she gave an involuntary shiver—but whether it was of pleasure at his fleeting touch, or at the oddness of his words and expression, she was not sure. What *is* the matter with me? she thought angrily. The unaccustomed alcohol, the danger of the situation, the attractiveness of this strange man... they were combining to make her lose her head, and if ever she needed her wits about her, it was now! There was an oddly speculative look in MacGregor's eyes that made her very uneasy.

As if reading her mind, he stepped back a pace and formally held out his hand. 'I'm sorry—I've completely forgotten my manners. My name is Lachlan MacGregor—Mack to my friends.'

'*Mack*? What kind of a name is that?'

'Nicknames are common out here among the miners, but they're not very original, I'm afraid. Most Scots are called Mack, and the Irish tend to get called Mick or Paddy. It's a fair bet you'll end up as Blondie, for instance.'

'I should most certainly hope not!' she bristled. 'My name is...' she hesitated for only a split second before glibly coming up with the name of her old nanny, '...Miss Page. Miss Emily Page. And, if you don't mind, I would prefer to call you Mr MacGregor.'

'Well, I'm damned if I'm calling you Miss Page! So you call me Lachlan and I'll call you Emily. Is that settled?' It was. 'And before we go any further, can I thank you for your timely intervention, lass? You undoubtedly saved my life this afternoon.'

'But it's I who should be thanking *you*,' she said honestly. 'If the dray had gone over the cliff-edge...'

'No, that wouldn't have happened,' he assured her with a grin. 'I couldn't have lost the best-looking cargo I've ever carried, could I?'

Her mouth dropped slightly. Had he—perish the thought!—known all along that she was hiding in his dray? She remembered now that he had expressed no surprise when she had cried out in fear, that his first reaction had been to reassure her... His eyes gave nothing away.

'We'd best get going,' he said quickly, as though to forestall any questions. 'I wouldn't put it past William to be busily setting up another little surprise for us further down the track right now.' He would have taken her hand to help her up on to the clapboard, but she turned away slightly to evade his grasp.

'You seem to know William Price rather well.'

Something about her statement seemed to amuse him. 'I suppose I do.' She would have asked more, but he put his hands round her waist and swung her up. Then he collected the rifle and handed it to her. 'You look to have a fair idea about what to do with a gun, so keep your eyes open, lass, and keep this at the ready. We'll be on the flat soon, and a great deal safer—but until we're off this bit of track we can't be too careful. There are a hundred places up ahead that would be perfect for another ambush.'

He did not climb up beside her but took the horses' heads for a while, leading the still-nervous animals carefully up the trail, muttering soothing noises as they started at every sharp crack of rock beneath the heavy wheels.

Melissa sat rigidly clutching the rifle in her hands, her eyes darting over any rock conceivably large enough to hide William Price and his men. It was only ten minutes, but it seemed more like hours before the road ahead flattened out to a tussock-covered plain, with scant cover available to would-be highwaymen. At last Lachlan walked back to climb up beside her and take the reins and, with a huge sigh of relief, she went to put the rifle down. 'You'd better keep that ready,' he told her. 'We've a long way to go before we can get to the nearest settlement.'

'How soon can we get to a police station?' she asked anxiously. 'We must report what happened as soon as possible, before Mr Price makes his escape!'

Lachlan chuckled. 'William won't be escaping anywhere—he'll be heading quite legitimately for either Canvastown or the Arrow. And there's no point in reporting any of this to the police, lass. If you did, there'd instantly be a dozen people ready to swear that he was elsewhere. I'll not waste my time, and I suggest that you do likewise.'

'But it was attempted *murder*!' she spluttered. 'I witnessed it! Wouldn't the police take my oath on that?'

He shrugged. 'I doubt it. The word of people like you and me means very little against that of men like William and his friends. Look—just take my advice, and try to forget that any of this ever happened.'

He spoke with such an air of finality that she could only sit in stunned surprise. What kind of country was this where a crime as serious as attempted murder on a public road could be regarded so casually by its victim as to go unreported? And Lachlan MacGregor seemed the least likely of men to be intimidated by anyone; he was such a hard, tough-looking character... A sudden and very logical thought occurred to her. It was highly likely that he had his own nefarious reasons for not wanting to become involved with the law, and under the circumstances it could be tactless of her to insist on his doing so. But she did rather object to his including her with people of his sort! Everything considered, she decided that she had done the right thing by not telling him her real name. It had been an instantaneous reaction, but it had helped to distance her from this dangerous man, in this dangerous situation. Why she had let him kiss her in that manner back at the pass she could not explain, except that she had been confused and taken by surprise. Now her own behaviour embarrassed her so much that she would, had she been able to, have asked him to put her down by the road there and then and she would find her own way to Arrowtown. Unfortunately, that was simply not possible. As soon as she could, as soon as she got to Arrowtown, she would ensure that they parted company. She could not imagine having anything to do with a man like MacGregor in the future.

They rode in silence for some time, and she gave a start of surprise when he spoke again. 'Where are you headed?'

'Arrowtown.'

'As far as that?' He raised one eyebrow at her in surprise. 'And were you planning to spend the entire trip there in the back of my dray?'

'I don't know...I suppose so,' she stammered. 'I must admit I hadn't thought it through properly. Is Arrowtown very much further?'

'Another two days' hard travelling—a bit more, perhaps, after this rain.' He looked at her stricken face, and his own was not unsympathetic. 'So you didn't know that? Why'd you do it? No money, eh?' She nodded, and he continued kindly, 'I've been in that situation many a time myself. You needn't have feared asking me for a ride, lass.'

She smiled at him gratefully. 'Thank you so much! You see, I didn't know what else to do after my money was stolen on the ship this morning, and...' She broke off at the look of incredulity on his face.

'Are you telling me that you sailed into Dunedin harbour only today? And that you set straight off for the goldfields?'

'Er...yes,' she said cautiously. She was at a loss to understand his marked reaction—surely other people did the same thing every day of the week? 'You see, it's very important that I get to Arrowtown as quickly as possible.' She stopped herself from saying any more, sensing his rising disapproval.

He contented himself with saying only, 'Not as quickly as all that, surely?'

She did not answer, keeping her eyes fixed firmly on the hills ahead, but she was aware of his scrutiny.

At last, in a rather more conciliatory manner, he asked, 'Did you never think of giving Dunedin a try, lass? The Arrow's a damned hard place for a woman, and there's plenty of custom in Dunedin—and good money besides. You'd do very well there, believe me.'

'Thank you for the advice,' she said tartly, and he smiled slowly, not in the least offended.

'You don't have to take it—but I'm guessing that this is your first goldfield, and you may not know what you're letting yourself in for.'

'Perhaps I had better explain,' she said carefully. 'I'm not going there for the gold. I have business interests in the town, which is why I'm so anxious to get there quickly. I'll be able to pay you for the transport as soon as I get to Arrowtown, I promise.'

That disturbing look was in his eyes again as he said briefly, 'I'll take payment in trade, if you prefer.'

'Oh. Well, yes, all right then,' she said automatically, caught rather off balance. She was not too sure what the term 'in trade' meant, but she had heard it before, and guessed it to mean some kind of business consideration. A night or two's accommodation, perhaps. She sincerely hoped that the Regency *had* adequate accommodation to offer—so far, very few things in this country had been quite what she had expected.

They had risen to a tussock-covered plain, and the two tired horses, perhaps knowing that the day was

coming to an end, had bravely sped to a trot. The sun
was beginning to set over the mountains, turning the
snowy peaks to glowing embers, and the dark purple
shadows were stretching long over the hills. As they
rounded a bend a strong cool wind coming directly off
the mountains caught them, and she wrapped her arms
round herself to keep warm.

Lachlan noticed, and leaned over to pull out a blanket
behind her. 'Here—put this round yourself. It can get
bitterly cold up here at night even at this time of the
year. But we're almost at the inn.'

The blanket smelt strongly of horse, and she had her
suspicions as to its usual use, but she snuggled gratefully
enough into its prickly warmth. As she thanked him, he
turned to smile briefly at her and she caught her breath
suddenly, her eyes widening.

'What's the matter?'

'Nothing...' She bit her lip in agitation, wondering
if she would give offence if she continued. 'It's just
that...I keep thinking that you...look like someone
else.'

'Like William, you mean?'

'How did you know? I am sorry...I don't mean to
be insulting.'

'I'm not insulted, lass,' he said calmly. 'It was William
who was generally held to be the best-looking one in the
family.' He waited for a moment to let that sink in before
explaining, 'He's my half-brother.'

She stared hard at him, convinced that he was having
some sort of strange joke at her expense, but he met her
gaze levelly and without guile, and once again it was like
looking into William Price's dark grey eyes. She shook
her head in distress. 'If you *are* brothers, then, why did
he try to kill you?'

'For reasons that are none of your concern,' he said,
mildly enough. 'I'm sorry that you had to get involved
in all this, but it's a situation that began a long time ago
and has nothing to do with anyone but the two of us.'

'But is he unbalanced?' she asked, ignoring the re-
proof. 'I did wonder when he heard about his mother,

and he...' She broke off, aware that she had just committed a *faux pas* of considerable insensitivity. But he
was staring at her now with such concentration that she
could only falter on. 'Please forgive me—I didn't mean
to say that, and you shouldn't hear it from me...'

'Hear *what*? Come on, lass—out with it!'

'Well...when I was in Dunedin, I came close to accepting a ride from William. You first saw me as I
was...leaving his carriage.'

'I had noticed, yes,' he commented grimly.

'He was reading his mail just before that, and...one
of the letters was about his—his mother's death. It was
his reaction to it that made me think that he must be
completely unbalanced.'

Lachlan gave a short, humourless laugh. 'I'd imagine
he'd be delighted at the news.'

'He was,' she said, surprised. 'I just feel dreadful at
telling you about her death this way...'

He looked at her distantly, his mind obviously preoc-
cupied. 'What? Oh—no, don't feel badly about that. She
was no relation of mine.'

'But...!' She sat up straight, indignant. 'You said...
And you don't have the same surnames. How can you
be brothers?'

He laughed out loud and looked away. 'Haven't you
worked that one out yet? One of us is legitimate and the
other one isn't. I'm sure it's obvious which one is which.'

If he had intended embarrassing her into silence, he
succeeded, and she sat in a miserable huddle alongside
him as they continued to drive through the lengthening
shadows of the evening. For his part, Lachlan appeared
to completely ignore her, lost deep in his own thoughts.
The light had faded from the mountain tops when he
pointed to what looked to be a large pile of stones
squatting low on the skyline, a pinpoint of light from a
single lamp gleaming palely in the twilight.

'Jamieson's Inn. We'll be putting up there for the
night.'

'Really?' She looked dubiously at the small win-
dowless building with the roof that she could now make

out as being of turf. 'Does it have enough room for guests? It looks...'

'Small? I suppose it is, but buildings this far out don't usually come much larger. There's not much timber, you see, and so people aren't aiming for much more than a simple roof over their heads. But it's warm and cosy enough inside, you'll find.'

'Are all the inns that size out here?'

'There are a few larger ones, where the coaches meet and they have to put up a lot of overnight guests. But most of them are this size.'

As they drew up outside the tiny dwelling, she wondered yet again just what the Regency Hotel in Arrowtown would look like.

CHAPTER TWO

THEIR HOST came out to greet them. He was a tiny, wizened old man who reminded Melissa of nothing so much as a spritely garden gnome, and who was clearly delighted to have some company. He greeted Lachlan warmly by name and nodded affably enough to Melissa. 'I thought you were about due to pay another visit, Mack. How're the roads after all that rain this mornin'?'

'Not bad at all,' Lachlan answered easily. 'Miss Page and I had a very uneventful trip. Didn't we?' He gave her hand a warning squeeze as he helped her down from the clapboard.

The old man looked at her approvingly. 'Nice, Mack. Very nice. Ain't she?'

'She is indeed, Pete. And hungry, too, I should think. What's in the pot for dinner tonight?'

'Enough,' the old man rejoined. 'Outhouse is round the back if'n you want it, miss. Carryin' your usual, Mack?'

She fled behind the cottage, her cheeks aflame at both the old man's want of delicacy and his assumption that she was some sort of property of Lachlan's. Not, she thought, that Lachlan had bothered to correct his mis-apprehension. There was an outhouse not far from the stables, as well as a pump, and beside that a wooden trough that was clearly used to bathe in. As she washed her hands and face, she thought of how long it had been since she had been able to wash herself in more water than a small basin could hold. That had been the very worst aspect of the four months she had spent on board ship, with the only fresh water being taken on at Cape Town and Sydney.

Lachlan, coming round the side of the cottage with his horse, saw her running the pump-water longingly over her arms, and said briskly, 'I'll fetch you some hot water in a moment.'

'Hot water?' she said blankly.

'For a decent bath. It's the very first thing I always want when I've been at sea for a while. You'll be completely private out here—old Pete's already well into a bottle of my best whisky, and he doesn't like to drink alone, so you can take your time.'

'That would be wonderful! Thank you!' She was touched by his unexpected thoughtfulness.

He shrugged. 'Pete's cooking's not bad, but it's the bath-tub I myself come here for—it almost makes putting up with Pete worth while.'

'What do you mean?'

'You'll see,' he replied darkly.

She understood his partiality to the 'bath-tub' soon after, as she lay luxuriating in hot water to her neck, watching the first stars coming out in the deepening sky. Clean skin, clean hair, the smell of a hot stew on a still evening... What more could I ask for? she thought, blissfully soaping her toes. From the cottage, she heard the occasional clink of bottle against mug, and with increasing frequency Jamieson's raucous shout of laughter at something Lachlan had said. She wondered if they were talking about her, laughing at her naïveté in stowing away on the dray, but she felt too relaxed to be annoyed.

As the aches and stiffness were soaked from her body, so too were the tensions and problems of that long, confusing day washed from her mind. Why should she concern herself with Lachlan's feud with his brother— if brothers they truly were—if he himself was so insistent that she not become involved? He seemed prepared enough to take her on to Arrowtown, which was all that should concern her now, and after which she thought it unlikely she would see him again. Besides, he seemed to be quite capable of looking after himself. From that distance of several hours, the kisses she had responded to earlier seemed much more explicable. He had taken advantage of her disorientation and her tipsy state;

the situation had been one that could never be repeated, despite Mr MacGregor's obvious expectations!

Feeling quite blameless now and much happier, she was just about to sink under the water again when she remembered that Lachlan had mentioned wanting a bath after she had finished with the tub. Standing up, she tipped the last cool bucket of water over her head and stepped out, shivering. The night air was cold on her bare skin and her fingers were shaking slightly as she buttoned the bodice of her blue muslin dress. It was actually a morning gown, but it was the prettiest dress she owned, and her dinner companions were unlikely to know the difference.

In the dim interior of the cottage, a big roaring fire was ablaze in the hearth, and whether the faces the two men raised to her were flushed from the heat or from the near-empty bottle of whisky on the table, she could not tell, but the look of open appreciation on their faces—or, more important, on Lachlan's—was most gratifying. They both rose to their feet at her entrance, and remained staring at her for so long that she became embarrassed.

'May I dry my hair by the fire?' she asked, motioning awkwardly at the hearth.

The men came back to life. Lachlan took down the pot of water hanging over the flames and went outside without speaking. Melissa knelt before the fire, brushing her hair furiously until it flew up around her in a silver halo. Plainly fascinated, old Jamieson staggered over to stand beside her, and this she found very unnerving, although she tried not to show it. At last the old man stretched out a grimy finger and tenderly stroked her hair as it fell down her back.

'Can't ever recall seein' a woman wi' hair like yours, 'n that's a fact,' he pronounced. 'What a lovely lassie you are, to be sure.' He turned and spoke over his shoulder. 'Ain't that right, Mack? Ain't she a beauty?'

She had not heard Lachlan come in, but he was seated again at the low table, his broad shoulders resting against the stone wall, his long legs stretched out in front of him, watching her steadily. He had changed his shirt, and his hair clung damply to his forehead, and once more she felt that strange slow pounding of the blood in her ears. Except that, this time, there was no whisky to blame for it. She fumbled to pin her hair back into its customary chignon, and heard Jamieson give a sigh of disappointment.

'Leave it loose,' Lachlan said quietly. 'Please.'

Her hands dropped to her sides as their eyes met, and she felt the blood rise to her face at his intense gaze. She had to look away, but the link between them remained, as invisible and yet as tangible as silk.

Lachlan broke the silence first by grabbing for the pot of stew just before Jamieson spilt it all over the table. 'Steady on there, Pete—it smells far too good to be thrown out!' He set the pot upright, and, taking the ladle from the old man, began to dish it out into the three bowls set on the table. Jamieson mumbled his thanks and sank down to reach for the whisky bottle again.

They sat on hard benches, and they ate with wooden spoons out of cracked pottery basins, and yet Melissa thought that she had never in her life tasted anything as good as the mutton and potato stew. There was a great deal more left in the pot, and, feeling positively gluttonous, she took a second helping as large as her first; breakfast on the ship did seem a very long time ago. Jamieson seemed content with his mug of whisky, and they finished their meal in an atmosphere of mutual satisfaction.

Afterwards, Lachlan made tea, moving knowledgeably around the room, having to stoop slightly to avoid the low roof. He set the pot of tea by the fire and came back to sit at the table. 'That's the bottle gone now, Pete. How about calling it quits for the night?'

Jamieson shook his head vehemently. 'Na. 'Nother bottle, Mack. Night's still young.'

'You've had enough, Pete.'

In answer, the old man pushed out his mug aggressively, and with obvious reluctance Lachlan pulled out another bottle from beneath the table. At Jamieson's insistence he filled his own mug again, although it was clear to Melissa at least that he did not wish to drink any more.

She left the table to curl up on the thick sheepskin rug by the stone fireplace, sipping strong bitter tea and watching the flames slowly dying in the grate. Apart from the soft gleam from the oil-lamp on the table, there was no other source of light in the cottage. Outside, a rising wind howled quietly through the cracks in the stone walls and rustled the turf roof. The men at the table seemed as reluctant as she was to break the mood of peaceful reverie. Eventually a loud snore announced that Jamieson would not be drinking any more that night. Quietly, and with great care, as if the old man were no more than a small child, Lachlan picked him up and placed him on one of the small bunks against the walls, covering him with a blanket.

Melissa spoke first, her voice sounding strange after the long silence. 'Why do you give him whisky to drink when he gets ... like this?'

'Because, if I don't give him the good stuff, he makes his own out the back, using Lord knows what,' Lachlan said quietly. 'He damned near killed himself with the gut-rot once. Also he's not a well man—something to do with his stomach—and he claims that the drink makes a change from the laudanum.'

'I ... didn't realise. The poor man.'

'Ay.' She stood up, and they faced each other. He held out his hand. 'Shall we go outside for a bit?'

The moon had risen, full and heavy and yellow. The massive black shapes of the mountains loomed all around them, and up above, the stars of the southern sky gleamed frostily. She pulled her shawl round her shoulders against the wind rippling off the mountains and waited for Lachlan to make the first move. She sensed rather than heard him coming to stand behind her, and then his hands gently closed on her waist and turned her round to face him.

He said nothing, his lips seeking hers in the darkness. She accepted his kisses coolly at first, almost primly,

telling herself sternly that while this was most pleasant,
she would not let it get out of hand this time; that she
knew enough now to control her unruly responses. But,
as if he sensed her reserve, he took his time—holding
back as if to tantalise her, seeming to know just how to
touch her and when. In no time at all she became aware
of her own ragged breathing, her fingers which had
somehow crept under his shirt and were now running up
the hard length of his back, pulling him close. Just when
she thought she could bear it no longer, he bent and
picked her up, not removing his mouth from hers. He
was carrying her in the direction of the stables, and she
managed to break away for long enough to ask him
rather unevenly where he was taking her.

'Somewhere a wee bit more comfortable,' he replied,
with a ripple of amusement in his voice.

Now, for the first time, she felt a sharp stab of alarm.
She was not quite sure what he expected from her, but
she knew it would be more than she was prepared or
able to give. He laid her down on a pile of loose straw
on the stable floor and was at once beside her, his breath
coming faster as he began to kiss her face and throat,
his hand travelling up beneath her skirts. Abruptly she
felt a rush of such exquisite desire for him that she knew
to hesitate a second more would be sheer folly. 'No!'
she gasped, pushing away the hand that was causing her
such delicious agony.

He raised his head to look at her, puzzled. 'Emily,
what's the matter?'

His use of her pseudonym gave her strength at last.
He had the wrong name, the wrong woman! She tried
to get up, but his hands lightly restrained her. 'Let me
go!' she ordered, her passion rapidly evaporating as she
realised her perilous situation. He released her immediately, and they both got to their feet. She began to
pluck nervously at the pieces of straw sticking to her,
shaking slightly with shock at what she had started. She
dared not look at him.

'All right. How much?'

'I—I beg your pardon?'

'I said, how much? I'm sorry, I must have misread the signals or something. I thought we'd agreed...that you wanted...' He shook his head angrily, his voice harsh. 'Look, whatever your price is, I'll pay it. Just let's get on with it.'

'My...price? Good grief!' Melissa hissed at him. 'Just what do you think I am?'

He stared at her in frank surprise. 'Lady, we both know what you are. That's not the issue here.'

'Oh, but it is! How dare you insinuate that I am to be bought!'

'Aren't you?' he said quietly. 'And how else were you intending to pay for you transport to the Arrow but on your back?'

'You despicable animal!' she spat, revolted. She saw the white flash of his teeth in the moonlight as he grinned, and then he began to move closer. She was suddenly afraid: he was so very big and she was completely defenceless. Backing away, she bumped into the chopping-block by the hitching-rail, and her fingers convulsively closed round the handle of a small kindling axe. 'Don't you dare touch me!' she warned, but he kept coming and, in her panic, she reacted instinctively to protect herself. She had intended only to feint a swing of the axe in his direction, to demonstrate that she had a weapon, but unfortunately he happened to lunge at her at the very second that she happened to bring the axe up over her head. There was a sickening moment of impact, and he dropped like a stone to the ground. She threw the axe down as if it were suddenly red-hot, appalled beyond measure at what she had done.

'Oh, Mr MacGregor! I'm so sorry! Are you all right? Please get up!' she babbled wildly to the prone man at her feet. There was no response. She sank to her knees beside him and, with an enormous effort, managed to heave him over on his back to look at what she had done. She felt with her fingers round his head until she felt the enormous contusion on his left temple, and realised that she must have hit him with the blunt edge of the axe. Her relief was immediately superseded by rising panic as she discovered that he did not appear to be breathing. Where does one feel for a pulse? she wondered. She tried desperately to find one at the base of his throat and was vastly relieved when, after a few seconds, he gagged under the pressure of her fingers. 'Mr MacGregor? Are you alive?'

He demonstrated his revivification by uttering a string of words so obscene that she had never heard of most of them. Then he lurched to his feet and staggered as far as the trough, where he collapsed again, his head under the water.

Wringing her hands frantically, she flew to his side, convinced that he would compound her problems by drowning. She put her hands on his shoulders, the broad, hard, saturated shoulders that she had been caressing just minutes before, and pulled. He did not move. She pulled harder, and this time his head came up, spraying her with water. He took one huge, gasping breath and submerged his head again, quite oblivious of her efforts to restrain him. She stood back, waiting in an agony of self-reproach, until he came up for air again. Then she repeated her apology.

There was a long silence as he knelt looking down at the moonlit ripples on the water, his forearms braced against the wooden sides of the trough. 'Lady, you've got one hell of a way of getting your point across,' he said finally and completely without rancour. 'Any other woman might have been content to slap my face. But you—you feel obliged to beat my brains out instead.' He started to laugh, but broke off with a sharp gasp of pain, holding his head in his hands. 'Oh, God!'

'It was an accident,' she whispered, mortified by the pain she had caused. 'I really didn't mean to...' She fell silent, wondering if he could even hear her.

He was frowning slightly, rising unsteadily to his feet. 'You don't believe in half-measures, do you? You know, you remind me of a mate of mine... Hell, you even *look* a bit like him...' His speech was becoming slurred. She took him by the arm and started to lead him in the direction of the stables in the hopes of finding some blankets. 'Most immoderate damned woman I ever met,' he was enunciating with some difficulty, when he suddenly pitched face-forwards.

She tried to catch him, but he was much too heavy and she merely succeeded in breaking his fall. 'Mr MacGregor! Lachlan, speak to me!' Caught underneath him, she stroked his wet hair frantically, willing him not to be dead.

'I'm cold...so cold...' he muttered.

Indeed, he did seem to be freezing in his soaking shirt. She managed to unwrap her shawl and drag it over him, but he was still shivering, so she pressed herself against him in an effort to transfer some of her own body heat. Would it be safe to leave him, she wondered, to go and look for blankets in the cottage? She suddenly realised that somehow her bodice had become unbuttoned, and that the man in her arms was displaying a perfectly coherent interest in that part of her anatomy. 'Mr MacGregor!' she hissed in fury, removing his exploring hand. 'I don't believe you're in any pain at all!'

'Oh, but I am, my sweet, soft, bloodthirsty Miss Page,' he muttered happily against her breasts. With a snarl, she fought free at last, but he reached out and caught her ankle as she tried to get away. 'Won't you stay and give a little comfort to a man in need?' he wheedled.

'Oh, you—you...! How could you take such advantage of my sympathy!' She kicked him in the ribs, which hurt her much more than him since she had somehow lost her shoes, and she was forced to hobble back to the cottage door, sharp jabs of pain darting through her toes. She turned to glare through the darkness at the man lying on the ground where she had left him, his body shaking. 'You are a maniac, sir!' Unable to restrain himself any longer, Lachlan burst out laughing. Tears of humiliation stung her eyes as she shouted at him, 'I hate you! I hate you! I hope you freeze to death out there!' Her abuse met only another outburst of helpless laughter, and, defeated, she turned without another word and made what she hoped was a dignified exit into the cottage.

* * *

Despite her every resolution to the contrary, and tired as she was, Melissa spent a miserably wakeful night. Her bed was a narrow wooden bunk pushed against the wall, through which small draughts whistled and froze those parts of her not well wrapped in the prickly, smoke-scented blanket. The thin mattress was filled with some kind of tussock which, while it did not appear to harbour any bed-bugs, still felt itchy. And, to make matters worse, when she did doze off it was to dream of Lachlan's hard, demanding hands on her skin, and she would wake to stare endlessly into the dark, rigid with anger and humiliation. So it came as a shock when she was jolted out of a late, deep sleep by the sound of the innkeeper pushing wood into the newly-lit fire.

'Mornin', miss.' He nodded to her as she blinked owlishly at him, trying for a moment to remember where she was. 'An' a nice mornin' it is, too.'

She remembered, and sat up, feeling dreadful. Of necessity she had lain down fully clothed, partly for extra warmth and partly because there was no provision in the one-roomed inn for any privacy. Now her stays were making her rib-cage ache and her muslin dress was a crumpled mess.

The old man shuffled around his cottage, seemingly quite unaffected by his excesses of the previous night, putting the used plates and mugs on the table into a bowl to be washed.

'What—What time is it?' she asked hesitantly, more for something to say than for any other reason. Through the half-open door she could see brilliant sunshine, but it felt like no more than five minutes since she had last been awake.

'Late, miss—dawn's an hour gone. Mack'll be champin' at the bit to be off, no doubt, but p'raps it were no bad thing for yer to 'ave a lie-in, seein's how you came such a long ways yesterday.'

An hour past dawn meant five o'clock in the morning. With a stifled groan, she eased herself off the bed and stood to straighten her dress as best she could. As the coldness of the dirt floor seeped through her feet, she woke up enough for the rest of what Mr Jamieson had said to sink in. 'Is—Is Mr MacGregor still here? He hasn't . . . left already, has he?'

Her brief hopes were dashed when the old man shook his head with a chuckle. 'Mack go off without his breakfast? That'd be the day! Nah—he'll be in any second now, demandin' his tucker.'

'Do you mean that you haven't seen him this morning?' A horrible thought occurred to her. What if he had died during the night, and his body was still lying out there, stiff and cold and undiscovered? She had barely covered the short distance to the door when it swung open to reveal Lachlan, very much alive and carrying two full buckets of water.

'Good morning, Miss Page. Did you sleep well?'

She was saved from answering by Mr Jamieson, who brushed past her to stare up at Lachlan with a look of horror on his face. 'What the . . . ?'

'It's all right, Pete.' Lachlan turned away to put the buckets of water by the fire and thus spare them the sight of the huge purple contusion on his forehead. 'It doesn't feel as bad as it probably looks.'

'Yer can't let it go undressed, Mack!'

'The skin's barely broken, and I heal fast. When's breakfast?'

'But . . . how'd it happen?'

'I walked into a door,' Lachlan said so briefly as to discourage any further questions. He looked across to where Melissa stood in awkward silence. 'Can I have a word with you, please, Miss Page? Outside?'

She managed to nod, and he turned without another word and went back outside, leaving her staring at the closed door and pulling on her fingers nervously. This cool, brusque man was alarmingly different from the passionate man of last night, and all the things she had thought of during her long hours of wakefulness to say to him seemed impossible to utter in the clear morning light, with Mr Jamieson likely to be within earshot.

The old man, mumbling to himself, had meanwhile poured some water into the pot over the fire and added a mugful of oatmeal, moving impatiently around where she stood indecisively in the centre of the small room. 'You kin tell Mack his tucker'll be ready in a few minutes,' he told her at last, and she took the hint and moved towards the door. 'Oh—an' give him this, will you, miss? It's something the Maoris round here use to stop sores festerin'.'

She took the small jar he held out and went outside. The bright light made her wince for a moment—the sun was well up now, but the morning dew still clung to each leaf and blade of grass, giving vibrancy to the dusty colours of the tussock plains. All around towered the mountains, harshly red, and the air shimmered with the promise of a hot, still day.

Lachlan was waiting by the trough, and Melissa took a deep breath before going over to join him, nervously smoothing down her dress as she went. He looked up as she approached and, although it should not have made any difference, she was relieved to see him smile. Her instinctive reaction was to smile back, but she suddenly and vividly remembered what had happened on that very spot the night before. This man had touched her, had made her into a different woman entirely with his soft, searching kisses and his knowing hands. She could not afford to be so vulnerable again. Averting her eyes, she took her stand on the far side of the trough.

'Mr Jamieson asked me to give you this . . . for your head.' She thrust the jar of ointment at him. 'What did you want to say to me?'

'Just that the coach to Dunedin comes by here in another hour. I want you to be on it.'

'But I'm not *going* to Dunedin,' she said calmly, albeit through gritted teeth. 'I'm going to Arrowtown!'

He sighed, and leaned forward. 'Look at me, Miss Page.' She looked up reluctantly. He was holding up a banknote a foot from her face. 'Do you see this? It's a ten-pound note, Miss Page. That represents enough money to get you back to Dunedin on the coach and pay for accommodation until you obtain gainful employment. Do you want it?'

'I wouldn't touch a penny of yours!'

'Are you quite sure?' he asked patiently. 'Old Pete's not a bad old fellow, but he can't and he won't keep you for free. How are you going to pay him for last night's board? The same way you paid me?'

She flushed. 'All right, I'll take your grubby money, but only because I have to! But I'll be taking the coach to Arrowtown, if it's all the same to you, and I'll pay you back as soon as I get there!' As much as it cost her, she held out her hand for the note.

'I'm sorry, but I can give this to you only if you're going to Dunedin—and I don't need repaying. Just your assurance that you won't be coming back out this way again.'

'But I'm going to Arrowtown!'

He shrugged, and put the note back in his shirt pocket. 'You're obviously very determined, and that's your business, but don't ever say you weren't warned. You'll be coming with me on the dray, then.'

'I will not! Continue travelling with you after what happened last night? You amaze me, Mr MacGregor!'

'And *I'd* have thought you'd find it more amazing that I'm prepared to give you anything at all after last night.' He looked down at her feet with a small smile. 'I hope you've a stouter pair of walking-boots than those, Miss Page.'

'Give me the money, drat you!'

'Why should I? You haven't earned it!'

'If you were a gentleman . . .'

'Which I'm not, and I've never claimed to be. But you affect to be a lady, Miss Page, and that's quite different, isn't it?'

'Stop calling me Miss Page!' she could not help snapping helplessly.

'Why?' he shot back. 'It *is* your name, isn't it?'

'Yes, of course! I mean . . .' She stopped, flustered by the look in his eyes—not unfriendly, but very disconcerting, almost as if he *knew* . . . but of course that was impossible! He was only trying to upset her, to force his

will on her just as he had tried to force his body on her
only hours before!

'Breakfast! Move yerselves!' Mr Jamieson's impatient voice broke the tension between them, and she
quickly turned away, glad of the interruption.

Breakfast was huge bowls of lumpy, steaming por-
ridge, washed down with mugs of acrid tea. Melissa and
Lachlan ate in silence, Lachlan replying only monosyl-
labically to Jamieson's chatter. As soon as he had finished eating, he got to his feet and picked up his jacket.

'I'll get the dray ready while you think about what I
said, Miss Page.'

'You put that stuff on yer head I gave yer?' Jamieson
asked. 'Don't want the ladies goin' off yer 'cos of a nasty
big scar, do yer? Eh?'

Lachlan muttered something indistinct but clearly rude
before slamming the door behind him. Jamieson did not
seem to take offence at all, and sat chuckling and shaking
his head in what appeared to be admiration. 'What a
lad, eh? What a lad!' He looked across at Melissa and
surprised her with a broad wink. 'Fancy him, doncher?
I kin tell yer do!'

'What? Oh . . . Good heavens, no! Whatever gave you
that idea?'

'Aw, come on now, lass! Sittin' there last night you
were, battin' them big eyes at him, anyone could tell!
Mind you, from what I hear tell 'bout that big lad, you're
not the first!' He laughed lewdly. 'Though I don't
suppose he were too much use to yer last night, wi' a
skinful of booze an' a sore head!'

Melissa stood up so quickly that she overturned the
bench she had been sitting on. Seizing her carpet-bag,
she ran outside without another word, anxious only to
get away from the horrible Mr Jamieson and his disgusting insinuations. As she stepped outside, she was
aware of a difference; a rumbling in the air and slowly
swirling dust above the track some twenty yards from
the front of the inn. She went to where Lachlan was
harnessing his horses to the dray.

'What was that?'

He was concentrating on the buckle he was doing up. 'That was the coach to Dunedin. You've just missed it.'

'Oh, no! But why didn't you . . .?' Her words trailed off as she realised what he had done.

'You hadn't changed your mind about going on to the Arrow, had you?' he asked innocently. 'It'll be two days before there's another coach to Dunedin.'

'You're detestable! I should have *killed* you last night!'

He looked shocked. 'All you seem to want is my money or my life, Miss Page. I think you might be in the wrong profession!'

She did not deign to reply, but turned on her heel and set off up the track in what she hoped was the direction of Arrowtown. Her shoes were solid enough, and her carpet-bag was not excessively heavy. If she could put enough distance between herself and Mr MacGregor, she would be bound to meet another vehicle with friendlier occupants or, failing that, she was quite prepared to walk all the way if need be. Anything had to be better than spending another minute in the company of that man! She had not been walking for very long when she heard the sound of the dray behind her. A quick glance over her shoulder proved that it was MacGregor and not some other, possibly more helpful, person at the reins. She moved over to the side of the track in the vain hope that he would pass her by. He did not, of course, and simply reined in the horses to a slow plod at her own pace.

'Getting tired, Miss Page?'

'Not at all, Mr MacGregor. Please don't let me delay you.' Dear God, she thought, is there no end to this man's ability to torment me?

'Oh, I'm in no hurry, lass.' And the irritating man continued to drive patiently alongside her, stopping the horses occasionally when they drew ahead.

By now, her boots were beginning to rub against her feet. The four months of shipboard life had accustomed her to little more than a leisurely stroll on the decks twice a day, and her lack of fitness, combined with the stiffness in her muscles from yesterday's hours in the back of the dray, soon combined to make every step an effort of will. It was decidedly warm now, and little rivulets of perspiration were running down her back and face. The road had begun to climb again, and even MacGregor's horses were beginning to strain a little on the steeper grade. It took a full hour, but at last she stopped and threw her carpet-bag to the ground in frustration and weariness.

Lachlan was beside her at once, throwing it into the back of the dray, holding out a hand to help her in. 'Come on, lass—you've made your point,' he said kindly enough, when even then she did not move.

'What point?' she asked bitterly.

'Damned if I know, but you've made it. If you want to get to the Arrow so badly, I'll willingly take you; and you've nothing to fear from me.'

'I think I have.'

He shrugged. 'It's me . . . or the next driver who comes along. He might be better—or a great deal worse. Two men were murdered in a gully ten miles on from here last week—bushrangers, they thought, but they haven't been caught yet. That's why I always travel with a rifle nearby, and apart from yesterday, I've never had any trouble. But a lone, unarmed woman . . .'

'Then lend me the money to get to Arrowtown!' Did he know, she wondered, what it cost her to beg? She would never forgive him for this!

'On the coach you'd be a little safer, sure—but not as much as you'd think. Come with me, and then at least I can be sure you'll get to the Arrow safely.'

'You have no responsibility towards me!'

'Well, I happen to think I have, lass. Let's get back on the dray, and I'll tell you why.'

She shook his hand off her arm, still obstinately refusing to look at him. 'Very well, I will travel with you, Mr MacGregor. On one condition.'

'Which is?'

'That you don't speak to me unnecessarily for the rest of this journey. I'm not interested in you, or what you happen to think about anything, in fact! Everything I say you—you twist to suit your own deviant purposes, and the only way we could ever travel together is if you restrict yourself to the bare essentials of communication, and no more! Are you capable of doing that, Mr MacGregor?'

Any normal, self-respecting man would have been deeply offended by such a speech, but typically Lachlan merely threw back his head and laughed out loud. 'I promise to try,' he managed to say at last. 'But I think you could regret this, lass.'

'That's impossible,' she assured him as she permitted him to help her up. 'And if you do persist, Mr Mac-Gregor, I shall put my hands over my ears and sing very loudly—all the way to Arrowtown, if need be.'

He looked most impressed by this threat, and took the reins obediently. They rode in heavy silence for several hours. The road became even steeper and rougher, but the horses plodded on steadily, and they had covered many miles by the time Lachlan pulled them over to the side of the track in the late afternoon.

'Why have we stopped here?' she asked, as he climbed down and began to rotate his shoulders, cramped after so many hours of driving.

'Can't you hear?' Melissa listened intently and, over the sound of the wind whistling through the tussocks, she could hear something different. 'It's the stage-coach to Dunstan. If we didn't get out of its way, we'd likely get flattened. They don't stop for anything!'

As she watched, the stage-coach appeared over the brow of the hill behind them. The four matched greys pulling it were slick with sweat, heads still held high even after the long haul up from the foothills. Piled high with luggage, its ornate red panels gleamed in the sunlight, and the high yellow wheels threw up a shower of rocks as they passed by at breakneck speed. The ground trembled even through the wheels of Lachlan's heavy dray, and Melissa watched the stage-coach disappear with mixed feelings—on that vehicle she would soon have been at Arrowtown. On the other hand, such a pace on these roads must be dreadfully dangerous. She said as much to Lachlan as they resumed their journey.

'Ay, it's true it can be a dangerous trip,' he agreed. 'They opened this road—the Mountain Track, it's called—only a few months ago. The Cobb & Co. coaches used to take it more slowly, but now there's a rival coach-line, and so all the drivers race to see who can get to the goldfields first. It's a slower trip on the way back to Dunedin.'

'But don't the passengers object to travelling like that?'

'It's the passengers they race for, lass. When men are so desperate for gold that they spend months travelling half-way round the world to get to it, they'll take any coach that offers to get them there a half-day faster. It seems crazy to me, but I guess that's human nature.' He stopped suddenly and pretended to look guilty. 'My apologies—I've just expressed another unwanted opinion!'

'Just as long as it's your last, Mr MacGregor,' she said loftily, and he laughed.

They passed several miners, some walking heavily laden, some with a mule or a horse to carry their load. Just as the light was going that night, they pulled up at a large hotel, standing oddly alone in the wilderness. A number of other travellers were there, and they ate a huge communal dinner before falling into deep, ex-hausted sleep on palliasses around the fireplace. It seemed that Melissa had only just shut her eyes when Lachlan was gently shaking her awake in the half-light of dawn and directing her to the kitchen, where large mounds of bacon and eggs and buttered bread awaited the early travellers.

The road on the second day was, if anything, even worse. Melissa had to dismount several times to help lighten the load on the dray, and once they stopped to help another driver whose dray had become stuck in the gravel of a river-bed. She walked up and down on the bank while she waited, watching the men unload every box from the dray in mid-stream and carry them to dry land. This was an adventure in summer, she realised, but in winter such travel could be an ordeal. She tried to imagine the roads covered with the twelve-foot-high

snowdrifts she had heard of that could isolate Central
Otago for months at a time. Lachlan had also shown
her the wreckage of a stage-coach at the bottom of a
ravine. He said the accident had happened only weeks
before—mercifully everyone had managed to get out in
time, and the horses had been cut free. It was such a
wild country, with hundreds of tales of drownings in
flooded rivers and deaths on mountain tracks, and she
had witnessed for herself enough to be grateful for
Lachlan's knowledge of the roads and his expertise with
his horses.

They spent the second night in a hotel on the high
plains of the Dunstans. In the pale hour before dawn
when Melissa came outside after breakfast, Lachlan was
already transferring his consignment to the backs of a
dozen mules, ready for the day-long journey over the
Dunstan Range to Arrowtown. She stood for a while
watching him checking the loads, and reflecting that none
of her fears about him had proved to be justified; he
had been the soul of politeness and consideration ever
since Jamieson's Inn and now, just as the journey was
drawing to a close, she found herself almost regretting
her original pact with him. Sometimes she caught him
looking at her with a strangely amused expression, as if
he were having some secret joke at her expense, but she
had not been able to fault his behaviour. Determined
not to part from him with any rancour, she moved
forward with a bright smile.

'I hadn't realised until now that you were carrying so
much alcohol. Is it all going to Arrowtown?'

'Morning, lass. Yes, it's all bound for Arrowtown—
and all to the same bar, what's more. And this will keep
them watered for no more than three weeks.'

'It must be a huge bar you supply!'

He shook his head, laughing at her. 'Very modest,
even by Arrow standards, I'm afraid. You'd be
disappointed.'

She did not like his laughing at her naïvety, and
withdrew again behind the cool façade she had maintained up until then. 'I hardly see that that sort of thing

would cause me any disappointment or otherwise, Mr MacGregor. I'm not going to Arrowtown to interest myself in the drinking-habits of miners!'

'No?' He stopped what he was doing and looked at her with keen interest. 'You've yet to tell me what you *are* going to the Arrow for.'

'Because it's none of your business!'

'You mean you're still angry about that night at Jamieson's? That was an honest mistake, lass—and I think I've surely paid the price for it by now.' He ruefully touched the subsiding but still livid bruise on his head as he spoke. 'And haven't I been well behaved these past few days?'

She bit her lip in exasperation. She had long since given up waiting for an apology for that night, suspecting that Lachlan did not hold himself particularly to blame. It was his high-handed, cheerful arrogance that she found so hard to accept, and if ever she challenged it, she ended up sounding like a fishwife. 'I shall be delighted when this journey is finally over and I won't have to put up with your rudeness any more!' she told him sincerely. 'Just how soon can we be on our way?'

'Just as soon as you get your bag, Miss Page.'

Riding at the rear of the pack-train over the Dunstan Range as the sun rose would always remain one of the most cherished memories of Melissa's life. They moved so slowly up the precipitous slopes that she was able to dismount and comfortably walk whenever she chose. On the saddle of the range, the wind bit cold but the view was unsurpassed, the world looking like a multi-textured carpet laid out at her feet.

Lachlan rode well ahead, turning round often to check that the train of mules and Melissa were still following safely, speaking to her only to tell her when they reached the Arrow River. It was grey and fast-moving, but little more than a shallow stream, which surprised her; she had somehow expected that a river whose name was now known world-wide for its gold workings would be much more impressive. They forded it several times, working their way up the deep, steep-sided valley to the township, and for the first time she saw miners working, panning and sluicing the river-bed.

Her heart was racing with excitement when at last Lachlan turned to call, 'Arrowtown round this bend!'

And there it was—a dusty, sprawling blanket of many hundreds of tents and a few rough wooden and stone huts. The settlement looked as if it had only just sprung up (which indeed it literally had) and could just as quickly disappear. The Arrow wove through the gorge lined with cliffs that were almost sheer on some faces, seemingly quite undisturbed by the makeshift settlement perched temporarily on its boulder-strewn banks. The 'town' was nothing like Melissa's worst fears—she had simply never imagined anything like this waiting for her at the end of her journey.

Lachlan led the mules around the side of the encampment to where there were some buildings that looked as if they were intended to be stables, and dismounted. In a daze, Melissa slipped off her horse and untied her bag from the back of the saddle.

Catching sight of her expression, Lachlan made his way down the line of mules and put a steadying hand on her elbow. 'It's not what you expected, is it, lass?' His voice was so unexpectedly sympathetic that she could not trust herself to speak, and only nodded assent.

'Have you got somewhere to go?'

'The—The Regency Hotel. Do you know where it is?'

She heard the faintest intake of breath and caught the odd mixture of emotions flickering over Lachlan's face, but his voice was unaltered. 'Straight behind you, about two hundred yards. I'll walk you to it.'

'No...thank you. I'd rather go alone. Goodbye, Mr MacGregor.' He made no effort to farewell her and she did not try to analyse the expression on his face as she turned and walked away. She picked her way through the maze of tents and camp-fires, trying to keep to a straight line.

It was a dreadful walk. She had to skirt round a number of fires, the men lounging around them refusing to move their legs from her path. The smell of a hundred cooking dinners overlaid a more acrid aroma of unwashed humanity. It was an almost entirely male encampment; once she heard a woman's laugh from inside a tent, but otherwise she had to tolerate a male barrage of whistles, catcalls and personal remarks. She kept her eyes lowered, trying to ignore them all. Then there was a clearing amid the tents, and she raised her eyes to the building in front of her. The last vestiges of the dream she had been clinging to, of a little whitewashed hotel, vanished as she took in the rickety unpainted wooden shack with its loose canvas roof. A slightly lopsided sign over the doorway proclaimed it to be the Regency Hotel. There was no mistake. This was the inheritance she had travelled half-way round the world to see!

Feeling decidedly weak at the knees, she steeled herself to walk inside. The door creaked open on its hinges to reveal a dark and smoke-scented interior. There were no windows, and it took her a moment to adjust to the darkness after the glare of the early evening sun. An oil-lamp gleamed dully on the wall and she could, by its grudging light, make out a bar at the end of the room, with tables and benches before. She could see no back door leading to a kitchen or any sleeping arrangements—the 'hotel' consisted of just this one room. Above her head, the canvas roof flapped in a gust of wind. She wondered if she was entitled to throw a hysterical fit.

There was the sound of bottles being moved around, and then a man stood up from where he had been kneeling behind the bar. He was young, of medium height and build, and although he now sported a short fair beard, Melissa knew him immediately.

'David!'

'Can I help you?' he asked, his voice puzzled as he peered through the murky light to see who it was. Recognition dawned on his face as she stepped forward under the lamp. 'It's...not Melissa, is it? It can't be!' He flung his arms round her and gave her a rib-crunching hug. 'Little Melissa! Good heavens, after all these years... Let's take a good look at you.' He reopened the door behind her, letting the light stream in. Admiration shone in his eyes. 'You've turned into a real little beauty, haven't you? Whatever happened to the pigtails and little fat legs?'

'I'm not the only one to have grown up,' she rejoined, gently tugging at his beard. 'You weren't even shaving when I last saw you.'

'Fourteen years ago, it must be. I wasn't more than thirteen when I left England.' He looked her up and down in concern. 'You look very tired. How did you weather the trip out here? It's pretty arduous, isn't it?'

'It was interesting, David. I've got lots to tell you. But I must admit I hadn't expected . . . this.' She gestured to include the dirt floor and the rough wooden walls of the shanty.

David sighed. 'Believe me, coz, it was much worse when we got here. Uncle Toby was a . . . well, he drank rather a lot; couldn't even organise himself, let alone a grog-shanty in a place as rough as the Arrow. He drank himself to death less than a week after I got here. I'd stayed to look after him when I realised he was sick, and then after he died and you were named as co-beneficiary, I thought I'd better stay on and find out what you wanted done with the place. I'd expected you to *write*, though— not turn up in person! Although it's marvellous to see you, of course!' he added hastily.

'Eight months.'

As she raised her eyebrows in surprise, he said defensively, 'As I said—we've done what we could. At least it's got a roof of sorts, and tables and chairs, and we're only just starting to make a profit now because we've put all our money into buying decent liquor. Uncle Toby used to brew up this dreadful stuff in cans—and drink most of it himself, anyway! We left the sign on the place; poor old Toby used to call it his "hotel", and after he died I didn't have the heart to change the name, misleading as it is. So . . . how soon do you think you'll be up to travelling back to Dunedin? I'll arrange somewhere for you to sleep tonight, and perhaps tomorrow . . .'

'I wasn't planning to go back so soon!' she protested. 'It's taken me over four months to get here, and I'd like to stay a little longer than one day!'

'No. That's quite out of the question.'

She was somewhat taken aback by the flatness of his tone. 'But I thought...I thought I had a half-share in this place?'

'Yes, you have, that's true, but Uncle Tobias made his will before...' He stopped and began again. 'I want to buy you out. I wrote to the solicitors in London telling them that, but you'd obviously already left. I've not much money at the moment, because we've just spent a lot on new supplies. I'm not sure what sort of value to put on this place, but if you tell me what you want for your share, I'll send it on as soon as I can get the money together.'

'I don't know, David...'

He misunderstood her hesitation. 'Three hundred pounds? Does that sound enough?'

'It sounds far too much! That's a lot of money!'

'It will be worth it if you don't have to stay in Arrowtown, coz, believe me!'

'Really?' She was puzzled by the note of desperation she detected in his voice. 'Why don't you want me to stay, David? Why am I so sure that there is something you're not telling me?'

He sighed in exasperation. 'Don't let's argue about this now. You can see what it's like here, and it's no place for a lady. So just be a good girl and don't bother unpacking.'

'Will you please stop talking to me as if I were a child!' she said furiously.

'Then stop acting like one!' David retorted, his face flushed.

'Take care, Davey—you're in trouble if you make her lose her temper,' warned the man standing in the doorway, a crate under each arm. Melissa's heart lurched at the sound of the deep, lilting voice.

'Mack, you're back already!' David greeted him, obviously relieved to have a diversion. 'Put those down and let me introduce you to someone very special.'

'I've already had the pleasure of meeting your cousin,' Lachlan said. He took off his hat and came to stand in front of her.

Melissa wished the floor could open up and swallow her. She should have expected Lachlan and David to have met before! So Lachlan was the wagoner who supplied the Regency—and if David had told him about her, the two men must know each other well. For how long had Lachlan known who she was while she had kept up that ridiculous pretence? She could not bear to think about it! She stared fixedly at the top button of his shirt while she tried to compose herself. For three days now she had tried to pretend to herself that he barely existed, but that was no longer possible. Now he was much too close, much too big—even the curling hairs on his chest seemed larger than life.

He put his fingers under her chin, bringing her eyes up to meet his, which to her mortification were brimming with laughter. 'Welcome to Arrowtown, Miss Edwards,' he said, and placed a light kiss on her cheek.

She drew away abruptly. 'Why didn't you tell me you knew? All this time you let me pretend . . . let me make a fool of myself . . .'

'I started to suspect only after the . . . mishap . . . at Jamieson's,' he said almost apologetically. 'You look and sound so much like Davey, and everything else about you seemed to coincide with what he'd told me about you—but you'd made it very clear you wanted your privacy, and I didn't want to offend you any more than I already had, lass!'

David had been following this exchange with a look of total incomprehension. 'How did you two come to meet?' he interrupted.

'I gave Melissa a ride in the dray from Dunedin,' Lachlan told him calmly. 'Drink, anyone?'

'Who else was with you?' David seemed to be quite agitated by that small piece of information.

'Just the two of us. Champagne, I think, don't you?' Lachlan went to look behind the bar, and David followed him suspiciously.

'How'd you get that bruise on your head?'

'That's where your little cousin hit me on the head with an axe. And to stop you asking why, Davey, it was for the same reason you're thinking it is, so save the lectures, lad.'

'Christ, Mack, you're damned impossible!' David exploded. 'My cousin, of all women, and you have to...'

'I didn't know she was your cousin,' Lachlan defended himself cheerfully. 'You always said she was little and fat with freckles. Now look—you two haven't seen each other in a long time, so sit your poor weary cousin down and explain to her what I'm doing here while I get us all a drink.'

Obviously still furious, David pulled over a bench for Melissa and then sat down heavily beside her. 'I'm so sorry about all this, Melissa.'

'Is he always like this?' she asked quietly, half appalled and half intrigued by the easy, overbearing way Lachlan had disposed of David's perfectly righteous anger. She was by now desperately curious to know what the relationship was between the two men.

'I'm afraid so. He's... Well, I suppose I'd better tell you what's going on here.'

'Please.'

'You see... You own half this place, and... I've sold half my share. Well, not exactly *sold*, because the place isn't worth anything, but I needed someone to help me run it, and Mack and I have been partners since our mining days at Ballarat.'

So that was it. Unwittingly she had become a business partner with the last man in the world she would have wanted! That explained Lachlan's interest in her and the casual protection he had extended on the trip here, but she still could not shake off her earlier suspicions that Lachlan MacGregor was not the only reason David wanted her out of Arrowtown. She looked over to where

Lachlan was standing watching them alertly. 'Do you think I should go back to Dunedin now?'

'That's your decision entirely, lass.'

David glanced at him angrily and she knew for a certainty that something more was troubling him.

'This is your fault, Mack! You should have taken her straight back to Dunedin! What was the idea of bringing her all the way out here and not even telling her who you were?'

'If I'd told her who I was, I think she'd have gone straight back to Dunedin! But she had her heart set on coming out here, Davey, and it seemed hardly fair to deny her the chance of seeing what she'd come so far to claim. I think I did the right thing...don't you, lass?'

Melissa looked at him thoughtfully, surprised to find that, after all that had gone between them, he should prove such an ally. Unless, of course, he had his own reasons for wanting her to stay...

'David, I'd like you to be honest with me, please,' she said slowly. 'Is there any other reason—apart from the rigours of life here, and Lachlan—why you don't want me to stay?' When neither of the men answered, she made a stab at the answer. 'Is it anything to do with William Price?'

Her suspicions were all confirmed when David's head snapped up. 'What do you know about William Price?'

Lachlan cast her a very reproachful look. Very briefly he outlined what had happened at the place he called Jessop's Pass, when William had tried to kill him. Even told as sparsely as Lachlan told it, the story was still chilling, and by the time he finished, David's face was white.

'Melissa, you've got to go back to Dunedin immediately! If he's threatened you... If anything were to happen to you...'

'Then I'd go back to Dunedin,' she said promptly. 'I don't understand what this feud is all about, and Lachlan wouldn't tell me, but whatever it is, I can promise you I don't want to get involved!'

Lachlan had been busy wrestling the top off the bottle in his hand. It came out with a loud pop, and out of the corner of her eye she saw David flinch. 'Champagne all round,' announced Lachlan, slopping it into the three beer-mugs on the bar. 'Come and get it before it gets cold.'

'What shall we drink to?' she asked, as they sat at one of the tables, mugs in their hands.

'To Melissa,' Lachlan offered, raising his glass, a challenge in his eyes.

'Yes, of course,' said David. 'A safe trip back, coz.'

'I don't think so,' she said, and clinked her glass with theirs. 'How about a toast to our new partnership?'

CHAPTER THREE

AN HOUR later Melissa was still arguing with David. Lachlan, to her surprise, had kept very much out of the argument and sat playing absently with the cork from the second bottle of champagne he had opened, listening, but contributing nothing. It was left to David to do battle with her—and he was losing ground fast.

'All right!' he shouted at last, leaping to his feet. 'Stay if you must, but I'm warning you, Melissa, you'll regret it! The life here's much too hard for any lady of your background to tolerate—you'll soon be begging to go back!'

'My background? David, you've no idea how life was for me in England these past years. I've had to fend for myself in every way since my parents died. I don't mind hardship, I don't mind hard work and hunger... but I couldn't live any longer in the prison that my life had become. If you're so worried about Mr Price, I promise to leave Arrowtown at the first sign of trouble, but please let me stay here awhile and try to find my feet in this country? I don't want to run back to Dunedin like a coward, because I believe you when you tell me I can't cope with life here.'

'You wouldn't be a coward at all,' David said tersely. 'It's just that... it's inappropriate for you to stay in a town like the Arrow.'

'Why? Because then people will think that I'm a prostitute?' David winced at her bluntness. 'I've already had to correct one man who thought I was for sale, and I'm quite prepared to do so again.'

'Strewth,' Lachlan said admiringly. 'There won't be a man left standing in Central Otago!'

She decided against expending energy in trying to deflate Lachlan MacGregor's blithe self-confidence—she knew it would be a fruitless endeavour.

'Mack's right; there are two hundred men out here to every woman, and there's no such thing as a "respectable woman" on the goldfields, either. A saloon girl, a dancing girl—that's what everyone will think of you as being. Is that what you want? Because that's exactly what will happen!' David sat down beside her again, his face flushed and unhappy, and he took her hand. 'Lissy, you're my little cousin, and all I want is your safety and well-being. For many reasons it's not safe for you here. Please go back to Dunedin.'

This final, soft appeal to her emotions affected her more than anything he had said thus far. The concern and affection in her cousin's eyes was so real that she had to hesitate. 'If I *did* go back, what would I do? What sort of a job would I get?'

'Job?' David looked appalled. 'You shouldn't have to work, Melissa! The Regency brings in quite enough to be able to keep you in Dunedin, if you're careful. The two of us had planned to keep it running for a while yet, because we're making more steady money from this bar than we've ever made before. And when we sell it, well, then you'll have a little nest-egg to keep you safe.'

'A nest-egg,' she repeated. 'That's exactly what the solicitor in London told me I should look for. To keep me safe in my old age.' She shook her head slowly. 'But I'm only twenty-three, David.'

He was looking at her blankly, but when she glanced across at Lachlan, she saw in amazement that he understood exactly what she meant. He leaned forward. 'You're a piano-teacher, aren't you?'

'I used to be, yes.'

'We need someone to play the piano here.'

'No, we don't,' David said sharply. 'And besides—we don't even have a piano.'

'The Carousel has—or, rather, had. I'll be right back.' Lachlan picked up his hat and strode out, leaving Melissa to stare perplexedly at her cousin.

'The Carousel was another bar,' David explained. 'The miners took exception to the piano-player last week and took the place apart, and him with it. That kind of thing happens a lot here. Why the hell Mack seems intent on encouraging you to stay here, maybe being subjected to the same sort of treatment, I don't know!'

'Have you been friends for long?' Melissa asked.

'We met in Ballarat, in Victoria. I was living off the cards in those days; not very successfully. I couldn't meet some gambling debts I'd run up, and was in a bar having my face rearranged by my creditors when Mack decided to intervene.' Despite his annoyance at his friend, David's voice softened perceptibly. 'He didn't know me from Adam then, but he's always been one to rescue drowning kittens and underdogs. He was a miner and I was a gambler, but we liked each other right from the start. He talked me into coming to mine with him on his claim in Ballarat for six months, and then...there was some trouble in Melbourne, and I booked our passages to Auckland. I wanted to come and see old Uncle Toby, so...here we are.'

'What sort of trouble in Melbourne? With William Price?'

'William? No, nothing like that,' David said much too quickly, and Melissa remembered that he had never been very good at hiding his emotions. 'But, listen, coz,' he continued carefully, 'if you really are set on staying here, it would be best if you didn't mention what...er...what William Price did on your way out to the Arrow. It would cause trouble, you see, and that's something we have to avoid. Do you understand?'

'No.' She looked searchingly at his taut face. 'I don't understand at all. Why should he be allowed to get away with what he tried to do to Lachlan? And to me? It was attempted murder, David!'

'No, coz, you can't say that,' David hushed her anxiously. 'It might have *looked* like that...'

'Of course it looked like that! That's what happened!' she said incredulously. 'What's the matter with you? Why don't you want William to be punished?'

'Melissa, *please*!' he implored her. 'Just listen to me! I can't tell you why for a number of reasons. You'll have to trust Mack and me when we ask you to act as if nothing has happened, and to try to forget it if you can. It's more important than I can possibly say. Please, Melissa?'

She hesitated for a second and then reluctantly nodded. 'Very well, if it's so important, I promise I won't say another word. But can you at least tell me something about William Price? Lachlan told me that he owns a bar here in Arrowtown?'

'The Pink Palace. It's one of about five that he owns in the goldfields. He's a very wealthy man—most of it is family money from England, but he also makes a fortune from his bars. Here at the Regency we just sell drinks, and settle for a modest profit. William also sells... Well, he sells women, and out here that's a commodity that lonely men are prepared to pay a lot of money for,' he ended, his face red with embarrassment.

'I see.' The reason for William's apparently kind offer of transport suddenly became clear to her. 'I almost accepted a ride from him in Dunedin. Do you mean that I would have ended up...'

'In one of his bars. Yes, that wouldn't have been the first time he'd have picked up a young woman fresh off the ships like that. And, from what I hear, once you work for William Price, you never get away.'

She shuddered at the thought of her lucky escape. 'And he's here—in Arrowtown?'

'Fortunately not. His bars are all run by managers, so we very rarely see him. And there's a rumour that he's gone back to England to settle the estate now that his mother's died. With luck, we might never see him again,' he ended fervently.

Melissa prayed that that would be true. It would make life so much easier for her here if she could manage truly to forget the dreadful journey to Arrowtown.

They sat in silence for a while, and then David said, 'Lissy, I have to ask you something. What... What

happened between you and Mack on the way out here?
Was that true about how he got the bruise?'

'Yes, it was. I didn't mean... It *was* an accident,
David. I didn't mean to hurt him.'

'It's all right, really,' David soothed her quickly. 'I'm
pleased you did—it's high time somebody did.'

She blinked. 'You're pleased that I hit him? David, I
almost killed him!'

David sighed. 'I'm sure it was no more than he deserved. I know he's my best friend, and I'd happily go
to hell and back for him, I really would, but he's just
been asking for something like this! He had a bad experience with a woman in Melbourne, and since then
he's been completely impossible where women are concerned. With luck, you've knocked a bit of sense into
his head, and he'll think twice before trying to seduce
every woman he meets! I think you did him a favour, if
the truth be known.'

'Oh.' Melissa gave a short, mirthless laugh. 'I had no
idea he was so much of a womaniser! I didn't realise
that... any woman...'

'I'm sorry, coz. I had to tell you.' David gave her hand
a warm squeeze. 'But I think he'll have got the message
to leave you alone now, don't you?'

Far from being reassured, Melissa felt an uncom-
fortable gnawing sense of guilt. Lachlan had not been
entirely to blame for what had happened at Jamieson's.
And David's description of him as a ruthless womaniser
did not tally with the Lachlan she had come to know of
late as a considerate and even kindly man. It was, all in
all, a most confusing situation to find herself in.

The door was suddenly flung open, and half-a-dozen
burly men appeared, dragging a piano. They pulled it
across to stand near the bar, its heavy base digging deep
grooves in the packed dirt floor. It was garishly decorated with lashings of gilt, and there was a large hole in
the wood above the keyboard that looked as if a fist had
gone through it. Once it was in position, Lachlan opened
the lid, and the men all looked at her expectantly.

'Melissa,' David said warningly as she moved towards it, 'I think you ought to think about this first.'

But she had never been one to resist an open piano, and, as if drawn by strings, she tentatively put out a hand and played a few notes. It needed tuning, but it was not too dreadful. A chair appeared behind her as if by magic, and she sat, fingers poised. 'Any requests?' she asked lightly, to break the anticipatory silence. She had no idea why she should be so nervous of playing before these rough men, who were no doubt all tone-deaf anyway, but she sensed that this was an audition of sorts, and an important one, too.

'Do you know "The Rose of Tralee"?' suggested one man.

She ran her fingers over the keys and then started to play the tune. After the first few bars, she began to hum along and then broke into song, her strong contralto filling the small room. As the last notes faded away, she looked up at the man who had requested the song. 'Was that all right?'

But he could not speak, his Adam's apple bobbing up and down with emotion, and he only nodded enthusiastically.

'Ay, fine miss, fine!' applauded the others. 'Can you play "Oh, Susanna"? How about "Clementine"?'

The Californian goldminers' songs had been popular with some of her pupils in London (although Melissa privately thought them rather vulgar), and she was able to oblige them. These songs they sang robustly themselves, almost drowning out the tinny notes of the piano. More and more requests flowed in, and she eventually realised that there were a great many men propping themselves up against the piano, mugs in hand, breaths redolent of whisky and beer as they bellowed out their favourite songs. Looking over her shoulder, she saw the place was in fact crammed full of miners. David and Lachlan were in their shirt-sleeves, working efficiently behind the bar filling the mugs as they were banged down on the counter. Lachlan, catching her eye, winked encouragingly, and she smiled back, oddly pleased by his approval. At last she grew tired, her back and fingers aching, and she got to her feet.

A chorus of good-natured complaints arose, but David was at her side in an instant. 'Melissa, come and rest. You must be exhausted!'

She blinked at him wearily. 'What's the time?'

'Late.' He led her over to a woman who was sitting talking to a group of men at one of the tables. 'Coralie, can you take my cousin to her tent now?'

'Sure thing, David. Melissa, isn't it? I'm sure you'd like a bite to eat as well, wouldn't you, honey?'

Her accent was unmistakably American. She was about Melissa's age, with a pretty, cheerful face, and a truly remarkable bosom rather perilously supported with a green corset. A yellow skirt that was far too short to be decent completed the outfit. Her dark hair was artfully curled down her back and decorated with a couple of pink feathers. Somehow she did not look in the least out of place in the Regency.

Melissa had not realised how stiflingly hot it was in the bar until she stepped out into the night air. She had been perspiring in the heavy clothes she had worn for travelling, and now felt grimy as well as tired and hungry. She followed Coralie blindly across the camp to a small tent pitched near a low-burning fire. Crawling inside, she found her carpet-bag and the clean soft blankets that someone—bless them!—had thoughtfully laid out. By the time Coralie returned with a bowl of stew, she was already fast asleep.

And so the routine of the next few months was set. At night she played in the hot, crowded bar; sometimes singing, sometimes simply playing as the miners themselves sang, and sometimes accompanied by an impromptu orchestra of fiddle, harmonica or an accordian. She enjoyed these times the most, for then they would play old English, Scottish or Irish airs, sweet and wild. Sometimes it was a polka or a waltz, and the saloon-girls would partner the diggers in a hilarious parody of a European ballroom, occasionally in their exuberance spilling out of the Regency and on to the stony banks of the Arrow, twirling and pirouetting about the tents. She worked long and very hard hours, occasionally even serving behind the bar. To her surprise, she found that she actually grew to enjoy the bantering contact with the customers as her confidence grew, and as they came to know her.

Her days were spent in sleeping late, taking walks in the hills around the camp and sitting and gossiping with the six saloon-girls from the Regency. They had welcomed her warmly and without curiosity, and she in turn liked their open, no-nonsense approach to life. The painted, laughing women in the outrageous clothes who served behind the bar and danced the night away with the diggers were completely different from the tired women who sat in the morning sun outside their tents, sipping coffee and wryly discussing the world and its inhabitants.

Melissa found them an ideal source of information about the camp: there seemed to be nothing that the women either did not know or could not find out. They knew which diggers had struck it lucky and which were having to go back home penniless. It was expensive to live in Arrowtown, where everything—food, clothing, equipment—had to be brought in over the mountains by pack-horse. Most of the diggers were lucky, however, and some of the ways they found to spend their new wealth were quite astonishing; Melissa had seen for herself how a miner in the money would sometimes order the best French champagne for the house by the crateful. It was no wonder that Lachlan had to make the trip into Dunedin at least once a fortnight for supplies, in addition to the beer they bought from a brewery up the Molyneux River.

There was an astounding array of entertainment available—other 'grog-shanties' like the Regency, as well as gambling houses, beer-halls, gin-palaces and even a music hall. Most of the 'hotels' were unlicensed and sold liquor seven days a week, despite the occasional forays of officialdom from the police based at Dunstan. The miners had money to spend, even in the wilderness. Melissa was pleased to find that, as the establishments of Arrowtown went, the Regency was regarded by the saloon-girls as a good place to work. As David had told her earlier, the women were employed only to serve drinks to the customers, and a blind eye was turned to any other services they might elect to provide. She gathered that things were very different in some of the other bars—the very mention of William Price's name was enough to make the women spit on the ground in disgust. She became used to the colourful expressions and raciness of the saloon-girls' conversation, and while she could not approve of their way of life, she did come to understand that, for most of them, it was the only life they had ever known, and was often an escape from appalling poverty and hopelessness. At least here in the goldfields they were independent and had money in their pockets, and were also in demand as wives for the many miners who had decided to settle down as farmers or businessmen in the Colony. There, but for the grace of God, go I, she thought, and tried her hardest not to judge them.

She knew that David did not like her talking to the other women, fearing that they would be an unhealthy influence on her, but she was astute enough to realise that, for all their frank ways, the women still regarded her as an outsider and exercised a measure of discretion in what they talked to her about. David was also worried that she would be upset by harassment from the diggers, but in fact she found that she was treated with increasing respect by the men. After a few days, the comments and whistles subsided and she was soon able to move about the camp without fear of unwelcome approaches. She commented on this one day to Coralie, who burst out laughing.

'Your reputation went before you, honey!'

'I beg your pardon?'

'Our big Scotsman is the one you have to thank! After you left the Regency that first night, he told everyone who had given him that crack on his head. We'd all been trying to find out who'd had the nerve to cosh him, and the men were real impressed to find out it was *you!* No, don't look like that,' she said, as she saw Melissa's face. 'Mack's a real discreet lad—made it clear it was because he hadn't treated you like the lady you are. That *was* how it happened, wasn't it?' Her eyes twinkled mischievously as she analysed Melissa's expression. 'Don't you worry, honey—now rumour has it you'll defend your honour to the death if need be, and if you've got the guts to thump someone Mack's size, anyone else'd get carried out feet first. You see?'

Melissa saw. Another instance of Lachlan's kindness, and not something that made it easier to cope with him. If only he would show her something of the anger and aggression that he had that night at Jamieson's Inn, she could justify her low opinion of him. But she soon found that he had a reputation for fairness, and a dry, self-deprecating wit that made him universally liked and respected by the miners. He also had a penchant for practical jokes, and she discovered that she was held to be completely blameless for hitting him over the head with an axe for his impudence. There were few reasons for them to be alone together these days, anyway. The business decisions regarding the hotel were always made in David's presence, and, moreover, Lachlan was away so often on the Dunedin run that she saw him only for one week out of every two. But still, he unsettled her. He had only to get in the same group of people for her to be uncomfortably aware of his presence. She had only to hear his voice with its faint American inflection for her heart to skip a beat. He was not a man to be ignored—but she did try her hardest.

Until the golden autumn day that she was down beside the part of the Arrow that was commonly used for washing clothes. She had been in the camp for six weeks, and had developed a daily routine of coming here, enjoying the mild feeling of satisfaction that this simple housekeeping ritual gave her in an otherwise unordered world. She had finished her washing, and the small pile of wrung-out clothes was sitting on a rock beside the river while she cooled off by paddling in the water, her dress up round her knees, watching the silvery ripples about her ankles.

'Hello.'

She started, not having heard Lachlan approach. He was sitting on the bank, watching her, and she was suddenly very conscious of her bared legs. 'Hello,' she replied shyly, feeling like a little girl. She scrambled out and came to sit a short distance from him, modestly pulling her dress down as she did so. It was the same blue dress that she had worn at Jamieson's, and, as she saw him looking at it, she knew he remembered it, too.

He felt in his back pocket and pulled out a thin, folded newspaper. 'Have you seen this?'

It was a copy of the *Lake Wakatipu Mail*, the small Otago paper that kept them in touch with events both local and abroad, and she took it eagerly. The front page was devoted entirely to the celebrations planned for a nearby mining town when it changed its name from Canvastown to Queenstown that month. 'The Camp', as it was called, had, unlike most of the other mining towns, sprung up around several established farms and consequently possessed a strong element of family and community spirit that was largely lacking in the other male-dominated encampments. As part of their move towards respectability, the people of Canvastown had decided on a name with more dignified and permanent connotations—and were throwing a town-wide party to celebrate.

'It sounds marvellous fun,' Melissa said wistfully, as she read the list of events planned for the celebrations.

'It does, doesn't it?' he agreed. 'I've been planning to go over for some time to register a claim on the Shotover—would you like to come with me tomorrow?'

'Is David coming?'

'It's you I'm asking—not David.'

'I couldn't possibly go with you unchaperoned,' she said firmly. 'What if we had to spend the night? And, besides, it wouldn't be proper.'

Idly he picked up a pebble and turned it over and over in his long, strong fingers. 'Are you so worried about your reputation?' he asked at last.

'It's *your* reputation I'm worried about,' she responded tartly, and he raised one eyebrow in amused surprise.

'So sanctimonious, Miss Edwards? I seem to recall that you weren't always so prim.'

She flushed. 'You took advantage of my ignorance on that occasion!'

'You knew what you were doing.'

'I did not! But...that is hardly the point. You can hardly expect me to travel alone with you to Canvastown after...what happened!'

'And what happened?' He waited a moment for her to answer before continuing, 'Nothing happened, did it? And nothing will happen this time, either.'

'I can't believe you.'

'Look, lass, you'll be perfectly safe with me—you have my word on that. You might not take that seriously, but I do. I'd like you to come with me; I like your company, and I think you'd enjoy the trip. I have no ulterior motives, believe me.'

He seemed sincere, and she was sorely tempted—it would be wonderful to leave the camp for a while. But she knew she could not go. 'I'm sorry, but the answer is still no.'

'Very well. What if I ask Coralie to come with us. Will that satisfy you?'

Despite herself, she giggled, trying to imagine Coralie in the role of chaperon and failing completely. 'No, it would have to be David.'

With a heavy sigh of defeat, he got up. 'David it is, then. We'll be away at dawn. I'll have a horse saddled for you beside my tent.'

He walked away without looking back, leaving her in a small glow of triumph. She had won, for once! He was not so hard to handle, after all; all she had to do was be firm and stand her ground, and he would give way. It was easy.

* * *

It wasn't quite so easy, as she found when she met him outside his tent in the soft light of dawn the next morning, her blanket-roll in her hands. He was saddling the second of his two horses, and he took her bundle to secure to the back of the saddle.

'Hello, girl,' she said softly to the mare he was saddling for her, fondling the soft nose, relishing the prospect of riding a horse again.

'Her name's Maud.' Lachlan indicated the other, larger, mare with a nod of his head. 'That's Maggie. I've got no side-saddle, I'm afraid,' he said, looking at her wide skirts. 'You'll find it much easier in a man's saddle, anyway, with the kind of terrain we'll be going over. Do you have a pair of trousers?'

She gasped at the very suggestion. 'Trousers? Certainly not!'

'Then you'll need some.' David's tent was pitched next to his, and he bent down to reappear with a pair of David's moleskins. He held them up for her inspection. 'These look reasonably clean, and you and David are pretty much of a height.' As she hesitated, he added in exasperation, 'You can always put your skirt on before we get to Canvastown, lass. Come on now—don't be coy! We've got a long way to go!'

She was back in a couple of minutes, clutching her discarded skirt to her front and feeling extremely self-conscious at the shape of her lower limbs being so revealed.

Lachlan, however, seemed to find it much more amusing than titillating. 'Very stylish! Just take off that silly bonnet of yours, though, will you, and put this on.' He carefully placed one of David's wide-brimmed felt hats on her head in place of her soft cotton bonnet, and nodded to himself in approval. He wrestled her skirt from her reluctant hands and added it to the bed-roll.

'Where's David's horse?'

He smiled slightly as he tightened the girth. 'David's a bit indisposed this morning. I'm not sure he's coming with us.' He looked past her to David's tent. 'Morning, Coralie.'

Melissa was shocked to see Coralie clamber out of David's tent, clad only in a rather stained pink satin wrap; she had no idea that David was one of Coralie's customers.

'Mack,' Coralie greeted him with a yawn.

'Is David all right? Is he coming?' Melissa demanded, and without waiting for a reply, bent down to peer into his tent. Then she rather wished she had not. Her cousin was lying stark naked on his back, snoring erratically and smelling strongly of liquor and vomit. She hastily backed out, her face scarlet.

'Not a pretty sight, is he?' Coralie sympathised. 'You shouldn't have kept him up so late last night drinking, Mack. You know he can't take it.'

'Belt up, Coralie, there's a good lass,' Lachlan said equably, as Melissa turned to glare at him accusingly. His hand shot out and grasped her wrist as she began to back away. 'Up you get, Melissa.'

'No! You...I...!' She pulled back from his grasp, but when it became clear that that was ineffectual, she resorted to trying to twist her hand free. He released her immediately to grab her wrist and unceremoniously hoist her on to Maud's back.

He put a restraining hand firmly on her stomach. 'Now—stay there.'

She hesitated, aware that to jump off in her present situation would necessitate another unseemly struggle and even more physical contact with him. Far from coming to her aid, Coralie had wandered off unconcernedly to the far side of the camp towards her own tent. Melissa watched her go, and cursed her own gullibility. She should have known that he would pull something like this!

Lachlan swung himself into his saddle, taking the reins of her horse to ride close in case she should try to break free. He picked a way for them through the camp and across the river, and all the time she rode beside him and hated him for his arrogance, his rudeness and his deceit!

'What's the matter, Melissa?'

'Nothing's the matter.'

'Yes, it is. Your face is as long as your boots, lass. It's going to be a grand day, and I'd hate anything to spoil it, so why don't you tell me what the problem is, and maybe I can do something about it?'

She shook her head defiantly, but he looked so sincerely concerned that she could not help but burst out, 'It's David. With—With ...'

'With Coralie?'

'Yes.' She bit her lip, embarrassed to speak to him about such a thing. 'I—I didn't know they were...lovers.'

He shrugged dismissively. 'Then you're the only person in the camp not to know—they've been together for a long time now. What's the problem?'

'But Coralie is a ...' She could not say the word, and she could see that Lachlan was determined not to help her. 'You don't care, do you!'

'It's none of my damned business,' he said flatly. 'And neither is it yours.'

'But all this time he's been lecturing me about how I must and mustn't behave here, and all the time he was... He's no better than you are!'

His hand shot out to grasp her wrist as she began to dismount. 'No better, maybe—but he's no worse. Now calm down, lass, and remember where you are. I know we seem amoral to you, but most of the diggers here have left a home, a family, loved ones to come here. You'd have to be made of stone not to get lonely sometimes—to need someone else. Can't you understand that?'

'Of course I can!' she snapped, wrenching her hand back and making a great show of readjusting her sleeve. 'I lived for years by myself in an attic. But I never...I never found I had to...'

'Well, maybe you never had the opportunity,' he said softly, mischief in his eyes. 'Until now.'

'I—I don't know what you expect from me on this trip...' she began, but he shook his head.

'As I told you before, your company, that's all. Now, lass, let's make a bargain, shall we? It seems we can't

exchange more than a half-dozen words without getting
into an argument, and I don't think it needs to be like
that. Shall we try our damnedest to be friends now?' He
put out his hand.

After a moment she took it, but without much conviction as to the viability of their pact. For all his ge-
niality, Lachlan was as easy to sway as the mountains
around, and, given her own stubbornness, she had no
great hopes of matters improving between them.

He turned to urge his horse on again. Then, as they
began to climb the steep track cut into the mountain, he
turned back to grin at her, and at the sight of the laughter
shining in his eyes, she felt the hard knot of anger in
her stomach start to dissolve. What was it about him
that affected her so? Despite herself, she felt the ends
of her mouth twitch upwards and she had to clamp them
firmly down again.

'Are you a good rider?' he asked.

'I used to be, but until I came across the Dunstans, I
hadn't ridden in years.'

'This gets a lot more interesting than the Dunstans,'
he promised, and he was right. After half an hour of
following the path, it literally disappeared, and she had
to follow Lachlan blindly as he led the way through damp
narrow gullies lined with ferns and ponga trees and then
up across bluffs so steep that she could only close her
eyes in terror and leave it to his sure-footed horses to
pick their way. They dismounted only the once, in order
to traverse what looked to her to be a sheer rock-face,
and when she tried to remount, her legs had turned to
jelly. Lachlan was at her side in a second, helping her
into the saddle and not commenting on her set white
face, and for this she was grateful. She was determined
not to display her more cowardly side to him, of all
people. She was congratulating herself on her silent self-
control until they reached Arthur's Point, where they
had to cross the lower reaches of the notorious Shotover
River.

'I'm not going over that!' she quavered in terror.

A suspended bridge of rope and wood, some thirty yards long, swung menacingly over a sheer-sided, deep canyon. Below that raged a faster torrent than she could ever have believed possible, its surging fury seeming to batter the narrow rock walls as if seeking to break free of their confines. Droplets of spray settled on her face even where she stood high above, and a shimmering rainbow appeared to span the banks in a duplication of the precarious looking man-made bridge.

Lachlan looked up from putting hoods over the horses' heads. 'Of course you're going over that—even the horses manage it!'

'Yes—but you're blindfolding them!'

He reached for his neckerchief. 'Well, if you think it will help...'

'No!' Her knees finally gave way, and she sat down abruptly on the ground beside Maud. Even the ground seemed to vibrate with the power of the thundering water just yards from her feet. She hated this country—no matter what men did to it, no matter how many people lived here, it seemed that there was no way whereby this wilderness could ever be tamed or civilised. Usually that very feeling of her own insignificance thrilled her, but on this occasion it had gone too far and she found herself heartily wishing for the gentle delights of the English countryside where rivers were more sedate and knew their place. Generally, the nice safe bridges could be crossed without fear for one's life.

'You don't like heights very much, do you?' Lachlan asked, coming to sit beside her.

'Are you surprised—after the time I nearly went over that cliff at Jessop's Pass?'

'No, that was a nasty experience for you. I just don't understand why you're allowing yourself to be defeated as easily as this. What has happened to your usual policy of charge in and think later?'

'I've met my match, I suppose,' she said miserably. 'Please don't laugh at me, Lachlan—I can't cross that river.'

He did not answer, but raised his hand in salute to a prospector coming down the track towards them. The man gave them a cheery greeting before deftly blind-folding his heavily laden mule, just as Lachlan had done, and then setting off without any hesitation whatsoever. Melissa watched, holding her breath, as the rope-bridge swung and lurched, but within a minute the prospector was safely on the other side and removing his horse's blindfold.

'You see? It can be done!' Lachlan appealed to her, but she remained unconvinced until, at last, with a sigh of resignation, he tethered Maud to a rock and took Maggie's reins. 'Well, I can't force you! I'll be back before dark.'

'You wouldn't go without me!' She sprang to her feet, trying to see if he was bluffing, coming to the rapid con-clusion that he was not.

Five minutes later she was hanging on for dear life to the damp hand-ropes, swinging wildly above the foaming water. As the bridge could take the weight of only one horse at a time, Lachlan had gone ahead with his and now stood waiting for her on the other bank. His voice floated encouragingly to her over the loud roar of the river. 'That's it lass—take it one foot at a time. You're almost there!'

She realised that she was forgetting to breathe, and took in a great shuddering gasp of air. Sweat trickled down the back of her neck and she dared for a moment to release one of the hand-ropes to wipe away the sweat escaping from under her hat-band to her eyes. Behind her, Maud whinnied nervously, gently nudging her arm with her nose. Somehow the horse's reliance on her gave her courage. Looking steadily in front of her and not down, she inched her way forward until she was at last able to scramble up the last few yards and throw herself into Lachlan's waiting arms.

'Good girl! I knew you could do it!' He hugged her tightly.

'I don't believe it! I can't believe I didn't fall in!' she exulted.

He dropped a brotherly kiss on her forehead. 'You're a game wee lass under all that twittering, aren't you?' he said, in such an admiring tone that she decided against disagreeing.

They mounted and rode on over easier country, enabling them to ride side-by-side. As they went, Lachlan began to engage Melissa in conversation, pointing out places of interest, telling her the names of some of the birds and plants they passed. He was an informed, charming conversationalist when he chose to be, and she began to enjoy his company thoroughly. It was growing to be another hot, cloudless day and the sun was approaching its zenith when at last they reached the brow of a hill, and there, like a glittering sapphire in the sun, Lake Wakatipu lay below. The mountain range that was so justly named the Remarkables towered above, their almost perpendicular sides appearing to plunge dramatically into the ice-fed waters at their feet. It looked like her idea of the Norwegian fjords, the Swiss Alps and the wildest parts of the Scottish highlands all put together into a landscape of such intense beauty that it literally took one's breath away.

The township of Queenstown nestled whitely on the shore. There was the inevitable collection of tents dotted around the outskirts, but in the heart of the town were many substantial wooden and stone buildings, as well as cob-cottages made of tussock and mud-bricks. It came as a surprise to Melissa to remember that not everyone in the world lived in draughty tents or shanties with canvas roofs. There was even a large jetty projecting well out into the lake, where the ferry, which was Queenstown's link with the rest of the country, was moored. Despite its isolation, she found herself envying the people here for living in paradise and yet still being a little closer to civilisation. Melissa went behind a rock to change back into her skirt and bonnet, and then they descended to the township.

They led their horses down the main street, which ran directly down to the lake-front. Strung across the street was a large banner proclaiming 'Welcome to

Queenstown'. Bunting and Union Jacks hung from every available space, and a number of people were busily setting up trestle-tables further down the street. Children—the first she had seen since leaving Dunedin—darted around excitedly, startling the horses and getting in the way of the grown-ups. They stabled the horses and went to find the Claims Office. When they did, it was to find its door firmly closed and a sign hanging from the handle stating that the office would not be open until two o'clock that afternoon—some three hours away.

'Everything's closed for the celebrations,' someone explained, and Lachlan looked at Melissa with a small frown.

'It could make it too late to get back today; I don't want to be travelling that route in the dark. Still, we are here for the celebrations, so let's go and see what's happening.'

They were drawn by the noise to an area that had been set up on the outskirts of the town and were able to witness a number of the diverse competitions in progress—from sheep-shearing to wood-chopping—all the competitors being enthusiastically encouraged by the spectators. Then there was a tug-of-war to be held between the citizens of Queenstown and the visitors, and someone slapped Lachlan on the back.

'You should be worth two of the opposition! How about giving us a hand?' He was a jovial-looking man of middle years who could not have been anything other than a farmer and who was yet another Scot.

Within a few minutes, Lachlan was lending his back with a will with the other visitors against a dozen citizens. His side eventually lost, although there were some good-natured suspicions voiced aloud that the match had been thrown in deference to the hosts of the celebrations. At any rate, the result was a popular one, and the losers were generously applauded as they rejoined the crowds.

They agreed to stroll around the lake-side for a while, before the celebrations started in earnest, and made their leisurely way along the shore until the sound of the crowds in the township became nothing more than a cheerful murmur. At length they came to a large flat rock that projected out over the lake, and simultaneously turned to walk out on to it. Heedless of the dust on her skirt, Melissa leaned over to dabble her fingers in the clear blue water while Lachlan sat beside her, studying the mountains soaring above. After a while, she turned to look at him in amusement.

'You seem to be mesmerised by those hills! What are you thinking about?'

'I'm thinking what a grand country this would be for farming. All that land, all that grass—and scarcely an animal in sight. It must be heaven to farm here. Hard— but heaven,' he told her.

'Farming?' She stared at him in surprise. 'No one could farm here, surely? It's far too steep and rugged— all the animals would drop off the hillside!'

He laughed at her. 'Not the sheep, lass—they'd thrive. And the cattle would do well enough in the high-country, too, if you were growing them for beef and not milk.' He proceeded to explain high-country farming to her, quoting herd-numbers and heads-per-acre with an enthusiasm that left her in no doubt about his background.

'Why on earth did you ever leave farming?' she asked, when he finally paused for breath.

'Farming? What makes you think I was ever a farmer?'

She was stung by the evasive look she saw in his eyes. 'It's perfectly obvious that you used to be a farmer,' she said sternly. 'What isn't obvious is why you're not now. What happened?'

He shrugged. 'I went off to see the world instead, lass. Many men do.' He grinned at her. 'And a few women, too.'

'But to end up running a bar! It's not something you enjoy doing, is it?'

'No. I hate it.' His instantaneous response came directly from the heart and seemed to take even him aback.

She was suddenly aware of the undercurrent of discontent beneath his good-humoured surface that she had exposed for a second with her innocent question. Intrigued, she persisted. 'Why don't you go back? Aren't you ever homesick?'

'Homesick? Ay, I get homesick even after nine years,' he said bitterly. 'Sometimes I...' He broke off and looked away, and she could see that he was struggling to compose himself.

At once she felt contrite at having brought him low like that, and impulsively put a hand on his. 'I'm so sorry—I realise that you don't like talking about yourself, but I know so little about you. Please forgive my curiosity if it was ill-mannered.'

He looked down at her hand lying in his, and smiled slightly. 'Nothing about you is ill-mannered, Melissa. It's I who am at fault. Sometimes I forget that you're from a completely different world from mine.'

She did not know quite what he meant, but said warmly, 'But I am in your world, now!'

For a moment he was very still, a strange expression in his eyes, and then he withdrew again behind the mask of easy banter. 'I hope not, lass. I'd hate to think you had fallen as far as that.'

He led her back to the township, and somehow it seemed perfectly natural to leave her hand in his as they walked. As if regretting his earlier evasiveness, he now became more forthcoming about the claim he was staking. 'It's on the upper Shotover—damned near inaccessible—and it will be a pig of a site to mine. But I keep coming back to it; it *feels* right, somehow. I've never had that feeling about any other claim. After California and Ballarat, I swore I'd never go mining again, and I still don't know that I shall.' He shook his head at his own folly. 'But mining is a funny thing—like drink or gambling, it can get in your blood sometimes, and even though you know you shouldn't, you keep coming back for more.'

'I've often thought you had a hint of an American accent,' she remarked. 'How long were you in California?'

'Five years or so. And you—did you live all your life in London?' He had successfully diverted the conversation away from the topic of himself once more, and they chatted companionably enough all the way back to the township.

Once there, they could not help becoming drawn into the festivities now taking place in the streets. Plates were thrust into their hands and piled high with steaming pork, potatoes and the famous eel-meat from the Molyneux River, all cooked Maori-style in a huge *hangi*—a deep pit in which the food had been slowly baking since early that morning. In no time at all they were separated and seated at different tables down either side of the main street, surrounded by Queenstowners all determined to enjoy themselves and to extend the very best of their hospitality to the town's visitors.

Even here, there was an acute shortage of women, and so Melissa was immediately engaged in conversation by several of the town's womenfolk, pleased to see a new female face. She was thoroughly enjoying herself, and was busy admiring the very new baby of the banker's wife next to her, when Lachlan appeared at her side.

'We have a problem, I'm afraid. I've just seen the officer in charge of the Claims Office suffering a surfeit of celebration. We'll have to spend the night here and put in the claim tomorrow morning.'

'Is there a hotel where we...I mean *I*...can stay to-night?' she asked, anxious that he not misunderstand her question. The prospect of staying overnight in this delightful place dismayed her not at all, but she knew that she had to be very careful not to put herself in yet another compromising situation with Lachlan. After this morning's episode in Arrowtown, his behaviour had been impeccable, but she was coming to know him well enough to know that it was not a situation she could realistically expect to last.

'I've asked. All the hotels are completely full.'

He looked so sincerely concerned that she dismissed any suspicions she might have harboured as being quite unworthy. Then she became aware of the woman beside her patting her arm and saying something.

'. . . and my daughters would love the company of another young woman. There's always room in our house for one more,' she finished.

'Thank you! How very kind,' Melissa said to her, and turned to Lachlan. Was she imagining it, or was the look on his face just a trifle *too* polite? She smiled sweetly at him, and, as if reading her suspicious mind, he raised his eyebrows in mock offence and excused himself.

The small band were just starting to tune up their instruments, as the food was cleared away and the tables pushed back to make room for the dancing. As she covertly watched Lachlan helping the townsfolk to do this, a young girl came up, obviously urged on by a couple of giggling companions, and shyly spoke to him. Melissa saw him smile down at her and gallantly take her arm. As the band began to play a lively reel, he put his arm round her waist and they were one of the first couples to start the dancing. For such a big man, he was light on his feet. He bent his head courteously to hear something the young girl said, and the unabashed admiration on her face was clear enough.

He seems to be very used to that kind of feminine reaction, Melissa thought sourly, wishing that the other girl would do the decent thing and leave him alone. Jamieson had been quite right when he had talked of Lachlan's attraction for, and to, women. All he had to do was smile, and they came running. Lothario! She realised that she was biting her nails, and took her fingers out of her mouth. She was not jealous, she told herself—it was simply discourteous of him to leave her alone like this after bringing her all the way out here! The polite cough behind her was turning into a paroxysm, and she turned to see that there was not one but a number of gentlemen waiting to request a dance. For the next couple of hours she hardly had her feet still as she twirled and skipped with a succession of admiring partners to every country dance she knew, and many she did not. Lachlan, too, seemed to find a partner for each dance, despite the dearth of women. Over the head of the banker's wife he gave her a broad wink, as an enthusiastic partner steered her determinedly up the street in a polka, and mouthed the word 'supper' at her. She nodded agreement, her earlier fit of pique entirely gone.

When at last the band stepped down to enable everyone to have supper, Lachlan was there at her side, steering her away from the crowds to a quiet spot down beside the lake. 'Enjoying yourself?' he asked, a laugh in his voice as he took in her flushed cheeks and sparkling eyes, and the hair beginning to come loose from the coil at the nape of her neck.

'I can't remember when I've ever enjoyed myself so much!' she gasped, fanning herself with her hands in an ineffectual effort to cool herself.

They found a quiet seat on some boulders well away from everyone else, and he returned to the supper-tables to reappear a couple of minutes later with two glasses of wine.

Night was falling in one of the long golden twilights typical of Central Otago, and there seemed little chance of the festivities in the street winding down for many hours yet. Lamps had been lit and placed around the lake-front, and the lights on the ferry tied up at the jetty threw long streamers of gold across the mirror-still water.

'I can still hardly believe that this place is real, and not some wonderful dream,' she said at last, turning to him and realising that he must have been watching her for some time.

'How strange. I was just thinking the same thing about you,' he said quietly, and the look on his face mesmerised her so that she could not pull her eyes away again. He reached out to brush her hair away from her face, his hand lingering on her cheek, and she knew for a certainty that he was going to kiss her.

Abruptly remembering her abysmal record of resistance to physical contact with him, she managed to turn her head away just in time. 'How—How very kind of

Mrs Barker to offer me a bed for the night,' she said unevenly, desperate to break the spell he was weaving between them. 'Where are you planning to sleep?'

He grinned, and moved back from her, acknowledging defeat for the moment. 'I'll be sleeping down here on the beach, I expect,' he answered cheerfully, squashing a mosquito on his arm neatly with his thumb. 'All alone with these little beggars for my only company.'

'I did try to make it very clear to you in Arrowtown that I would come here only with a chaperon,' she retorted. 'If you have any ideas about taking advantage of the situation, Mr MacGregor, I suggest you forget them!'

He looked both hurt and completely innocent. 'What a nasty mind you have, Miss Edwards!'

'Not at all. But my cousin has warned me about you.'

'I'll bet he has! But I find it amazing that for once you're actually taking some notice of someone else's advice.'

'I knew it! I knew you couldn't stay pleasant for much longer!' She began to get to her feet, but his hand was out, restraining her.

'Calm down, lass! Must you always be so damned touchy? Why not call it a truce and have another glass of wine and stay awhile?'

She hesitated for a moment, but his tone was so reasonable that she slowly sank back to the ground. 'I don't want another glass of wine, and I want you to take your hand off me,' she said petulantly. He obeyed instantly, and they sat in silence as the darkness gathered around them. It was very difficult—almost impossible—to sustain anger in these surroundings. When she turned to say as much to Lachlan, it was to find his eyes resting on her again. 'Why do you keep staring at me so?'

'I've told you—you're a beautiful lass. I like looking at you.'

'There are prettier girls back on the Arrow,' she bridled.

His eyebrows shot up in surprise. 'Fishing for compliments, Miss Edwards? That's not like you.' Then, before she could think of a suitable retort, he took her swiftly in his arms and kissed her.

She resisted for only one short second before melting willingly, sensuously against him. The feeling she had felt before—that of losing such delicious, delirious control of her body and her senses—took her over completely, but this time she almost welcomed it. It might be wrong, she knew it *was* wrong, and she would regret it later, but for this brief moment it was sheer heaven to be so desired and desirable, to want and be wanted with such fire. When at last he drew away, she took a deep, shuddering breath to compose herself. She knew that she should keep her wits about her; she knew that now he would suggest they find a more private place for their lovemaking. Now was her opportunity to decline firmly. But as she looked into his tender, shadowed face, she felt her lips aching with the loss of his, and suddenly she was not sure if she could refuse him this time.

'I'm sorry,' he said slowly. 'I didn't mean to do that at all.'

She blinked in surprise. 'You...didn't?'

He shook his head decisively. 'No. You're special, Melissa—much too special for some furtive coupling in the dark after a few drinks. I made that mistake once before with you, and I'm not about to repeat it. You deserve more than that.'

'I expect I do,' she agreed breathlessly, and turned away, her face flaming.

He took her chin in his fingers and turned her back to face him. 'I've offended you again, haven't I?'

She shrugged his hand away. 'Must you always be so...*blunt*?' she asked. 'My experience with the opposite sex has been negligible up until now, and you...I just don't know what you want of me.'

'That's why I'm being blunt,' he said gently. 'You're so very out of place here, so vulnerable, like a butterfly in a sandstorm. I don't want to hurt you and I don't want to frighten you away, but if I don't try to hold you, you're likely to flutter off again. I don't ever want you to misunderstand me again—so that's why I'm telling you as plainly as I can that you have nothing to fear from me.'

She could not doubt the sincerity of his words, but still she hesitated to believe him completely. The more she learned about this man, the less she knew, and the secrets he held from her, and the deeply-hidden violence she had once sensed in him, made her wary. Yet she could see nothing in his eyes but his desire for her to trust him.

'I...don't know,' she said at last. 'After this morning... Just what are your intentions? Are they honourable?'

'Absolutely,' he said promptly. 'At the moment.'

'And later?'

'That's entirely up to you, lass.' The tension had left his eyes, and he was laughing at her again. 'I'm putty in your hands, but can I suggest in the meantime that we call a truce? I'd very much like for us to be friends.'

'Friends?' She thought for a moment, and then nodded. 'Very well.' He took her hand and shook it like a man's. As he smiled down into her eyes, she felt suddenly and absurdly happy. 'I think it's time we went back to the dancing,' she said, to cover her confusion. 'We'll be confirming all the local prejudices about Arrowtowners being uncouth and uncivilised.'

'An excellent idea! Let's show them how we Arrowtowners can dance, then.' He helped her to her feet, keeping her hands in his. Then his eyes left hers to look over her head, back to where the band in the street had struck up again. She saw his face tighten.

'Oh, hell!' he said resignedly.

She turned. Making his way towards them, his face like thunder, was David.

CHAPTER FOUR

MELISSA STOPPED playing and took a sip from the glass of water that was always kept beside her piano in the evenings. It was stiflingly hot in the Regency tonight, despite the thin crisp ice on the ground outside. The men round the piano who had been bellowing out their favourite songs turned away to push through the crowded room to the bar for more refreshments. From a corner, voices rose above the hubbub in a quarrel over a game of cards that was taking place, and she looked anxiously at David working alone behind the bar. Lachlan had been gone for a week on the run to Dunedin, and she knew that David disliked being left as the sole man in charge of the Regency. Lachlan had greater physical presence than her cousin, and an earthy diplomacy which was invaluable in defusing the tense situations which so often arose among men who had drunk and wagered too much.

Coralie went over to where the argument was becoming louder, and soon her ringing laugh told them that she had managed to patch up the matter between the antagonists. Melissa saw David visibly relax. With a rowdier element now on the Arrow, Lachlan's absences were becoming times of increasing stress for them all. On the other hand, they had yet to have any serious trouble in the bar, and business had never been better. Lachlan had been serving behind the bar the previous week, when an event had occurred that was still being talked about, and which had already grown into one of the camp legends.

Among the many 'characters' at the Arrow was a massive Swede, who dwarfed even Lachlan in stature. He spoke very little English, and a misunderstanding had arisen at the Gold Office one day, when he had claimed that his gold was being under-weighed. He had almost killed the Gold Commissioner, and it had taken half a dozen men to subdue the giant. As there were only weekly visits by the Otago Constabulary to round up offenders, he was 'locked up', which meant that he was chained to a heavy log in a special 'gaol tent' situated in the middle of the camp, thus making all the Arrow miners jointly responsible for the prisoner. He appeared to be docile enough until he became both lonely and thirsty later that night. The miners singing round the piano had stopped in mid-song as the door of the Regency was ripped off its hinges and the Swede walked in, the log under one arm. There had not been a sound from anyone as he strode up to the bar, heaved the log on the counter and bellowed 'Visky!' David had stood rooted to the spot in shock, but Lachlan had perhaps recognised a kindred spirit and, shoulders shaking with laughter, had passed him an entire bottle without a word. No one had dared to intervene until the Swede had drunk his fill and then shambled back to the prison tent, his log still under his arm. To save wear and tear on the hotels' doors and bartops, he was released every night by common consent and restricted only by day until the constables came to collect him.

Over the heads of the miners at the bar, Melissa caught David's eye and indicated by sign language that she was going out for some fresh air. He merely acknowledged her with a curt nod before turning away, and she frowned slightly in frustration. It was four weeks now since he had found her and Lachlan together at Queenstown, and he was still brooding over the incident. He had been tired, hungry and furious then, his mood hardly sweetened by a massive hangover. She had been cowardly enough to excuse herself and flee to the township to find Mrs Barker, the banker's wife who had offered her hospitality for the night. What had taken place between the men she was not sure—they were both tight-lipped and uncommunicative the next morning, although she sensed that they had battled it out and come to some sort of understanding. David had retained all his anger at her until they were back in Arrowtown the following

afternoon, where, in the privacy of the deserted
Regency, he had given vent to all his feelings.

'How could you do it?' he had shouted at her. 'I've
warned you about Mack! How could you just go off like
that after all I've said, without me...'

'You were in no condition to come with us,' she said
as reasonably as she could manage. 'And I wanted to
see the Queenstown celebrations, David. I'm not a small
child, and you're not my guardian or my warden. I make
my own decisions.'

'Do you? Or did Mack make this one for you?'

'It was my decision,' she said firmly. And, she thought,
if she were to be completely honest with herself, she had
to admit that it *had* been her decision to leave Arrowtown
without David. Lachlan might have bullied her on to a
horse, but at any time she could have turned round and
returned to David. Her cousin's assumption of authority
over her had irked her then—now it positively angered
her.

'But you do realise what all the diggers think about
you now, don't you?' David said tersely. 'They all think
you're Mack's mistress. Is that what you wanted? For
everyone to think that you're no better after all than the
other women here? You had to fight so hard in the beginning to make a place for yourself in the camp—and
now you've gone and ruined it all!'

'I don't care,' she said defiantly and not quite truth-
fully. 'And if the men do think I'm Lachlan's mistress,
they're quite wrong. But I haven't noticed any change
in their attitude to me.'

'Because they think you're under Mack's protection.'
He sat down wearily at one of the tables. 'And that will
keep you safe enough—until he withdraws it.'

'Do you think he will?' she could not resist asking.

He was silent for a moment, looking at her steadily,
and then he shook his head. 'No. For all his faults, he'll
stand by you for as long as you need him. But your reputation has been shot to ruins now, coz—I hope you
understand that!'

'And I hope you understand that nothing happened between us at Queenstown. I know what you told me about Lachlan, but he had no intention of taking advantage of the situation, believe me!'

'I do believe you,' he said surprisingly. 'Mack told me the same thing, and he either tells you the truth or he tells you nothing at all. But the fact remains that you ignored my advice; you disobeyed me . . .'

'I didn't realise that I was your chattel!' she burst out indignantly. 'How dare you talk to me like that! I wouldn't presume to interfere with you spending the nights with Coralie!'

He looked genuinely indignant. 'That is quite different—I'm a man!'

She would have said much much more at this blatant display of bigotry when the door opened and Coralie herself walked in, ready to start work for the evening. Melissa and David, unsure whether she had overheard anything, fell silent, although their resentment and anger still hung in the air. She had tried to make amends by not seeing Lachlan alone any more, and for his part Lachlan did not appear to seek her out unduly. He continued to treat her only as a good friend and business partner, and none of them referred again to the Queenstown incident—but still David brooded.

The moon was hidden by a layer of heavy clouds, and the only light in the blackness came from the dozens of small fires dotted around the camp. Some of the quieter souls among the diggers were enjoying a leisurely brew of tea, or a late supper, or were simply sitting round the warmth of their fires, talking and singing. It had all become remarkably familiar to her over the past few months; the life might be hard here, but she had made a niche for herself, and some friends as well, and for the first time since her parents had died she felt oddly secure. It was partly due to her newly-found confidence and resourcefulness, but increasingly it was because of Lachlan and the strength and stability she drew from their new friendship. Just to know that, whenever he could, he would be there to support and care and make her laugh...

Yes, she thought in surprise, she was happy now, for the first time in many years.

Outside the Regency, she slipped over the ice-coated stones and almost fell. She had only a thin shawl for warmth, and decided to go back to her tent to fetch the heavy winter jacket Lachlan had bought her on his last trip to Dunedin, along with a pair of wool-lined boots. They had been meant to fit a small man, but Melissa did not need convincing that warmth would prove to be of greater importance soon than feminine trappings—it was not yet winter, and already the wind could cut to the bone.

As she thought of Lachlan, her hand went up automatically to touch the glossy green pendant on its thin leather band. He had surprised her with it the week before, tying it around her neck as she practised at the piano one morning. To her stammered thanks he had said nothing, but his smile told her that his gift was very special. It was greenstone, the New Zealand jade, and it hung like a cool caress at the base of her throat. She never took it off. He had bought it from Matt Pohatu, the Maori drover who always came across the Dunstan Range with him after the dray was stabled at the Dunstan Hotel. The two of them would load Matt's horses and mules with the liquor supplies and make the tortuous trip over the mountains to the Arrow. Matt's extensive family were also miners of the greenstone found so plentifully on the West Coast, and her pendant was a truly beautiful piece, flawless and lucid—and a constant reminder of the man who had given it to her.

A figure loomed quickly out of the darkness. She had hurriedly stepped aside for the man to pass, before she realised who it was.

'Matt? But it's late at night to be travelling! Where's Lachlan?' A thin prickle of fear ran down her spine as she saw the look of exhaustion on his tense perspiring face.

'Melissa—come quick! Trouble!' he gasped, his chest heaving.

She ran behind his solid form to where the mule-train stood waiting patiently on the outskirts of the camp, still loaded with the Regency supplies. She recognised Lachlan's horse Maggie, and her heart stopped as she saw the big body slumped over the saddle. At Melissa's sharp exclamation of horror, some miners from nearby tents came to see what had happened, and between them they carefully eased Lachlan off his horse and into a nearby tent. Someone brought a lamp, and by its light they laid him on a blanket on the ground. She whispered a quick prayer of gratitude that he was still alive, but when she lifted his thick jacket away from his body, the front of his shirt was drenched with blood. He opened his eyes as she bent over him, and in their grey depths there was a flash of recognition before they glazed over with pain and he fell back into unconsciousness.

'What happened to him?' she demanded desperately.

Matt looked sick with shock; he and Lachlan were close friends, and it was plain that he was as surprised and horrified as she was by the severity of Lachlan's wounds.

'I—I don't exactly know. We were crossing the Dunstans in the late afternoon. It was getting dark, and then suddenly one shot—only one—and until Mack dropped off his horse...I didn't even realise what had happened.'

'Bushrangers, d'you think?' someone asked behind them.

Matt shrugged, his expression confused. 'Mack had a rifle, as usual, but I don't carry one—I've never had the need for one before. It was a difficult bit of track we were on, and we were both concentrating on getting all the mules across, so I suppose we would have been easy pickings for anyone who wanted the mules. But I didn't see or hear anyone after the shot. It's almost as if...it was just Mack they were after.'

His voice trailed off, and Melissa looked at him in bewilderment as though the answer lay somewhere in his face. Lachlan had no enemies, that she knew of. Only...

But William Price would be well on his way to England by now. Who else could it be?

She began to try to ease back Lachlan's shirt where it was most heavily stained with blood, and where she guessed the wound must be. Someone handed her a small knife and she resorted to cutting away the material, reluctant to move him any more. Just below the left shoulder-blade was a hole—a surprisingly small hole—through which the blood was steadily seeping. She tried to stanch it with her shawl, for lack of anything else to hand, but it stained the thin silk within seconds. The sight of his blood covering her hands made her suddenly frantic.

'Please—can't someone do something? He's dying!'

Before anyone could answer, David's head appeared at the tent-flap, his face strained.

'Melissa, is he . . . ?'

'He's hurt badly. He's losing so much blood . . . and I don't know how to stop it. Can you find a doctor for him?'

'We're trying to find Splints Finney—if we're lucky, he might be in a condition to help.'

David did not sound particularly reassuring, and her heart sank as she realised why. Steve 'Splints' Finney was a likeable, knowledgeable man, and it was rumoured that he had once had a flourishing medical practice in his native Northumberland, but he was also an alcoholic, and they would be very fortunate indeed to find him sober enough to perform surgery. Sure enough, he was eventually found snoring loudly over a card-table in one of the hotels, and although he was taken down to the Arrow River and immersed repeatedly in its freezing waters, he could not be revived. In the tense silence after she had been told this devastating piece of news, she realised that the men crowded into the small tent around Lachlan's unconscious body were all looking at her expectantly.

'I can't do anything!' she burst out in frustration, angry that the mere fact of her femininity qualified her in their eyes to perform miracles, but even as the words left her lips, she knew that there was unlikely to be anyone else. The sum total of her medical knowledge might be nil, but then so was everyone else's. Unless she did something to help him, and did it soon, he would slowly—drop by drop—bleed to death before her eyes. 'What can I do?' she whispered to the faces watching her intently.

'I think the bullet must still be in him,' Matt ventured. 'It would need to come out.'

'I can get Splints's medical equipment for you,' offered another man.

She came to a firm decision at last. 'Yes, can you do that, please? And can you boil up some water too—and get some bandages, if you can.' She scrubbed her own hands thoroughly and sat quietly preparing herself, waiting for the equipment and the boiled water to arrive.

Lachlan's eyes were open again, fixed on her face, and she was frightened at the trust she saw in them. 'I'm going to try to take the bullet out of your shoulder,' she said quietly, taking great care to control her voice. 'I'm afraid it's going to hurt a great deal. Do you want any alcohol to help to deaden the pain?'

He closed his eyes in refusal, but did not try to speak.

The hot, boiled instruments arrived beside her. Her hands shook as she took up a pair of forceps, and they rattled for a moment against the sides of the metal dish they had been lying in. She willed herself to be still, and gradually the trembling ceased. David was carefully sponging away the blood from the wound, and she could see it clearly now. Such a small wound, and the forceps looked so large and unwieldy. Lachlan flinched as the instrument entered his body but managed to remain still, although the perspiration broke out on his forehead with the effort. Everyone in the tent held their breaths as she felt cautiously about for the piece of metal that must be there somewhere, but there was nothing. Lachlan was bleeding even more, and David was using up sponge after sponge in a vain effort to keep the wound clear for her to see. Suddenly Lachlan gasped in agony, and his head rolled to one side as he fainted.

'Thank God for that, poor beggar,' someone muttered.

Melissa felt her self-control start to snap, and with the back of her free hand she impatiently wiped away the tears smarting in her eyes. If he were going to die, it would not be because her nerve left her at this stage of the proceedings! But after another few seconds, she was in despair. Perhaps the bullet was not in there, after all, maybe it was too deeply embedded in his shoulder, perhaps all her clumsy groping around had done nothing but cause him to haemorrhage even more... She began to withdraw the forceps. Then she felt something. With infinite care, she found and withdrew the bullet, and it dropped with a clink into the dish beside her—small and malignant. There was a loud and collective sigh of relief around the tent.

Matt had been squatting silently by her side, a billy-can filled with some sort of warm mixture in his hand. Now he bent forward and carefully placed a mud-coloured sticky poultice over the wound. '*Harakeke*,' he told her, as she looked at it anxiously. 'Flax. It will help to stop the bleeding and keep the wound clean. You did a good job, Melissa.' When the poultice had been applied to his satisfaction, he and David lifted Lachlan's shoulders off the ground to enable her to wind the bandage over the wound. Matt was right—the bleeding seemed to have stopped, at least for the time being.

At last there was nothing they could do except to wait. Dawn was beginning to break, and those miners who had been waiting outside the tent for news went back to their own tents to catch some sleep. Eventually only Melissa and David remained to sit silently on either side of Lachlan, keeping watch. From time to time she would tentatively put out her hand and touch his wrist. He was so pale, the skin over his inner arm translucent. His pulse was weak but steady, and there was no sign of a temperature, although she guessed that it was still too early for that. The lines round his mouth disappeared when his face was relaxed, and he looked much younger. There was a small scar below his eye that she had never noticed before—how had he come by that? she wondered. Gently she brushed the thick fair hair back from his forehead to see that other scar she *could* account for. How long ago that night seemed now. How full of life and vigour and humour he had been then; how vulnerable he was beneath it all; how easily she could lose him!

A life without him... She was shocked at how desperately inconceivable that seemed to her. Had he truly become so much a part of her life, of her heart, in just a few short months? She took his hand in hers and closed her eyes, concentrating with all her might on transferring her own strength and will-power to his failing body.

Soon, his temperature rose alarmingly, and they had to keep swabbing him with wet towels to try to cool him down. Anxious miners kept a vigil outside the tent, waiting for news, sometimes passing through plates of food and mugs of tea, which largely went untouched by the two vigilant people inside. At last David fell into a deep and exhausted sleep, slumped over in a corner of the tent, and Melissa was left alone to watch over Lachlan. She held him down as best she could when he tossed about deliriously, terrified that he would start bleeding again. He cried out several times, but the words were unintelligible, and she thought he must be speaking in Gaelic, the language of his boyhood. The only word she caught was William's name, and he seemed to be reliving some kind of horrible event long ago, but she could not even begin to imagine what it was. She could only wonder helplessly at the hell that was possessing him, the mental torment that obviously pained him even more than his body did. Much later in the day, he grew still and his skin became cooler and dryer to the touch. He slept, and when he awoke, lucid and calm, he saw her beside him, her eyes on his face.

'Melissa...' And he smiled.

She gently pressed back the hand he stretched out. 'You mustn't move, Lachlan. The bleeding could start again if you do.'

'Did you take the bullet out?' When she nodded, he managed a semblance of his old smile. 'So I'm doubly indebted to you for my life. Whatever can I do, I wonder, to repay you now?'

She put one finger over his lips. 'Just hush, Lachlan MacGregor. All I want is for you to get well again—I need no other repayment.' The look in his eyes made her catch her breath—the tenderness and affection there was like a mirror to her own heart. When he captured her hand in his this time, she did not try to stop him.

'Melissa, I . . .'

He broke off as David appeared at the tent entrance, a dinner-plate for Melissa in his hand. 'So—you haven't kicked the bucket yet, MacGregor?'

Lachlan's chuckle ended in a gasp of pain. 'No,' he said at last, when he had overcome the spasm. 'Despite someone's best efforts.'

'Did you see who it was?' David asked.

'I don't know,' Lachlan said slowly. 'I thought, just before he fired, that I saw him clearly—that in fact he'd *wanted* me to see him. But maybe I didn't—maybe it was just the delirium putting that picture in my mind.'

'*Who was it?*' David demanded in exasperation.

'I thought it was Willy.' He frowned in concentration. 'In fact, I *know* it was.'

Melissa and David stared at him incredulously. 'But he's in England . . .' Melissa began.

'Ay, so we've all been told. And, besides, Willy couldn't shoot himself in the foot if his life depended on it. But I'll still swear it was him I saw.'

David shook his head emphatically. 'No. You've been delirious—you've just put William's face on whoever it was who shot you, that's all.'

'So why'd you damned well ask me, then?' Lachlan said grumpily, and promptly fell asleep again.

David and Melissa stared at each other in silence, and then looked at the man sleeping peacefully between them. 'You . . . don't think he's right, do you?' Melissa asked falteringly.

'No, I don't,' David said adamantly. 'He's been close to death, remember, and running a high fever. As I said—and he said himself—he's got his memory and his imagination all mixed up.'

'But if it *was* William . . .'

'But it wasn't,' David said quickly, and his fierceness took her aback. 'And I don't want you ever to say to anyone else that you even thought it could be. Do you understand?'

Although she did not, she nodded anyway. He seemed so desperate to believe that it was not William, and she was almost frightened to ask him why. But he was undoubtedly right, she thought—after all, William was quite likely to be in England by now, twelve thousand miles away.

Barely two weeks later, Lachlan was on his feet again, working hard to regain the full use of his left arm. He had been an appalling patient, restless and hating to be fussed over, but Melissa had enjoyed caring for him nevertheless. Her nursing had had to be interspersed with long hours in the Regency, but she was still able to spend most of her day with him. They had found so much to talk about—his childhood in the Highlands, hers in London, those countries he had visited and she had read about. She managed to obtain regular supplies of newspapers, including some from England that were only four or five months old, and they spent many happy hours reading them and debating points of politics and opinions. To her surprise, she found that his formal education had been considerably more extensive than hers, and she was forced to revise her initial opinion of him as a rough working man. She longed to know more about his background but was aware that what he told her about his past was carefully edited, and only what he wanted her to know. She had to be content with that, acknowledging that what he shared with her was more than he shared with anyone else, except possibly her cousin.

The police from the station at Dunstan had come and gone, none the wiser as to who had shot Lachlan, and she knew that he had not told them, or anyone else, of his belief that it had been his brother. As time passed

and there was still no sign of William Price, she began
to think that it had been a sensible decision after all.
The Pink Palace remained under a manager, with its
owner reportedly in England. No one else reported any
trouble with bushrangers, and after a while speculation
over Lachlan's attacker died down.

Life was becoming busier these days. Winter was fast
approaching, and that meant extra work for everyone
who was planning to stay on the Arrow, preparing tents,
fuel and food supplies against the likely snows. At the
Regency, they soon had to face the fact that they were
running low on supplies. Another packer brought in their
beer from a brewery up the Molyneux River, but if they
were to remain competitive with other bars, they had to
offer a full range of liquors.

The subject came up on the first day that Lachlan was
able to leave the tent unsupported. Melissa sat outside
his tent huddled in her new jacket, watching him shave
in the crisp morning sunlight. There had been another
frost the previous night and the ground under her feet
felt crunchy, but there was still warmth in the glittering
rays of light angling down into the Arrow gorge.
Lachlan's chest was bare except for the bandage she had
just changed, and his face was lathered. David was supposed to be holding the mirror up for him, but could
not stop himself from moving around impatiently as he
spoke. The two men were arguing.

'You can't be serious!' David was saying. 'How can
you even think of going back on the road? You're nowhere near being fit enough.'

'I'm as near as dammit, thanks to our expert surgeon
over there,' Lachlan replied, smiling across at Melissa.
She smiled back, silently agreeing with her cousin, but
feeling a great happy warmth inside her at the look that
Lachlan gave her. Now Lachlan turned an amused stare
on David, who was moving nervously from foot to foot.
'D'you mind holding that mirror still, lad? It's bad
enough trying to do this with one hand without having
to chase you around as well.'

'Let me do it, then,' David said in exasperation, taking the razor from his hand. 'Though why you bother is beyond me. What's the matter with a decent beard like every other man here?' With the razor on his top lip, Lachlan evidently chose silence as the best diplomacy and stood motionless as David rather inexpertly completed the job. 'There—how's that?' he asked, stepping back to admire his handiwork.

'As long as I've still got my nose, I don't much care,' Lachlan said ungraciously, bending over to splash water awkwardly on his face with his good hand. 'Ah—that is much better!' He towelled himself dry, while David took up the argument again.

'You're still too weak to travel, Mack, and I doubt you'll be strong enough for weeks yet. Let me do the first run. I know I've never done it before, but at least I know how to get there, and if you give me instructions, I should have no problems.'

Lachlan shook his head. 'Any other time of the year I'd quite agree, but what if we have an early snow? There is no way that one man can cope with a heavily-laden dray in that kind of situation. Besides, I should be able to ride well enough with one hand, and if need be, I can see a doctor in Dunedin. Go by all means, Davey—but don't go alone.'

David hesitated, and Melissa saw him look up at the mountains beyond the Arrow valley. There had been several layers of snow deposited on those peaks in just the past few days, and he knew well enough how treacherous the Otago weather could be. After a few moments of deliberation he sighed. 'Very well then. But if you were to come with me, who'd look after the bar?'

'We do have a third partner,' Lachlan reproved him. 'Or have you forgotten?'

'But...' David looked at her anxiously. 'Could you manage, Melissa?'

'Of course she could,' Lachlan answered for her. 'Coralie can take charge of the bar and help Melissa lock up and put away the takings. You know where we keep them, lass?'

She nodded. David had already shown her the small iron box that they kept buried in the earth under the bar. They took out only what they needed for food from the general store, or when Lachlan made the run to Dunedin to buy liquor and their basic supplies. There was almost a thousand pounds in the box now, which was rather too much to keep in the bar, but their next expenditure was to be a proper iron roof and comfortable seating. The money remaining would then be consigned to the armed care of the military, who did the weekly gold run to the bank in Dunedin. While there was a lot of rowdiness and frequent brawling in the camp, there was also so much wealth that theft was rarely a problem and they had never needed any of the security precautions that they took. There should be no problems, Melissa thought to herself.

The liquor shortage was so imminent that, the very next morning, the two men rose early and prepared for the long ride over the mountains. Melissa had risen before dawn to see them off.

'Now—are you sure I've told you everything?' David said with a worried frown. 'Do you have the keys? And do you remember where the money is kept?'

'Yes, David,' she said patiently.

'And I don't want you to serve behind the bar—let the other women do that,' he continued. 'And be careful that...'

'Yes, yes, I promise!' she broke in, laughing. To silence him, she put her arms round him and kissed his cheek. 'Now travel carefully, and I'll see you in a week's time.'

'Do I get one of those?' Lachlan asked hopefully, and she went over to where he was standing by his horse.

'Of course you do,' she said lightly. He bent to kiss her cheek, but she deliberately turned her head and he met her lips instead. It was a long and most agreeable kiss, broken reluctantly only when David spoke impatiently.

'If you two have quite finished, perhaps we can make a start sometime this morning.'

'Take care, lass,' Lachlan said, gently pinching her chin.

She nodded, her words catching in her throat at the affection shining in his eyes. Relieved as she was to have him mobile again, she was reluctant to be separated from him for even this one week. And now she knew for a certainty that he felt exactly the same way.

She watched them riding away, trotting briskly up the river bank until they turned up into the mountains. Lachlan raised his good arm in a salute of farewell, and then they were gone from her sight. David had not turned round once, she noted; no doubt he was expressing his still very real opposition to her deepening relationship with Lachlan. He was alarmingly serious these days; very different from the young scamp her parents had found such problems in bringing up.

He had come to live with them in London three years after his parents had died and, being four years older than Melissa, had grown to become the perfect idol for a small and sometimes lonely girl. But he had never acquired the comfortable role of big brother, although he was as dear to her as if he had been. Then he had become of an age to be sent away to school. He had hated it there, and had run away to sea when still little more than a child, and she had not seen him again until here on the Arrow. There had been a few infrequent letters from far places, but never a return address. Whatever he had done, whatever had happened, she regretfully concluded, had done much to repress the high spirits and engaging flippancy that she had always thought to be natural to him. Sometimes it still bubbled up, but these days he mostly seemed to spend his time worrying about her, and Lachlan, and their unlikely but persisting friendship. Their friendship. She supposed that was what it still was, but deep inside, she could not hide her hope that it promised to be so much more than that.

By now thoroughly restless, she decided to talk to Coralie, whom she had scarcely seen since the night of the accident. She walked along that part of the camp where the bar-girls had their tents pitched, smiling a good morning to the few miners who were starting to prepare their breakfasts over newly-lit fires. She had to pass close to the Pink Palace on her way, and her footsteps slowed as she saw the man dismounting from his horse outside the hotel. How could he be William Price? Unable to believe her eyes, she watched as the tall, elegant figure handed the reins to another man, and brushed down his impeccable jacket. He had his back to her, and she willed him to turn round, to prove that she had made a mistake. William Price was in England! As though aware of her eyes riveted on his back, William slowly turned and looked at her. For a long moment their eyes locked, and then he gave her a slow, cold smile. She felt the blood drain from her face as she at last managed to wrench herself away and hurry on, her eyes firmly fixed on the ground. So William Price *was* back in Otago—if indeed he had ever left!

When she came to Coralie's tent, the pair of men's boots sitting outside told her that Coralie was not alone, and, in an agony of impatience, she went to sit down by the river bank to wait. She wondered if she would ever come to accept the drinking and open promiscuity that was an everyday part of life here. It no longer shocked her as it once had, and her firm friendship with Coralie had at least made her more tolerant, but she still found it impossible to understand how the girl could conduct what was obviously a serious affair with David, and at the same time sleep with other men. Yet it was the deep affection they both held for David that had drawn them together in the first place—that, and the fact that they both greatly enjoyed each other's company. Coralie's detached, pragmatic, rather cynical view of life intrigued Melissa, and her own genteel, very disparate, background fascinated Coralie in turn.

After a while, Coralie came out to see her customer off, and, spotting Melissa waiting forlornly down by the river, came over, drawing her wrap around her against the morning chill. 'The boys are off, then?' she said blearily. 'Come and make us some coffee while I get dressed, and we'll have ourselves a chat.'

Melissa busied herself with filling the billy with water, and waited until Coralie emerged fully dressed and awake from her tent before making her announcement. 'I've just seen William Price outside the Pink Palace.'

Coralie's reaction confirmed all her worst fears. 'Goddamn him! What the hell is he up to here?'

'David and Lachlan should be well on their way by now...'

'If he's come back to the Arrow, it might not be Mack he's after,' Coralie interrupted, and bent over abruptly to pour out her coffee.

Melissa was sipping hers, when she became aware of Coralie's eyes resting speculatively on her. 'What is it? What trouble could William make, with Lachlan away?'

Coralie shrugged, her tired face unreadable. 'Who knows? The main thing is that Mack is with David, and the two of them are pretty good at looking out for each other—they've been doing it for years. The men will be all right.' She was looking at her so strangely that Melissa felt a sudden cold clutching at her insides and she wondered what Coralie was really thinking. Coralie put her mug down. 'Would you trust me to look after the Regency? Without your being here?' she said suddenly.

'Yes, of course. David and Lachlan trust you implicitly, I know...'

'Then why don't you leave me in charge, and follow the men out? Even if you just stay at the Dunstan Hotel and meet them when they come back from Dunedin.'

'To keep myself safe from William, do you mean?' Melissa shook her head firmly. 'They left me the Regency to look after. I'm not so afraid of William that I would leave my responsibilities.'

Coralie's eyes narrowed. 'You're being plain stupid, honey. Mack's said before that if ever William came back to the Arrow, you'd have to leave. And knowing William like I do, I think that's real sensible.'

Melissa stiffened. Coralie seemed to know rather more about this than she did. How could she know so well what Lachlan planned for her, unless... No! She dismissed the image of Lachlan and Coralie together from her mind. Coralie would have heard that from David, pillow-talking after too much whisky. 'Lachlan has never said anything to me about having to leave,' she said at last, defensively.

'Maybe because he didn't think the situation would arise,' Coralie said briefly, and poured herself out another mug of coffee. When she sat back, she sniffed the air. 'Can you smell something burning?'

As she spoke, there came the sound of frantic shouting from the far end of the camp. Melissa knew what it was even before she turned round. She picked up her skirts and ran, with Coralie close behind, but by the time she got to the Regency, there was nothing she or anyone else could do.

Sick with anguish, she worked as if in a trance, helping to take down the tents round the bar and move their owners' possessions to safety from the flames. The wooden sides of the building were tinder-dry, and the tower of fire roared high into the air, turning into an inferno within minutes. There had been no time to have even started a human chain to bring buckets of water up from the river, and in any case the heat was too intense to have allowed anyone to get close enough to try to douse the fire. Hours later, Melissa stood beside the smoking ruins of her inheritance, with tears running clean tracks through the soot on her cheeks, feeling utterly shattered. David had been so right to doubt that she could take responsibility for the bar! What an incompetent fool she was!

Coralie came up, and wrapped a blanket comfortingly round her shoulders. 'Don't take it so hard, honey— there wasn't anything you could have done to prevent this happening.'

'But how could it have possibly started? No one had been in the bar for hours. William...'

'No,' Coralie said firmly. 'You haven't a single shred of evidence, so don't go saying anything like that. It's so dry here—a few sparks from a camp-fire was probably all it took to get started. And if it's the boys' reactions you're worried about, they'll soon build another bar, and the diggers are always happy to help to build one of *those*! It'll be all right, honey.'

Melissa allowed herself to be led away to Coralie's tent, where the other bar-girls had congregated to commiserate with each other. She knew that Coralie was right. They could soon rebuild with the money hidden safely beneath the earth in the iron cash-box; a bigger, better Regency, with a proper roof this time, and perhaps even providing accommodation, just as a real hotel should. She began to feel almost cheerful at the prospect.

That evening, she and Coralie went back to the charred remains of the Regency with a spade, and the two of them gingerly made their way through the cooling wreckage, trying to work out the exact location of the cash-box.

'I reckon this was where the bar stood,' Coralie said, after a while. 'There's a lot of glass around here, maybe from the bottles or glasses.'

Melissa came over to see. 'Yes, you're right. So the box should be . . . here. The soil is freshly dug—can you see?' She used the spade to part the blackened fragments of wood, grateful even as she did so that, not having had a solid roof, the Regency made scant bones in its demise. Then her heart stopped as she saw the collapsed earth in the hole where the cash-box ought to have been.

'Are you looking for something, Miss Edwards?'

The light drawl brought her head up with a snap. Lighting a cigar with consummate care, one long-booted leg nonchalantly resting on the remains of the Regency sign, was William Price.

The look of smug satisfaction on his face was much more than she could bear. 'Where is it?' She almost screamed the words at him.

William shook out his match and threw it on to the charred wood at her feet. 'I have not the slightest idea of what you are referring to, my dear young woman,' he said calmly.

'Melissa!' Coralie grabbed at her arm as she lurched towards him, the spade gripped tightly in her fists. 'Stop it!'

'Give me our cash-box or I'll kill you, I swear it!'

He took a step backwards, a flicker of wariness in his eyes now. 'Coralie, my dear, kindly restrain your friend—she appears to be turning hysterical. I have simply come to offer my...condolences. And to enquire whether there was any assistance I could render to ladies in such distressing circumstances.'

Melissa drew herself up. 'You can go!'

'Thank you, William, but I think we'll be all right,' Coralie intervened hastily. 'Melissa's just had a nasty shock, haven't you, honey?' She shook Melissa's arm warningly.

Melissa glared sullenly at the ashes on the ground, reluctant to admit that a confrontation was to be avoided at all costs. She had no evidence at all—no concrete evidence.

'Well, Miss Edwards?' William asked her gently, baiting her.

She turned on her heel and walked away, her fists clenched in impotent rage, not trusting herself to speak to the taunting man crowing over the ruins of her hotel. Behind her, she could hear him calling Coralie back.

Later, Coralie and the other bar-girls came to see Melissa at her tent, and she felt even worse, were that possible, to see the unhappy, tense expressions on their faces. They all sat around her small fire, and she waited while they made themselves comfortable.

It was Coralie who broke the silence first. 'We're real sorry, honey, but we've got some more bad news for you.'

'What has he done now?' After her earlier outburst, she had calmed down and felt much more in control, reasoning that losing her temper like that had accomplished nothing but to play her right into William's waiting hands and given him the satisfaction of knowing how much he had hurt her. She must never do that again. Her resolve was strengthened by the sight of Coralie looking so weary and strained. There had to be something for Lachlan and David to come back to, and it was her responsibility to hold together what she could in their absence.

'He's given us orders—all of us—to start work tomorrow night at his bar. Or else.'

'How can he give you orders? You don't work for him!' Melissa said indignantly. 'The men will be back in another week...'

'Another week will be too late. He's determined to stop the Regency from opening up again, don't you see? A bar's no good without bar-girls, so we're all to move over to the Pink Palace.'

'And—if you don't?'

No one spoke, but one of the women slowly ran her finger across her throat in an all too explicit gesture.

'Surely not! Not even William would do something like that!' Melissa exclaimed.

'Well, I'm not going to find out whether he would or not,' said one of the women determinedly. 'I need to work, and if the Regency isn't opening up again, I don't know if I've got any choice.'

Another woman shook her head. 'I wouldn't work for William if his was the last bar on the earth. I'm clearing out.' She spoke with such feeling that Melissa asked her why. The woman looked away, picking her words carefully. 'Mack and David—neither of them gave a damn what you did or who you were with, as long as you worked occasionally in the bar, and that suited us—it meant what we earned we got to keep. Right?' There was a murmur of assent from the circle of women. 'But William's girls have to do what he wants, go with whomever he tells them to, as often as he says. You got no choice, and he takes most of what you make, anyway. Those are his rules, and he's got the men paid to make sure no one gets away with breaking them. You understand?' Melissa did, and she felt sick to her stomach at the thought of these women entering into such slavery. 'I'm going to Cardrona,' the woman continued. 'That's one place I know of where that William doesn't own a bar—yet.'

'I'm with you,' another of the women said. The rest looked undecided as they got to their feet, but they all looked unhappy.

Coralie waited until the others had gone before she sat down again. 'Got any tea left in the pot, honey?'

'Yes, of course.' Melissa reached for the mugs. 'I take it there's something more you've been told to tell me?'

'Yeah, there is.' Coralie took the mug she held out and looked at her with unmistakable pity in her eyes. 'William wants to see you. Right away.'

'Why should he? We've got nothing to say to each other.'

'What I said before—about all of us going to work in William's bar. That included you, too.'

Melissa stared at her incredulously. 'I'd never play the piano in his bar! What can he be thinking of?'

Coralie took out a small tin box and carefully extracted a cigarette. As she lit it with the twig from the fire, Melissa sensed she was stalling for time, and forced herself to remain silent. 'It's not the piano he wants you to play, honey,' Coralie said at last, exhaling smoke. 'He intends making a few bucks out of you and really rubbing Mack's nose in it this time.'

'But ... I can't see how he can possibly think that he can get away with this! Everyone in the camp knows the Regency, knows that the three of us run it together. He can't force women to leave one bar and go to another, especially under his conditions. It's—It's illegal! He must be mad!'

'No. Mad he certainly is not. He's thought this through real carefully. It's Mack he's after, isn't it? And he wouldn't mind settling a score or two with you, either. So what's Mack going to do when he comes back to find his bar burned to the ground and his girl selling herself in his brother's bar?' She looked sharply at Melissa, who was sitting silently stunned. 'What's he going to do?'

'I don't know. I think ... I think he could kill him,' Melissa whispered.

'Yeah, he'll try, sure. Any self-respecting man would, and even an easy-going lad like Mack has a limit to what he'll take. So William's got a rock-solid reason for shooting him first. In public. In front of his mates. Like some mad dog.' She laughed bitterly. 'It's all going to work out perfectly for him—he's left nothing to chance.'

'Except me!' Melissa leaped to her feet. 'All I'd have to do is get to Lachlan first and warn him! Anyone here would lend me a horse, and I'm sure I could find someone to travel across the Dunstans with, and I'll be safe enough at the Dunstan Hotel until the men come back. That's it, Coralie! I'll leave at first light tomorrow morning.'

'If you do that, you'll make it about as far as the outskirts of town, I reckon,' Coralie said cynically. She jerked her head in the direction of the ruined Regency. 'See that man over there? The tall one with the leather jacket? He's one of William's men. If you try leaving the camp, you'll get precisely nowhere, same as if you try to talk to anyone else. If you want my advice, you'll stay put and do as you're told. And you've been told to go and see William.'

'He can come here if he wants to see me!' Melissa said with more spirit than she felt. 'I'm not his servant!'

'Don't fight him,' Coralie warned her. 'You can't win, and all that'll happen is that you'll get hurt real bad.' Her words were harsh, but her voice was far from unkind. Helplessly, Melissa turned and put her arms round the woman she had come to think of as a friend. Coralie hugged her back fiercely. 'Don't you go blubbering on me, Melissa Edwards! You're made of tougher stuff than that, and we both know it. You'll get through this somehow—I don't know how, but there'll be a way.'

'Not William's way. If I had to go to his bar to...work, I just couldn't. I'd really rather shoot myself, Coralie, really I would. What if he makes me...go with the men?'

'Look, honey, we all had to start somewhere, and it's never easy the first time. But you can take my word for it, the diggers here are real civilised in comparison to some of the camps I've been in. Sure none of them will be Mack, but just close your eyes and think about something else instead. And if that sounds heartless, I'm sorry, but if you—and maybe even Mack—are going to get through this alive, that's about all you can do.' With a parting hug she hurried out into the night, plainly wary of displaying too much emotion.

Melissa watched her go, her eyes dry. The man Coralie had warned her about had not moved from his position and was watching her unblinkingly, as if challenging her. There were hundreds of diggers around, many of whom she called friends, and friends of Lachlan and David, and yet there was no one she could ask for help. She was certain that if she went to any of them, the man watching her so intently would be at her side in an instant, and she was not willing to risk the consequences of that. She went into her tent, as much to evade that steady stare as for any other reason. To work in William's bar—the very thought was intolerable! And that William would or could force her to sell to a stranger what she had for so long delayed granting to the man she loved was something she could not even begin to contemplate. It will not come to that, she promised herself. She would not let it come to that.

She dreamed of Lachlan that night. They were dancing in the streets of Queenstown, and he was looking down at her with that teasing, tender expression she knew so well. She put her arms behind his neck to bring his head down to hers, but his cheek felt strangely cold and smooth, and it began to hurt her. She moved her face away, puzzled. There was a sudden loud click, and even in her sleep her brain registered the sound of a gun being cocked. She opened her eyes abruptly and there was the dark shape of a man leaning over her, a revolver pressed to her temple. She lay very still, hardly daring to breathe, while the sound of her heart drummed in her ears.

'Mr Price wants to see you. Now.' The man's voice was harsh and sneering, and even through her panic she realised that her fear gave him pleasure. Resentment made her calmer, and her heart slowed.

'Tell Mr Price, if he wants to see me, he can come here himself. At a decent time of the day. Now get out of my tent, and don't come back.'

There was a long and heavy silence while the man watched her for a sign of weakening. By an enormous effort of will she managed not to betray any emotion, and at long last the gun was removed from her face and he backed silently out. She spent the rest of the long night shaking uncontrollably, despite the blankets she wrapped round herself. Six more days. That was the soonest she could expect the men to be back. It was an eternity!

She spent the next day in her tent, coming out only to farewell the two girls who were joining a mule-train travelling to the nearby gold-town of Cardrona. She wished them luck, and waved goodbye until they were out of sight. Neither had suggested that she travel with them, and she knew that they were also uncomfortably aware of the tall swarthy man following behind her everywhere she went.

That night he came to her tent again. 'Mr Price wants to see you,' he repeated. 'And this time, I don't want any back-chat from you.' The cold muzzle slid down her neck and came to rest over her heart. 'Get up.'

'I want to get dressed,' she said coldly.

He snorted rudely. 'Get on with it, then.' They glared at each other for a long moment before, with a foul, muttered curse, he moved to stand outside.

She struggled into a skirt and blouse, her trembling fingers refusing to obey her. When she crawled out of the tent, he jerked her to her feet, his fingers digging into the soft flesh of her arm so that she gasped in pain.

'Move yourself! You've kept Mr Price waiting long enough!' he hissed, and thrust her before him.

They walked through the tents in the direction of the Pink Palace, the man behind pushing her viciously with the flat of his hand when he judged her to be walking too slowly. The camp was asleep in the early grey hours of the morning, the hotels and gambling-houses long since closed, but a chink of light shone beneath the door of Price's bar. The man with the gun opened the door and shoved her unceremoniously inside before stepping back into the darkness. The sound of the door closing behind her almost unnerved her completely, but she gripped her hands together and raised her chin, determined not to betray herself.

On a seat by the bar, his feet resting on a table, William Price waited for her in the pool of light given out by a single oil lamp. 'Miss Edwards, what a delightful surprise! I had almost given up on my man's powers of persuasion where you're concerned. Please do come in and make yourself comfortable.'

He pushed a stool over towards her with his foot and took another sip from the glass he was nursing in his lap. As ever, he was immaculately turned out, from his highly-polished riding boots to his exactly parted, gleaming hair. From where she stood she could smell his scent of expensive soap and tobacco, and kept her distance, as if the very air around him was polluted by his presence. He seemed perfectly aware of her revulsion, and indeed the low chuckle he gave made her think that he even enjoyed it.

'Please come closer, Miss Edwards. I can assure you that I don't bite.'

The way his eyes crinkled up at the corners when he smiled reminded her so much of Lachlan that she wondered again how she had ever doubted they were brothers. The straight nose, the firm mouth, the broad set of the shoulders...these were all Lachlan's. But the coldness in the grey eyes and the slight, permanent sneer were not. Somehow his similarity to Lachlan made his differences all the more pronounced.

She stared at him haughtily. 'You have no right to have me brought here like this. Would you kindly tell that creature of yours to leave me alone and let me go at once!'

'Oh, Lord,' he sighed with a weary smile. 'You're not going to act the wronged heroine on me, are you? I've had a long and stressful day, and I don't need you to start wailing and beating your breast. Now, please, Miss Edwards, just sit down and we'll have a little talk.'

'We have nothing to talk about.'

'Sit down!' he hissed suddenly, his face contorted with rage. She sat down quickly, and his expression disappeared as quickly as it had come. 'That's better. Now, can I get you a drink?'

'No, thank you. But I do want you to tell me why I've been dragged here in this criminal fashion—and why you burnt down the Regency.'

'Ah, the Regency. Yes.' William looked thoughtfully up at the ceiling which, unlike that of the now defunct Regency, was painted in gold and ornately decorated with bright pink damsels depicted in varying unlikely states of dishabille. A dusty chandelier hung incongruous and unlit above the rough wooden floor. She thought the place as false and pretentious as its owner. He stroked his upper lip thoughtfully, before saying in a slow, reflective manner, 'One thousand pounds is a great deal of money, isn't it, Miss Edwards? One could almost say a small fortune, perhaps?'

'You're talking about the money in the cash-box you stole from us?'

'I could well be,' he agreed, smiling charmingly. 'How would you like to have it all back—and with interest, besides?'

Her eyes narrowed suspiciously. 'Under what conditions?'

'So you're a businesswoman! What a pleasant surprise. You know, you would be amazed at how many people never learn that nothing comes for free in this world.'

'What are your conditions?' she repeated, impatient at his games. 'That the Regency doesn't rebuild? If that's what you want, then just give us the cash-box, and we'll go. There are dozens of other gold-towns, and I'm sure I can persuade my partners to go elsewhere.'

'Oh, Miss Edwards!' he chuckled. 'The Regency, poor old shack that it was, will never be rebuilt! That's not at all at issue here.'

In the silence after he had spoken, the meaning of his words sank in. 'Lachlan,' she whispered through suddenly dry lips. 'It's him you want, isn't it? You don't really want anything else—not really.'

'What a clever little girl you are. Clever...and beautiful too.' He leaned forward suddenly, bringing his face within inches of hers. She tried to back away, but he gripped her shoulder with slim white fingers that were surprisingly strong. 'And you are *beautiful*, Miss Edwards. Much too beautiful to be eking out an existence in a godforsaken place like the Arrow, wasting your good looks and affections on a penniless Scots peasant whose sole ambition in life is to keep one step ahead of the hangman!' He was watching her carefully as he spoke, and noted the unfeigned surprise that leaped in her eyes at his words. 'So...you didn't know that? How interesting.'

'No! I mean... What on earth are you talking about?' Had he not been looking at her so levelly, she would have disbelieved her ears. She had to remind herself that this was William Price talking—the man who had once tried to abduct her, who had laughed at his mother's death, and had tried to kill Lachlan on at least one occasion in cold blood. For her own safety, she must try to humour him and perhaps even find out the reason— if reason there was—for his bitter hatred of his half-brother.

William did not answer her question, but got up and went to the bar to pour himself another drink from the bottle of wine there. She noticed that his movements were slightly uncoordinated, as if he had been drinking heavily or was rigidly suppressing some deep emotion like anger; it could have been either. When he resumed his seat beside her, he took a long sip from his glass and then looked at her thoughtfully.

'How close are you to MacGregor?' he demanded abruptly. 'Oh, I know you've been away with him, and the entire camp has surmised that you're his mistress now. Except that my informants tell me that you spend your nights alone. And, having met you properly, I don't think you are his mistress. Am I right?'

She felt herself flushing, and ran her fingers through her hair nervously. To be spied upon! How...degrading! And William's perceptiveness was more than a little unsettling. 'My—My friendship with Mr MacGregor is my concern! It can't be any of your business, Mr Price!'

He sighed. 'Melissa—may I call you that, by the way? It can hardly have escaped your notice that I've made two recent attempts on MacGregor's life. Haven't you—in that sweet, dim, little female mind of yours—ever wondered why, for God's sake?'

She was too flabbergasted by his forthrightness to reply immediately, but he obviously expected her to, and sat patiently waiting while she found her voice again. 'Of course I've wondered! But no one could tell me why, and Lachlan and David have always refused to talk to me about it. I've always assumed that you're either a criminal or insane, and, quite frankly, tonight's events have made me even more sure that you are one or the other! What kind of a man are you who would want to kill his own brother?'

William was still for a moment after she had finished, and then he reached into his breast pocket and pulled out a yellowed pamphlet, which he carefully unfolded and handed to her. It was a 'Wanted' poster, issued by the Edinburgh Constabulary in July 1854 for one Lachlan Alexander MacGregor. He was wanted for the crime of murder and was regarded as being highly dangerous, and the public were warned not to approach him under any circumstances. There followed an artist's sketch of the wanted man, and although the sketched face was younger and bearded, it was unmistakably Lachlan's.

She handed the poster back in silence.

'Well, Melissa?' William prompted her at last.

'There's been some mistake...'

'There's been no mistake at all. Lachlan MacGregor killed my father—and his own.' He spoke flatly, his eyes hard, and she suddenly found herself without the words to refute him. He leaned back in his chair, and looked at her almost sadly. 'How much has he told you about his past? About his family?'

'Nothing, really,' she had to admit.

He raised one eyebrow in the expression of enquiry that she had thought to be Lachlan's alone. 'Didn't that strike you as odd? Given your...friendship and the months you've spent together?'

Feeling like a traitor, she nodded miserably.

'I shall have to tell you, then. My father...our father...was an important man. Certainly one of the most important men in Scotland. In his younger days he took as his mistress a common woman—the widow of one of the gamekeepers on his estate. Lachlan MacGregor was the result of that liaison. A year after he was born, my father married a woman of his own social position, and I was born within the year. I have no other surviving brothers or sisters. MacGregor might have been raised in a crofter's cottage, but he went short of nothing—my father in his misguided generosity provided everything for him, including the sort of education that only a gentleman's son is given. Do you know, he even expected me to go to the same school as my bastard half-brother? My mother stopped that, of course. Thank God she knew what was decent, even if he didn't! He even gave MacGregor complete management of the Highland estate—*my* estate. MacGregor should have been very happy with that; he was a very fortunate man. But it wasn't enough. He always wanted more. I barely knew him; I was mostly raised by my mother's family in London. But what I did know about MacGregor, I didn't like. There is a vicious streak to him—maybe you've never seen it, but it's there. And he is never satisfied, never grateful.'

Throughout this recital, Melissa was numb, gazing down at her hands.

'On his twenty-first birthday, he and my father had a terrible argument. No one ever knew what it was about, although I'm sure he was demanding even more from my poor, weak father. They were in Father's study for hours. The door had been locked, and when it was fi-

nally broken open, it was to discover my father dead of
stab-wounds and MacGregor passed out in a drunken
stupor, the knife in his hands. "My God," he said, when
we brought him round. "What have I done?" I'll always
remember that—he'd been so drunk that he couldn't even
remember stabbing a poor old man to death. We called
the police, of course, and he was taken into custody. On
the way from Inverness to Edinburgh, he overpowered
a guard and escaped.'

He now looked at Melissa, who was staring at him,
her face pale with shock. 'So...do you still ask why I
want to kill him? Why I've pursued him half-way round
the world? Is it so very strange to want revenge for what
he did to me and my family? Because something like
that affects everyone, Melissa. His mother died of a
broken heart at what her son had done. He left a naïve
local girl seduced and in disgrace. And my own mother
never got over the shock—when she died, it was a
blessing to all of us who had known how she'd suffered
in those years of widowhood.'

'But...you *laughed* when you heard that your mother
had died...'

'Did I? Then I'm sorry if you misunderstood. My poor
mother was so soft-hearted that she couldn't bear the
fact that I left my home just to seek MacGregor out and
take revenge for my father. Out of respect for her wishes,
I did nothing but have him trailed for years—she was
fond of him, you see, she liked his plain and rustic
manners, poor gentle lady that she was. But once she
died, it left me free to deal with him in my own way, to
seek justice in full for what he had done. So, Melissa—
as much as I loved my mother, MacGregor has so ruined
my life that I felt glad—yes, *glad*—when she died and
I could at last settle the score between us! I don't know
if you can understand that, but I hope you do.'

Shaken by his bitterness, stunned by the appalling
plausibility of his words, Melissa sat in a kind of numb
void, waiting for her emotions to return. She supposed
that she should feel grief and shame that someone who
had come to mean as much to her as Lachlan should

prove to be so false, so evil. But she felt...nothing.
There was something missing, something wrong with
William's story, for all his sincerity. She shook her head
in frustration, trying to think clearly. 'When did all this
take place? Almost nine years ago? Isn't it time you got
on with your life and let Lachlan go? Surely by now he's
paid the price for what he did?'

'*He's paid?*' William said incredulously. 'Do you really
think he has paid for all the lives he's ruined? The only
way he can pay is with his own life, Melissa, and I swear
to God I'll not rest until he's dead!'

Suddenly she knew what was bothering her. 'Then tell
the Constabulary, if what you say is true—if that
"Wanted" poster is genuine. Let them arrest him and
bring him before the courts. Why haven't you already
done that?'

'Don't you see? Because I want to—I have to—kill
him myself!'

'But then you'd be a murderer too! It would be you
being hunted by the law!'

He smiled coldly. 'Melissa, I have no intention of being
brought before the courts for avenging the death of my
father. MacGregor is going to die—but I have far too
much to lose to risk it all in what is a simple case of
natural justice.'

She got to her feet and began to pace up and down
the bar-room floor, trying to order the thoughts racing
through her head. William watched her alertly. At last
she stopped, and looked at him directly. 'I—I don't know
if I believe everything you say, but it does sound plau-
sible. Where do I fit into all this?'

He came to stand before her, his face earnest. 'I have
a plan—and you're a very important part of it.
MacGregor's come to trust you, to rely on you... All
I need you to do is come and work in my bar for a while.
Not for long—just until MacGregor comes back from
Dunedin. I'll take care of everything else.'

So Coralie had been right; William planned to have
Lachlan shot down in a situation he could engineer to
appear to be self-defence! A public, humiliating death.

Melissa closed her eyes as the room swayed around her, but she made herself go on, trying not to betray her rising revulsion. 'I'm not a bar-girl, William. I'll not act like one.'

'Of course not,' he soothed. 'I've made it my business to find out something about you, Melissa, and I do re-alise how out of place you are here. You were brought up to a very different life, weren't you? You should be in the great cities of the world, dressed in silks and furs, with all society at your feet.' Carefully he reached out and ran his finger down her face, down the slenderness of her throat, feeling the pulse leaping there. 'I do have the money from your cash-box, but taking it was merely a precaution on my part. I needed to be sure of you, you see. But now I know you better, I have a much better offer to make to you. A thousand pounds might seem like a lot of money, but believe me, it's really an insignificant return for the months of hard work the three of you have put in here. I don't need it—and I shall freely give it back to you—but you wouldn't need it, either, if you were to come away with me after all this is over. I can give you anything and everything you could ever want, Melissa. Life has so much—so very much—to offer a woman as beautiful and as spirited as you. You mustn't waste a minute of it.'

His eyes did not leave hers as his fingers fell lower, to trace the gentle curve where her breasts began. She brushed his hand away.

'Who else knows about Lachlan's background?' She hoped she managed to keep the tell-tale tremor from her voice. His touch was acutely unsettling, and she found herself horrifyingly responsive to his physical presence and the sensuality he exuded like a scent. Somehow her reaction to him frightened her more than anything else about him. It is his eyes, she warned herself; it is just his eyes that look so like Lachlan's. She broke eye contact and stared instead at his hand, now resting on her forearm. The long, slim white fingers were very different from his brother's.

'Who else knows? I'm not sure—just your cousin, David Frampton. And that whore who keeps him company—Coralie Jones.'

She stepped back as his words sank in. Now, beyond any shadow of a doubt, she knew that William had not told her anything like the truth. David and Coralie would never befriend and protect Lachlan as they did if he was in truth the murderer William had described. David might be impulsive and idealistic, but he was no fool, and Coralie was the most astute judge of human nature she had ever met.

'I've heard enough, William—enough of your lies! Even if you were telling me the truth, I wouldn't help you! What you're planning to do is both illegal and immoral, and I want no part of it!'

She tried to push past him towards the door, but he easily restrained her, holding her arms, shaking his head at her in disappointment. 'And I really thought we were getting somewhere. Has absolutely nothing I've said tonight sunk into that empty little head of yours?'

'Get out of my way, William!'

He responded to her push with a push of his own that slammed her back heavily against the wall and winded her momentarily. 'I've heard about your infamous temper, Melissa, but perhaps you haven't heard about mine. I can get very angry indeed if I don't get what I want.' He spoke calmly but through gritted teeth, and she was suddenly very afraid. He took her chin in his hand, wrenching her face up to meet his. 'So you don't want money and you don't want me, hmm? I rather think you've burnt all your boats, my lovely, because you've only got one option left now.'

'This is stupid, William,' she gasped. 'Let me go, please! I won't cause you any problems if you just let me go!'

He smiled chillingly. 'Aren't you pretty when you beg? No wonder my brother fancies you so much! By the time he gets back, I'll have personally ensured that half the miners on the Arrow have enjoyed you. I wonder how much he'll want you then?'

She tried to dart forward again, but his hands were on her upper arms, restraining her with a gentleness that was deceptive. He watched her face intently as his hands dropped to her breasts and quickly, lightly, flicked across the nipples under the thin cotton of her shirt. She gave an involuntary shudder even as she flinched away, and he chuckled.

'Not quite so averse to a bit of rough play as you make out, are you, my lovely?'

'Please—let me go!' she pleaded again, but he ignored her. His lips were on her neck now, cool and demanding, and she could feel the hard length of his body pressing against her, invading her. Summoning up the last reserves of her defiance she brought her knee up sharply, as Coralie had taught her to do. He was too close to her—the constricting bulk of her skirts took much of the force from her blow, but it was enough to make William recoil.

'Bitch!' he hissed, his face contorted with rage.

She did not even see his arm as it swung, and her head hit the side of the bar as she fell, dazing her. She lay on the ground, her head throbbing, the room swirling. Above her, through eyes dimmed with pain, she could see William slowly undoing his belt.

'I told you once that I owed you,' she heard him say as if from a great distance. 'It's time I repaid you, I think. With interest.'

CHAPTER FIVE

WHEN CORALIE came to see her that evening, Melissa was lying on her back in her tent, clad only in a light shift.

'William told me to come and get you,' Coralie said perfunctorily, peering into the dimness of the tent. When Melissa did not reply, she crawled in beside her and said warningly, 'You'd better come right away—he doesn't like being messed about by anyone, honey.'

'So I've discovered,' Melissa said quietly, not moving. The pain was so intense and had gone on for so long that she was now experiencing the strange sensation of feeling as if she was outside her body; as if the battered agonised body she used to inhabit no longer belonged to her but to some other poor strange woman. She had cried herself out at some stage during the afternoon, and now she simply felt very tired and very light, as if she were floating overhead somewhere...

Coralie reached over and gingerly pulled down the front of her shift, and Melissa winced as the material tugged at the dried blood on the welts criss-crossing her breasts and stomach. Coralie quickly averted her eyes from the bloody mess. 'Oh, my God!' After a moment, she looked back at her, her face set. 'So you fought back, did you? I did warn you, didn't I? I told you to do whatever he told you.'

'I had to.'

'Did you, indeed? And just what the hell did you prove by it?'

'Coralie, he would have done it anyway. Not because of anything I've done, or didn't do. Because of...Lachlan.'

After a moment, Coralie sighed. 'Maybe you're right. Did he...do anything else to you?'

'Coralie, I can't talk about it. I...' Her voice began to break. She screwed her face up in pain as the memories came flooding back, and so missed the quick flash of pity on the other woman's face as she reached her own conclusions as to what had happened.

'Hell, I'm sorry, honey. But it's over now, and at least he left your face alone—that would have taken longer to heal than the rest of you will. Can you get up now?'

'I haven't tried, and I don't want to. Please—just leave me alone.'

'I wish I could do that, honey, I really do, but William said you were to show up for tonight, and when he says jump, you jump.' She thought for a moment, and then asked, 'Do you want me to see if Splints has anything to help the pain? It'll help you get through the night.'

'No, I don't want anything like that. And I don't want anyone to know about—about what's happened. Some water, perhaps.' She sipped some of the water that the bar-girl held to her lips and then watched uninterestedly while Coralie sorted through her bag of clothes.

At last Coralie sat back on her heels, and shook her head in dismay. 'Nothing here that's even remotely right for wearing tonight. Haven't you anything else?'

'That's everything I own. I'll wear the skirt and blouse I usually wear in the evenings—if I go at all.'

'Oh, you'll have to go, all right,' Coralie answered tersely. 'But William isn't going to be too pleased if you don't dress right. Now let me see... the evening dresses are out—you can't wear stays with your ribs all cut up like they are, and your bosom's a hell of a mess. So, if you can't wear anything low cut, it'll have to be short, so's you show them a bit of leg instead.'

'You're joking!'

'I'm not joking—I'm trying the best I can to save what's left of your hide, honey, so just belt up, will you?' She looked at Melissa as if she were a child's doll to be dressed. 'Emily is about your size; a little shorter, perhaps. I'll go and see if I can get her to lend you something.' Within a few minutes she was back with Emily in tow, a couple of dresses over her arm.

'I just want to see what William did to you,' Emily said with candid curiosity. Burning with embarrassment, but not wishing to appear churlish, Melissa reluctantly showed her. 'Sweet Jesus!' Emily breathed in wonder. 'That's even worse than the hiding he ordered for Poppy, when he found she was keeping back some of her money. How's he expect you to work with your front all shredded like that?'

'I have no idea,' said Coralie briskly, bustling her out of the tent. 'Thanks for the loan of the dress.' She waited until Emily had gone before turning back to Melissa. 'I'm sorry about her, but I had to explain what had happened before she would part with the dress. Besides, it'll be all over the camp within the hour—which is no bad thing, I reckon.'

'No! I don't want anyone else to know!'

'Listen to me. I know how you feel, but don't you think it's better to have people feeling sorry for you and disgusted with William than to have them all think you've ditched Mack and thrown in your chips with his brother?'

'I suppose you're right,' Melissa said wretchedly, 'but, Coralie, I don't think I can take very much more of this.'

'I know, I know,' Coralie soothed. 'You've had a real rough deal of it, but like I said before, there'll be a way out of it somehow. Anyway, it seems to me that maybe the worst has already happened to you, hasn't it? So whatever happens now won't seem so bad—not after William. We've got another five days to think of something before Mack gets back, and the most important thing in the meantime is for you to keep yourself safe. I'll look after you as best I can, but the rest is up to you, so you *must* keep calm and keep your wits about you. Now, I've got a bit of muslin here to wrap round you so that you don't get blood all over Emily's dress, so up you get.'

The dress she had brought was a soft rose colour, with the front part of the skirt cut away to reveal the wearer's legs to well above the knee, and a short train at the back. Coralie had chosen it because it was strapless and the bodice came up fairly high, effectively covering the livid marks on Melissa's breasts.

Melissa felt that she might as well have been stark naked. 'My legs! I can't walk around like this with everyone able to see my legs!' she whispered, mortified.

'You've got real nice legs—what's the matter with them?'

'This dress is positively indecent!'

Coralie's mouth tightened in irritation. 'The other girls all dress like that, and you know it. Now shut up and try to get used to it. What shall we do with your hair?' She took a brush and struggled with the knots and tangles until Melissa's hair hung like a silver curtain over her bare shoulders and down to her waist. Then she sat back and looked at her work with professional appreciation. 'You don't need anything else with all that gorgeous hair. Hell, I wish I looked like you; without those drab clothes and that scraped-back hair-style you always wear like a schoolmarm, you're really something.'

'But I don't want to look nice! I shouldn't look nice!'

'It doesn't matter a fig what you want, honey. If you go into the Pink Palace looking like a lady, no man's going to be in a hurry to buy you a drink, and that's no good for William's business. But you go in looking like every man's dream woman, and William's in clover. You get my meaning?'

'What if a man wants...more than just a drink?'

'When the word gets round why you're there, chances are you'll have no problems at all,' Coralie reassured her, but she did not quite meet Melissa's eyes as she spoke.

They walked to the Pink Palace, Melissa hobbling partly with the acute pain she was suffering, and partly with the effort of trying to pull the train round to the front to cover her legs.

'You be careful with that dress,' Coralie warned her sternly, noticing what she was doing. 'Emily's very fond of that one.'

To Melissa's infinite relief, William was not at the Pink Palace when they went in, and there were only a few

customers as yet. A group of bar-girls—some of whom
she knew well from the Regency—were standing at the
bar, and they openly stared at their approach.

'Emily's been yapping!' Coralie hissed in her ear. She
steered Melissa to the bar and sat down on a stool. 'Give
the girl a large gin,' she ordered the sour-faced bar-man.
Melissa and the man both began to object at the same
time, but Coralie reached over and helped herself to a
glass and a bottle. 'Drink it up,' she told Melissa, filling
the glass to the brim and then pushing it over to her.
'It'll help, believe me.'

Melissa, who rarely drank alcohol, obediently pretended to take a sip, while Coralie turned to the other
girls.

'I guess you all know what's happened to Melissa?'
she demanded. When they nodded, she continued, 'Then
you all know she's new to the game. I'd take it as a
personal favour if you could all cover for her tonight
because she's in no condition to work—as Emily has no
doubt been busy telling you.'

Emily looked a little abashed, but one of the other
women asked curiously, 'But you're Mack's girl, aren't
you?'

Melissa managed to jerk her head in assent and then
sat rigid with shame and fear as the other women drifted
off muttering sympathetically. She had kept telling
herself resolutely that none of this was really happening
to her, that she would wake up soon and the pain and
humiliation would turn out to be only some frightful
nightmare. But with the mention of Lachlan's name, the
curtain of unreality had been abruptly thrown aside.

The Pink Palace began to fill up as night fell, and
soon the other women were busy serving drinks, encouraging the diggers at the gaming-tables, dancing with
them to the accompaniment of a small band. It was so
much like any evening at the Regency, and yet so hor-
ribly different. Melissa sat, still staring at the untouched
glass of gin before her, willing the dreadful night to be
over. A little later she began to think with some small
relief that Coralie was right; although the other girls were

all in great demand, she was not approached, apart from a few awkwardly muttered greetings from men she knew as customers from the Regency. She was about to think herself safe after a couple of hours, but then an incident reminded her how men's inhibitions tend to slip after hours of drinking.

It was Splints Finney, of all men, who came to her side and patted her arm rather unsteadily. 'Don't you worry, Melisha, my pet—we all know why you're here, and no one's going to take Mack's girl away from him, so don't you fret, now...' His hand slipped from her arm down to her exposed thigh and he looked at it resting there, blinking owlishly at it. 'What a pretty dresh... you're wearing...'

'Splints!' she begged, pushing his hand away in agitation.

He stared at her with blearily apologetic eyes. 'Shorry, Melisha...' and he swayed off, no doubt to collapse quietly in a corner.

The encounter shook her badly. If Splints, who had always treated her like his own daughter, could make advances to her... She did not have to turn round to know that William had come in and was standing directly behind her stool.

'Good evening, my lovely. And how are you feeling tonight?'

'You should know,' she said quietly, her teeth clenched.

He gave a light laugh that tinkled hollowly in her ears. 'Yes, I'm sorry about that—I did get rather carried away, I must confess. But my, my—don't you look beautiful tonight? Sometimes it takes a little pain to... bring out the best in a woman.' She turned to face him, bringing the glass of gin in her hand, but his arm shot out and pushed it back on to the counter, spilling it. 'You weren't going to throw that at me, were you?' he said smoothly.

The band was still playing, and all around, people were talking and drinking and singing. Apart from Coralie watching them, white-faced, no one had noticed the small drama they were playing out. William took a handful of her hair and absently ran it through his fingers, watching the light gleaming in it. Sickeningly she remembered Lachlan doing exactly the same thing, months ago on the dusty track to the Dunstans. But Lachlan's touch had been admiring, whereas William touched her much as a man would handle a possession—an object to be valued or destroyed at will.

'Why don't you come out to my tent, Melissa? Now that you've learnt the ground rules, I think we can advance to some more advanced play.'

'No!'

'That wasn't a request, my lovely,' he said mildly. He leaned forward and kissed her on the lips, and she sat rigid and unyielding beneath his hands. But then he forced her lips apart and thrust his tongue inside her mouth, and she could not resist it any longer. With a gasp of pain he leaped back, his hand over his mouth, moving his tongue experimentally to see if it was still in one piece. His eyes narrowed to slits. 'If that's how you want to play it...' Moving close to her so that no one else could see, he quickly reached out and savagely twisted her right breast. She sobbed with the agony, almost reeling off the stool, as he stood watching her in satisfaction, still nursing his injured mouth.

'You just refuse to learn, will you? I think we'd better get you a customer who will teach you a few manners, my sweet Melissa.' His eyes fell upon the man sitting next to her, and he grinned suddenly.

'Ernest, old chap!' he said jovially, clapping him on the back. 'How'd you like a bit of sport tonight?'

The other man turned to look at her. He was not a man she had ever seen drinking at the Regency. His eyes were dull with drunkenness in his large, slack-jowled face. He had huge, hairy hands clasped around his drink, and a huge belly.

He stared at her, and then mumbled, 'Couldn't afford the likes of her.'

'Oh, but I think you could, Ernest,' William assured him, enjoying himself hugely. 'She's a new girl, and in need of breaking in—so tonight she's free...on the house, so to speak. What do you say?'

Ernest ruminated for a moment, sizing her up, before pronouncing, 'Yeah, all right. Why not?'

'Good lad.' William seized her wrist and smiled vindictively into her eyes. 'She'll play a bit coy, Ernest, but it's all part of the act, so don't take any nonsense and just show her what you're made of, eh?'

Ernest wiped his mouth on his sleeve and stood up, jerking her towards him as she tried to shrink away, still not quite believing that William could be doing this to her. 'We'll be off then,' he muttered, and staggered towards the door, dragging her behind him. Suddenly the drinkers nearest the door fell silent, and she caught sight of Coralie trying to get to her side, frantically mouthing something. The crowd before them moved apart, and now she could see who was at the door.

Lachlan! Lachlan with a face white with anger and eyes so black that they were fathomless. Half a head taller than anyone else in the room, he stood silent and alone, staring at her as if he could not believe what he saw.

'Ah, the white knight has arrived at last,' William said softly.

The cry of relief died on her lips as she saw herself as he must see her: the tawdry, revealing dress, her hair loose over her naked shoulders, her hand in the possession of an ape of a man she had never seen before. She tried to signal to him with her eyes, but he looked away from her face with an expression of such disgust that her blood suddenly ran cold.

'You're not welcome in my bar, MacGregor. Get out!' William stood behind her, his voice triumphant.

'Not until I take what I came for,' Lachlan replied, his voice surprising her by its steadiness. He put out his hand to her and she started forward eagerly, but the man who held her wrist twisted it so that she gasped.

'She's with me, mate!' Ernest sneered. 'Get out of my way.'

Lachlan did not move until another vicious tug from her captor made her cry out with pain. There was a low, animal sound like a growl from deep in Lachlan's throat before he took a single long stride to where the other man stood. Seeing the look on his face, Ernest at once released Melissa to bring his fists up to protect himself, but Lachlan did not bother to throw any punches—he simply seized the other man by the collar and threw him bodily in the direction of the door. He lay there groaning piteously, and no one dared to help him.

Lachlan turned back to Melissa. 'Come with me.' Again he held his hand out.

Behind him she saw the man who had brought her to William the previous night, and she knew that he carried a gun. All William's planning was becoming reality now—all he needed to do was to provoke Lachlan just a little more and his man could shoot him and claim self-defence. Lachlan was on the brink of his own self-destruction; perhaps only seconds away from death. Her brain was racing wildly—she knew that William would not let Lachlan leave the bar alive; that if she went with him, William would intervene, start a fight... She came to a decision. 'I can't come with you,' she said quietly, hoping against hope that he would understand why, but he did not. The incredulity in his eyes hardened within seconds to a bitter cynicism.

William saw it, too, and it was not quite what he had wanted. He slipped a proprietorial arm around Melissa's waist. 'You heard the lady, MacGregor—she doesn't want to go with you,' he goaded him. 'You can't just walk into my bar and throw one of my girls' customers around like that! If you want the lady, you're going to have to pay for her now, just the same as everyone else.' He looked around for support from the other patrons, but immediately sensed that he was not going to get it; Lachlan was well liked by the Arrowtown diggers, and there was not a face that was not looking disapproving at the way Mack's woman was being used against him. William, for the moment, dared not push him much further. 'If you're not buying—get out,' he said at last, with less conviction than before.

There was a long, tense silence before Lachlan shrugged, a light smile surprising on his lips. 'Ah, what the hell! I'll have a drink before I go.' He moved past them to the bar, pulling a fistful of silver coins from his pocket and tipping them on the counter. 'Give me a large whisky,' he said to the bar-man. After a nod from William, the man pulled out a glass and filled it up. Lachlan swallowed it in one large gulp and slammed it back down on the counter. 'Give me another.'

Melissa had always known that he was a hard drinker, but she had never seen him drink more than he had that one night at Jamieson's. Now, for the first time, she had to watch helplessly as he set about getting very drunk in a very short space of time. Gradually the other customers began to return to their tables, and a quiet buzz of conversation started again. The band began to play rather tremulously, and Ernest was helped outside. But everyone kept their eyes on the big man at the bar drinking relentlessly. Standing beside William, watching Lachlan, she asked herself over and over why he had not simply walked out of the Pink Palace while he had the opportunity.

Suddenly she knew why. Lachlan knew that William had arranged this situation, and he believed that a fight was inevitable. He also knew that he could not win, and that he would be dead within the hour. But if he had given up, she had not—and she had nothing left to lose. Taking a deep breath, she walked up beside him and took the glass of whisky out of his hand. There was no sign of recognition in his eyes as he looked at her.

'Let's go now, Lachlan. Very carefully.'

At first, he did not move, and for one heart-stopping moment she thought he would refuse to go with her. But then he slowly put an arm round her waist and they turned towards the door. It looked a lifetime away as they made their way, Lachlan lurching slightly against her as they walked. After a few steps, William's henchman barred their way and she stopped, looking steadily at his chest, silently willing him, with all she had, to disappear.

'Let them go!' someone shouted, and there was a chorus of agreement.

'You've had your fun, Price,' someone else said. 'Leave off them now.'

From behind, William must have signalled, because his man stepped aside, his face surly, and they walked through the door. Outside, Melissa took great cold gulps of air and wiped the sweat off her face with hands that were shaking uncontrollably.

A couple of the diggers who had been habitués of the old Regency followed them out, and one of them said, 'We'll help you see Mack back to his tent, Miss Edwards. Mr Price probably won't try anything now, but you're better safe than sorry...'

She accepted their help gratefully, and they soon had Lachlan in his tent. He had not spoken to anyone, and it was left to her to thank the diggers.

'It's all right, Miss Edwards,' one of them said awkwardly, determinedly gazing at his feet—to avoid looking at her unseemly dress, she realised. 'No one in there likes seein' Mack being made a fool of like that. Reckon there'll be some score-settlin' on that account soon.'

His words seemed to her to be sadly prophetic. She bade him a good night and went into Lachlan's tent, determined to talk to him, to make him understand that, whatever happened tonight, he must not make the mistake of trying to take his revenge upon his half-brother.

Inside the tent, he was sitting with his arms on his knees and his head buried in his hands. She knelt beside him, her heart wrung with pity, taking both his hands in hers. 'Lachlan, listen to me...'

He looked up at her, and she was amazed to see a small, twisted smile on his lips. It was as if a different man entirely was looking at her through his eyes, and she suddenly felt she was trying to communicate with a total stranger. 'I've been a bloody fool, haven't I?' he said so softly that she had to strain to hear the words.

'No, I don't think so,' she replied, puzzled.

'Oh ay, lass, I have been. God, but you are so beauti-ful...I forgot how beautiful...'

His hand came up to snake through her hair, and she tried to pull away, alarmed now. She could feel the vi-olence literally coursing through him like a current, and she realised that it was all directed at her. He dragged her head back as he covered her mouth with his. It was a hard, hurtful kiss, and she fought to get free.

'No! Please, Lachlan... Not like this!'

'Yes. Exactly like this,' he replied, softly, savagely.

He threw her over on to her back beside him, his face tight with a blind passion that was not desire. She heard the stitches in Emily's dress tear as he pulled the bodice down to her hips and rolled on top of her. The pain of his weight on her breasts and stomach was almost in-tolerable as she tried to push him off, but her efforts were completely ineffectual. William had told her that he could be vicious—that he had murdered before! She tried even as she fought back to dismiss those thoughts from her mind. This was not Lachlan doing this to her—it was the other man, the man who had the fevered nightmares, who suffered in the private hell of his past...not the man she knew much better for his gentle, affectionate, good-humoured ways. *That* man would never knowingly be doing this to her...

His hands were under her skirt now, rough on her bare skin. He forced his way between her legs and she flinched violently when he touched that most tender part of her.

'Phyllida...' he groaned into her throat.

'For God's sake, it's me, Lachlan! Melissa!' But he was deaf to her, hurting her so that she began to sob with pain and fear and helplessness. She made herself go limp, so that the inevitable would not hurt her more than she could bear.

His lips moved down her throat and over her breasts. Then he froze. 'What the...?' He sat up quickly, pulling aside the tent-flap to let in more light. In the glow of the dying camp-fire he could clearly see the weeping sores of the lashes William had inflicted upon her; red squares on her white flesh where his buckle had cut. Abruptly she saw the insane stranger leave him, and it was Lachlan now who looked at her with shocked, sickened eyes. 'The bastard! God help me, I'll kill him for this,' he promised quietly.

'You can't do that!' She grabbed at his arm as he rose to leave, desperate to restrain him. 'That's what he wants you to do, don't you see? He'll be waiting for you to come—he's been planning this from the very beginning. Oh, please, Lachlan, don't play into his hands!'

He glared down at her, his face savage. 'He can do *this* to you, and you still want to protect him?' he snarled. The tears started to her eyes, and as soon as he saw them, his shoulders slumped and he sank beside her, shaking his head helplessly. 'I'm sorry,' he said quietly. 'I'm so sorry. I didn't mean to say that.'

'It's not my fault!'

'I know it's not. It's mine. Mine entirely.'

She did not understand how he could say that, and sat in anxious silence, looking at the hard, taut line of his back with the tears running unchecked down her face. At last he turned round, and she could see that the last of the violence in him had gone.

He reached over to wipe her cheek tenderly with his finger-tip. 'You're crying, poor lass. Do you know I've never seen you cry before? And, God knows, you've had more than your fair share of misfortune.'

His unexpected gentleness was her undoing. She took his hand and held it to her lips, great loud sobs beginning to rack her body as her self-control finally deserted her. More than anything else she needed his arms round her then, to comfort and reassure her that her world had not entirely come to an end, but after a moment, he politely disengaged his hand.

'It doesn't look as if you've had anything put on those welts—they'll go septic if they're left like that. I'll go and see what Finney has in his tent.' He left her without another look.

She had changed out of the hated, ruined pink dress by the time he returned, and, for the lack of anything else to wear, had put on one of his soft flannel shirts. Wordlessly he knelt beside her and unbuttoned the shirt again, carefully pulling it free. Then, with a small frown of concentration, he painstakingly applied a salve, spreading it over her cuts with such detachment that her humiliation was complete. He could have been tending to one of his horses, for all the interest he showed in her. On his own shirt she saw a small red stain of blood, either from herself or from his own wound opening up with the strain of throwing Ernest aside, but she dared not ask him about it. Afterwards, when he had covered her again with warm blankets, he stretched out beside her and they lay together, not touching, staring sleeplessly at the soft golden glow that the camp-fire outside threw on the roof of the tent.

At last she felt able to speak again. 'Why did you come back so early?'

'We met a Queenstown digger on the Mountain Road who swore he'd seen William there last week. It seemed improbable... but I'd had an uneasy feeling that something was wrong ever since we'd left, and I decided to turn back. We persuaded Matt to go with David, and he's showing him the way. I guess David will want to start rebuilding as soon as he gets back.'

'The cash-box, Lachlan. I'm afraid it's...'

'It's been taken by William. Yes, it's what I'd have expected him to do. Don't worry about it—we'll manage somehow.'

They lay in silence for a long time. He spoke again just as her eyes were beginning to close in exhaustion. 'When David gets back, I want you to go back with him to Dunedin.'

'No!'

'Yes,' he said wearily. 'Don't argue with me, Melissa. I want you to go.'

'But I don't want to leave you! I can't leave you!'

'For God's sake, grow up, will you, lass! This is the real world you're in now! There never was and there never will be anything between us, and you don't owe me a damned thing, so don't let any misguided sense of loyalty keep you here. Just get out of this while you can. Hasn't William told you what I've done?'

'I don't believe a word of what he's told me,' she said quickly, and was rewarded by a harsh, sardonic laugh that was so uncharacteristic of him that she was shocked into speechlessness.

'Don't you? So you don't believe that I killed my father in a drunken rage at being excluded from all the power, money and position that my younger, legitimate brother had by right? There are a dozen witnesses to prove you wrong, you poor, foolish lass.'

She stared at him, her eyes wide with horror. 'But ... you didn't ...'

'Didn't I?' he enquired, his voice low and brutal. 'Hell, you don't know the first thing about me.'

He watched unmoved as her face crumpled and she turned away to bury her head deep in her blankets. Her shoulders were shaking as she wept bitter, harsh tears, and he knew that she was crying for both of them, and for the loss of a future that could never have been, and a love that never was. It took a long time for her to cry herself out, but at last she slipped into the sleep of the exhausted, her steady shallow breathing disturbed only occasionally by a small sob.

Speaking to her like that had been one of the hardest things he had had to do in a life in which few things had come easily. It had been almost impossible to mask his true feelings for her while he had watched her fall apart, destroyed under the onslaught of his attack, but it had to be done, and he had evidently been successful in convincing her. The pain of hurting her so much rose in his gullet like bile, and he was shocked to find himself literally shaking with his hatred of the man who had caused all this. William was the only person Lachlan had ever really hated in his life. Even as small boys there had been an instinctive, mutual antipathy between them, and the few tentatively polite gestures of friendship Lachlan had made to his half-brother had been autocratically rebuffed by the younger boy. William had seemed to begrudge him everything. Raised by his mother's family in London from a very early age, he had loathed the times he had been forced to spend with his father on the Highland estate—Lachlan's territory. The closeness Lachlan had enjoyed with his father had been bitterly resented by William, and he had never lost an opportunity of reminding his half-brother of his mother's lowly status, of his bastardy, of what would happen to Lachlan and his mother when William came into his inheritance.

Lachlan had kept his silence, managing to convince himself that, despite his venom, William was harmless enough, until that warm summer afternoon when he had come across William and Cathy in the barn—just as William had known he would. Sweet, soft, foolish Cathy from the village, who had promised him her hand but had willingly given her body to the handsome and charming gentleman, up from London and in search of some summer dalliance. It had been Lachlan's twenty-first birthday that day, and he knew that the day had been no coincidence. Just as he was certain that William had engineered the whole, dreadful train of events that had followed that single discovery in the barn. Cathy. He tried to remember her face now, but found that he could not. Not like... He put his hands over his eyes in a vain attempt to blot out the scene that always rose before his eyes when he thought of *her*. But it was impossible now, just as it had been impossible for the last year.

He was back in the hotel room in Melbourne, lying on cool, white sheets, his tanned body dark against the ivory softness of the woman he held. Moonlight filtered through the lace curtains and lit upon the diamonds in her midnight-black hair as it lay across the pillow. Her arms clung to his back, her voice gasping and husky with passion in the darkness, her perfume surrounding him like a mist, taking him out of his very senses. And then...

'Damn! Damn! Damn!' He swore softly. It might have happened a year ago, but the pain was still as real as a physical blow. Phyllida had been William's paid whore

all along, and he had been a fool to have thought even
for a moment that such a woman could truly have felt
anything for a penniless, itinerant Scot like himself. But
he had been so consumed by lust and loneliness that he
ignored all the danger signals, had mistaken it all for
love, and had steadfastly told himself that she was
feeling—that she *had* to feel—the same way. William,
of course, had anticipated that he would. William was
always just one step ahead, always ready to take advantage of any weakness in the man whom he wanted
to bring to his knees more than anything else in the world.
And he had used Cathy, and then Phyllida...

'But not this woman!' Lachlan said aloud and invol-
untarily, and Melissa, lying beside him, gave a slight
start. He waited until her breathing had resumed its
regular rhythm before easing the slipped blankets back
over her shoulders. Why the hell had she chosen to wear
that damned pink dress? he wondered yet again. It was
Phyllida's favourite colour, and for one stomach-lurching
second in the Pink Palace it *had* been Phyllida standing
there before him, with William's hand round her waist
in a defiant gesture of ownership.

He had had the last drink of his life tonight—this was
the second time that the whisky had uncovered the anger
and hatred buried so deeply inside him. The second time
that he had seen Phyllida reflected in Melissa's face.
When Melissa had sobbed and pleaded beneath him, it
had been Phyllida he had been hurting, Phyllida's
beautiful, bought body he had been revenging himself
on. Not poor, brave Melissa. Poor raped Melissa.

Carefully, so as not to wake her, he risked a soft kiss
on her cheek. The last kiss he would ever give the woman
he had once dared to dream of asking to marry him.
But, between him and his half-brother, they had almost
broken her—and it was far from over yet. For one wild
moment he felt tempted to wake her up, to take her in
his arms and tell her everything. He knew she would
believe him, and that she would willingly, unquestion-
ingly, go wherever he chose to take her. He could have
been happy with her, with her high courage and her

strength and her unswerving loyalty. But William had
changed all that—now Lachlan had to make her hate
and fear himself; her very life might depend upon it.

Silently he put aside his blankets and found his rifle,
still strapped to his pack. Before he left, he took one
last long look at the woman sleeping alone on the ground.
If he managed to kill William, he would come back and
explain everything to her before the police came to take
him away. If he failed . . . then it was best to leave things
as they were. It might hurt her now, but in years to come
she might even thank him for it. He swung his rifle on
his back and left to join the shadows of the night.

He did not return the next day. When Coralie came to
see if she needed anything later in the afternoon, Melissa
asked if she had seen him.

'He's gone after William,' Coralie said bluntly. Then,
seeing the look of horror on Melissa's face, she added
sharply, 'Well? What else did you expect? That he'd just
sit back and let that louse get away with what he did to
you?'

'I don't need—or want—him to avenge me!'

'It's not you he's doing it for, honey—it's that male
pride.' She pulled the corners of her mouth down in disapproval. 'William was just using you to get at Mack,
and they both know it. Now Mack's not going to stop
until William's got a bullet in him. Damn fool men!'
She bent over to peer down the front of Melissa's
nightgown in the matter-of-fact way that Melissa found
so disconcerting. Since her encounter with William, her
wounds seemed to have become common property. 'Still
a helluva mess, isn't it? I reckon you might be scarred
for life. Pity.'

Melissa tied up her nightgown again. 'Do you know
where William is?'

'You're worried about that man of yours, aren't you?'
Coralie sounded slightly more sympathetic. 'William
cleared out last night after you took Mack off. The
diggers felt pretty strongly about what had happened,
and of course William knew what he could expect once
Mack sobered up. He's gone up north, someone said,

but you can never predict what vermin like him are likely
to do. Wherever he went, Mack was going, too—and I
hope he gets the bastard!'

'How can you say that?' Melissa demanded, aghast
at Coralie's vehemence. 'Then he'd be guilty of
murder...' She broke off as she saw the expression on
Coralie's face, and William's words came back sharply
to her. Coralie knew even more about Lachlan than she
did, and would surely have come to the conclusion that
any man who could kill his own father could have few
scruples about killing again...

Coralie made some flimsy excuse and bustled off,
clearly anxious to avoid being drawn into further
conversation.

Melissa spent the next three days in her tent, sleeping
and resting her battered body and mind. She saw no one
but Coralie, who faithfully appeared three times a day
with a meal, and who would bring her fresh salve and
bandages, but Melissa was grateful for her isolation. It
gave her time to think and time to come to some sort
of acceptance of what had happened to her—even if she
was sure she would never understand it.

From the very first, Lachlan had warned her not to
get involved in the vicious war between himself and his
brother. David, too, had tried to protect her by telling
her to leave the Arrow. She could see now, much too
late, that they had both been right. Whatever had happened between Lachlan and William—and she still found
herself believing that William had told her only part of
his story—had nothing to do with her. If she stayed, she
could not mend matters, and indeed might even make
them worse. She had to leave as soon as possible. Besides, it was clearly what Lachlan wanted her to do—he
had told her bluntly enough! A hundred times in those
days she asked herself whether he was in truth the murderer William had described to her. A hundred times she
sought for excuses, explanations... but despite them she
could not escape the conclusion that he was guilty. His
own words condemned him... and she had seen and experienced his violence for herself. It's all over, she told

herself again and again. He ended it, and I must accept that it is for the best. But still the small flicker of irrational hope persisted inside her.

The flicker went out on the fourth day, when Lachlan returned. She was still restricted to her tent by the stiff scabs stretched tightly over her healing cuts, and so he came to see her there. He put his head inside the tent, but came no closer. 'How are you feeling?' He addressed an area of canvas directly over the top of her head.

'Much better, thank you.' All the words of relief she been about to express at his return died on her lips as she saw his face. He seemed years older suddenly, with a harsh new set to his mouth, and eyes that were as flat and as hard as the stones in the Arrow. 'Did you... Were you...successful?'

'If you're asking whether I killed William, the answer is no.' He waited a moment before asking stiffly, 'Is there anything you need?'

'No, thank you.' He nodded curtly and left. It was like talking to a diffident stranger, she thought miserably. His manner now was totally devoid of all the warmth and humour of their old friendship, and for the first time she began to realise fully how much she was going to miss that time of her life.

He did not come to see her again, and it was not until two days later, when Coralie came by to tell her that David and Matt were coming into the camp, that she finally left her tent. She managed to dress herself with difficulty, and ran a brush through her hair with some agonised effort. A light drizzle was falling when she came out. It was the first rain in weeks, and she held her face up to it, letting the fine droplets fall in her mouth, welcoming their fresh, cold cleanness.

She found Lachlan and David on the site of the old Regency, talking quietly. One look at David's face told her that he knew what had happened in his absence.

He came forward quickly to take her hands, his face compassionate. 'Coz—you poor girl! If only we hadn't left you alone here!'

'I've almost completely recovered now,' she assured him. 'I've just been so worried about how you would take losing the Regency.'

But he took it as well as Coralie had predicted he would. 'It was always on the cards,' he told her cheerfully. 'There was nothing you could have done to have prevented it. Now we can build it bigger and better, and give the other bars a run for their money!'

Lachlan was much less enthusiastic, and she had the unmistakable sense that he did not want to start again, but he had worked hard in David's absence none the less. In spite of the weakness of his barely-healed shoulder, he had managed to clear the site of débris and had arranged for timber to be delivered from the timber-mill on the Molyneux River. This had put them into considerable debt, and they now had no assets but the liquor David had brought back with them, but somehow David's resilience was infectious, and for the first time their financial situation did not seem so dire to her. For the first time, too, the terrible weight of guilt that she had borne since the fire began to lessen perceptibly.

She and David were exchanging opinions on the desirable layout of the new Regency, when Lachlan cut in. 'How soon can you get Melissa back to Dunedin?'

'Not for a while yet, Mack. It's been raining heavily Dunedin-way, and the roads are likely to close soon. We would have to wait for a day or two to see if this is all the rain we're going to get before I'd risk taking the dray back again.'

'Then take her on horseback!'

'In this rain and in her present state of health? Have a heart, man!' David began, but Lachlan turned on his heel without another word and strode off towards the river, angrily kicking aside a piece of timber in his path. 'What's the matter with him?' David wondered. 'I've never known him to act like this before.'

'Some...dreadful things happened while you were away,' she said hesitantly, knowing that Lachlan would have held back the full story from David, and that part of which he was most ashamed. 'I think, in some way,

he blames me for what happened with William. He—
He didn't handle it very well, David, and...I think he
feels badly about that, and that he hasn't settled the score
with William yet.'

David's eyes rested on her sadly. 'I did warn you.'

'Yes, you did, and I should have listened to you instead of staying here and getting us all into this trouble.'

'Look, coz—this trouble existed long before you came
into it, so please don't blame yourself for that. Mack's
hit rock bottom, it seems to me, and he's the only one
who can sort this out—he and William. It has nothing
to do with you, and you'll be much better off going to
Dunedin. Winter's coming, and you'll be able to think
of us freezing out here while you're all snug and cozy
over a roaring fire. I'll probably be making the runs in
future, so I'll be able to come and see you at least once
a fortnight.'

She winced as he hugged her affectionately. He appeared to be positively relieved at the prospect of her
leaving them, and the more she thought about it, the
more appealing the idea did become. To forget the hard-
ships, the dangers, the dark mysteries of this dreadful
situation and to go to where people lived in warm houses
with properly ordered lives...to live a *normal* life again!

The next day it began to rain—a heavy, persistent
downfall that swelled the rivers, making mining all but
impossible, and stopping the building of the new
Regency. Transport in and out of the town became a
perilous business because of the slips on the track and
the flooded rivers. Life in the camp became a misery as
everything got wet: clothing, bedding, and the wood that
they had carefully collected for their fires. People
gathered together to share the heat from a few small
fires under makeshift canvas awnings, and to cook their
communal meals.

Coralie had left the Pink Palace the night that William
had disappeared, and the four of them spent their days
somewhat uneasily together at the half-built Regency.
They strung a large canvas awning between the newly-
erected sides and sheltered under it with their precious

firewood. In a normally arid climate like that of Otago, such heavy rain caught everyone unawares, and it did not take long before everyone and everything was cold and wet. There was little they could do but stare out at the rain, gamble or drink the long hours away, and tempers began to run short, with frequent outbursts of fighting. There always seemed to be at least three men sitting miserably chained to the huge log in the 'gaol tent' awaiting the judgment of the visiting magistrate.

Even David became increasingly terse as the opening date for the hotel began to look further and further away, and Lachlan was impossible to live with. He was testy and abrupt, withdrawn from all of them. He avoided even looking at Melissa, and any communication to her had to go via David, who quickly became frustrated and would stalk off elsewhere whenever Lachlan was around. Melissa and Coralie were the only two who managed to remain civil to one another, but since her time at the Pink Palace, even Coralie seemed a little more distant these days.

The atmosphere was so tense in the large, wet shelter that when Lachlan announced one day that he was going hunting for wild pig, there was a silent but collective sigh of relief among the others. They had no food left, and no money to buy any more from the general store, but the anticipation of a peaceful day was as welcome as the thought of a decent dinner that night. And Lachlan in turn seemed just as relieved to leave their company and head for the mountains with his rifle, despite the relentless, icy rain.

Coralie went to visit some friends, and David and Melissa spent a pleasantly companionable day playing cards. They started off with whist, but Melissa soon persuaded David to teach her his speciality, which was poker. Huddled under the Regency canvas, they played for stakes of building-nails while the grey sheets of rain floated across the sodden township and the water hissed and gurgled over and around the pebble banks of the Arrow. The afternoon passed slowly but interestingly enough, as Melissa discovered that she possessed a very

real talent for the game of luck and skill and guile. At
least, she thought, it takes my mind off my problems
for a little while.

Night had fallen by the time Lachlan returned with a
huge wild sow, which he had shot and dragged back to
the camp behind his horse. It was a grotesquely ugly
creature, and Melissa was careful to be elsewhere as he
began the task of butchering it. Apart from the pigs,
there were no other wild animals in the high country,
and the pigs themselves were not thought to be native
to New Zealand; they were known as 'Captain Cookers',
as it was generally held that they had escaped from
Captain Cook's ships almost a hundred years before,
although no one could say so with certainty. Whatever
their origin, they were now the sole source of meat for
the men in the camps, unless they were in sufficient funds
to purchase an expensive sheep from one of the newly-
established farms in the district. So, tough and gamy as
the pork was, it was still regarded as a great delicacy.

Soon hungry miners were crowding round the sow as
Lachlan expertly divided it between them, taking in exchange some flour, eggs, a few precious vegetables. When
he at last came back to the Regency camp, he was
carrying a pot of pork pieces in one hand, ready to set
over the fire, and in the other an armful of food supplies. He looked completely exhausted, but happier than
they had seen him for a long time—he was a man who
always found inactivity irksome, and there had been
enormous satisfaction for him in the day's long and difficult hunt.

But the lines of tension set in his face again as he
caught Melissa's grimace of disgust at his appearance;
congealed blood thickly coated his arms and shirt; his
trousers and boots were unspeakable. He unceremoniously dumped the food at her feet and stared at her defiantly. 'And what's the matter with you? A face like
that would turn milk!'

She knew that she should show some appreciation for
the food he had worked so hard to bring them, but his
irritation sparked off the frustration that had been

building in her for days. 'How can you bear to walk around in that disgusting state? Go and take off those filthy clothes before you come in here!'

His mouth tightened to a thin white line. 'Dressing for dinner, are we? How remiss of me to forget.' He dragged his shirt off as he spoke, and threw it outside to rinse in the rain.

'You animal! You crude, filthy, disgusting...' She broke off and quickly turned her head away as, with a martyred sigh, he removed the rest of his clothes. When she dared to look back at him, he had wrapped a blanket round his hips and was calmly pouring himself a mug of coffee beside the fire.

'There are plenty of vegetables there,' he threw at her over his shoulder. 'The sooner you get them into the pot, the sooner we can have dinner.'

'You mean you want your meat *cooked*?' Melissa retorted. 'Why don't you just take a raw bone and go and gnaw it in a corner like the savage you are!'

'I'll cook dinner,' David volunteered quickly, sure that there was going to be blood shed any minute. He and Coralie had been uncomfortably watching the whole, bitter exchange, and as they both moved to begin the preparations for the evening meal, he was obviously seeking to break the tense atmosphere. 'Mack, I've just remembered,' he said suddenly, his voice artificially cheerful. 'Isn't it your birthday today? What are you now—thirty?'

Lachlan took a sip of his coffee, his expression unchanged. 'Ay.'

'What do you say we celebrate? I'll open a bottle of your favourite...'

'No, thanks, lad. I'm off the drink these days.' Lachlan pulled his jacket over his shoulders and stretched out on the ground with his back against a pile of timber and his feet towards the fire, morosely nursing the mug of hot coffee in his bloodied hands. Something about him warned them all against speaking to him again, and they all busied themselves with other things for a time.

Melissa's hand hovered in mid-air over the carrots she was slicing as she suddenly remembered something that William had told her; it had been on Lachlan's birthday that he had killed his father. Was that part of the reason, she wondered, for his obvious depression today? He had been moody and difficult ever since the events at the Pink Palace, but today he seemed close to breaking-point. She felt her anger at him slowly evaporate as she studied him from across the fire. He was staring out bleakly at the ceaseless rain. The thick, rough-cut fair hair was slicked flat to his head and there was a smear of blood on his forehead, where he had wiped the water off with his hand. He looked tired and young, and suddenly very vulnerable.

He turned unexpectedly and met her eyes, and for just a second she caught a glimpse of the old Lachlan, the man behind the cold and aloof stranger. Then the hard mask was back, and he turned away, but now she knew that it *was* just a mask.

He still cared about her! Even as her spirits, always irrepressible, were rising again, she realised just why he had been acting in this way. She had thought it guilt at his attempted rape of her, together with his frustration at not being able to take his revenge on William. She knew now that, while that might be part of it, the real reason was to protect her—to drive her away from his side to safety. She knew him well enough to know what that must be costing him, but she was also sure that if she were to tell him that she understood, he would turn her away. If only he would talk to her!

Dinner that night was the most delicious meal any of them could remember having in months; thick, rich, meaty stew that was only a little too tough, cooked with the sweet potato called *kumera*, carrots, and the inevitable cabbage-tree leaves. Lachlan alone seemed to take little pleasure from the meal, and ate purposefully and in silence. Melissa watched him anxiously, the thought occurring to her that he looked like a man who was preparing for a long, lean journey. So his announcement after they had eaten took her less by surprise than the others.

'I'm leaving the Arrow. Tomorrow.'

David was the first to respond. 'But what about the Regency, Mack? We can't leave it now that it's almost built! Where'd we go?'

'I'm going alone. You and Melissa can have the bar—and the horses and dray. I won't be needing any of it where I'm going.'

'And where are you going?' Melissa found her voice.

His eyes flickered over her briefly and then away. 'My claim over on the Shotover. I've had a gutsful of running a bar and selling booze to drunken miners. Long before I ever came here I was a miner, and it's high time I went back to doing what I know best.'

'Don't you think you've sulked for long enough, Mack?' David demanded hotly. 'You didn't get even with your brother for what he did to Melissa, but is that reason enough to walk out on your friends like this? Especially now, when we need all the help we can get to get this bar going again!'

'I'm not walking out on you. You'll have no trouble taking on another partner, and there's enough money from that pig-meat to send Melissa back to Dunedin on the coach as soon as this rain eases up. You'll cope.'

David swore viciously, and leaped to his feet. 'You selfish bastard! Get out, then, if that's what you want. It won't be the first time you've disappeared like this—but this time I'll be damned if I'm picking you out of the gutter again! Or have you forgotten Melbourne already?'

'I'll never forget Melbourne,' Lachlan said, so quietly that Melissa hardly heard his words. 'But this is quite different.'

'David!' Coralie grabbed his arm as David looked ready to swing a punch, but Lachlan was already going, disappearing into the dark screen of rain without another word.

David slumped down beside the fire, looking suddenly very pale and shaking slightly. 'I don't understand him. Two years of partnership... I thought we were as close as brothers. Then he can turn round and treat me like a complete stranger. What's he playing at?'

'He'll have his own reasons, honey,' Coralie soothed, and her eyes met Melissa's over the top of David's head. She knows, too! Melissa thought, but Coralie shook her head slightly in warning before turning back to comfort David.

In the early hours of the next morning, Melissa was awoken by Coralie crawling into her tent, a small pack, or 'scrag', in her hand.

'I think I've got everything you'll need,' she whispered. 'It looks as if he'll be leaving within the next half-hour, so don't waste any time. And I thought you'd better take this, too.' She showed Melissa what she was carrying in her other hand. 'David's rifle. He won't need it—you might.'

'Coralie...' At the sight of the rifle, Melissa felt less sure of herself for the first time. 'Am I doing the right thing? What if he turns me away?'

'Then you just stick with him. He shouldn't be alone now, of all times, and it's right that you should be the one going with him. Sure, it won't be easy, and I reckon he'll be furious when he finds out that you're going to stay with him, no matter what he says—but it's in Mack's nature to need someone to look after and care for. A man like him should never be alone.'

'You know him so well,' Melissa said softly. 'Did you ever...?'

Coralie shook her head firmly. 'No. He never was interested in me that way. Can't say I didn't try, though—but he's never so much as looked at another woman since he first set eyes on you, despite what David might have told you. And a man like that ... they don't come along all that often.'

There was an oddly bitter note in her voice as she finished that made Melissa wonder how sincere David's affections were for Coralie. She had always secretly thought that the bar-girl was not quite good enough for her beloved cousin; now she began to wonder if in fact the opposite were true. She would have spoken, but Coralie forestalled her by patting her cheek in a gesture of affection quite extraordinary for a woman so measured in her emotions.

'You take care of that big boy of yours, honey. Good luck.' Then she was gone as quickly as she had come.

In the pack, Melissa found two pairs each of David's trousers and shirts, and a large, freshly-made damper wrapped with some apples in a square of muslin. There were a couple of pairs of socks, and ammunition for the rifle. She dressed quickly in the men's clothes, adding to her own jacket and boots and a wide-brimmed hat she had long ago 'borrowed' from David, leaving her own clothes in a neat pile for Coralie to dispose of later. She rolled her blankets in the approved manner to tie on to the outside of her pack, and left the tent that had been her home for the past four months without a twinge of regret.

It had stopped raining at last, and there was a cold grey dawn breaking. She sheltered behind the Regency walls, watching Lachlan's tent, and a few minutes later she saw him appear, carrying his pack, rifle, pick-axe and a spade. He stood still, looking in the direction of her tent, and for one moment she was sure that he was going to walk over and discover her gone. But then he seemed to think better of it, and shouldered his pack instead. He strode though the sleeping camp, his long legs carrying him swiftly. She followed him like a shadow, taking great care that he should not see her if he happened to turn round—but he did not once look back.

CHAPTER SIX

MELISSA MANAGED to keep up with Lachlan for most of that day as he walked upstream, through country she had never travelled before. After a couple of hours, he left the Arrow and veered off to the west, to the Harris Mountains. She would have lost him at this point had he not frequently stopped to remove his pack and flex his shoulders. While the wound he had received in his chest had healed cleanly, she knew that it still gave him trouble, and she guessed that the pack must be rubbing agonisingly on the tender skin. She was still somewhat weak herself, but with a much lighter pack she was able to keep the distance between them fairly even until night began to fall.

The terrain became steeper and rockier as she began to have difficulty in seeing where she was going in the gathering dusk. Her legs felt like rubber, and her breath was coming in great painful gasps when at last her knees gave way and she sank on to the ground, admitting defeat at last. Helplessly she watched the man far up the mountainside disappear from view. She was sitting just below the snowline and had not the faintest idea of where she was. At first she had thought that Lachlan was heading for the saddle between the Harris Mountains and the mountain called Coronet Peak, but they had forded the Arrow River several times, and with the lengthening shadows over the hills and valleys below, any landmarks she might have been able to recognise were indistinguishable. She was most definitely lost.

What should she do? In the dark, she might not find her way back down to the Arrow, and she could wander in the hills for days before she came upon a digger or a settlement. But to continue up the mountain would be madness! On the other hand, somewhere up there Lachlan was undoubtedly making his camp for the night.

She pulled her jacket collar up against the mountain wind and got to her feet, intending to continue to climb. With her head down and her hat partially obscuring her view, she did not see Lachlan before she walked into him standing in her path, just a few steps from where she had been sitting and thinking. She gave a sharp scream of fright, even as she saw who it was, and fell backwards, the rifle clattering to the rocks at her feet.

Lachlan swore disgustedly at her, and bent to pick up the gun. 'Come on, get up!' He extended a hand to help her to her feet, and then disengaged his fingers immediately. 'If you've had quite enough rest, I've made camp on the other side of this saddle.' He turned on his heel and strode off, leaving her to run to catch him up. When she had dropped behind by some distance, he stopped to wait impatiently. 'What made you think you could possibly survive out here alone?' he demanded harshly as she came up gasping to his side. 'I could have been anyone coming up on you tonight, and you . . .'

'I've got the rifle!' she panted indignantly, but he gave a snort of derision.

'And a lot of good that would have done you, flat on your back! This is the last thing I needed now—a damned useless woman holding me up. I'd have got at least as far as Skippers tonight if you hadn't been so slow.'

'You—You knew I was following you?'

'With the noise you were making, a blind man would have known! Now get a move on—I've lit a camp-fire up ahead and I don't want it to go out before we get back.'

She put out a hand to restrain him. 'You're not going to make me go back, are you?' He shook his head in exasperation, and for the first time, she sensed that he was not quite as angry at her as he would have her believe.

'You'd no doubt come after me again like some homeless puppy, damn you! Now give me your pack— we'll never get there at this rate.' He shouldered her pack before taking her hand and leading her firmly over the saddle, walking a little more slowly now. On the other side of the ridge, beneath the dubious shelter of a rocky outcrop, a low fire fought to stay alight.

It was almost pitch-black by now, and her ankles were twisted and swollen in her boots as she sank gratefully to her knees by the guttering flames. Lachlan threw a couple of branches on the fire, stripping away a handful of the leaves before he did so.

'Make some tea with this, will you? I'll set up a shelter.'

The leaves were from the manuka tree, sweetly fragrant. They made a bitter but quite palatable tea when the conventional variety was not available. She put it in a billy-can with a few scoops of snow, and placed it over the uncertain flames to stew. From her own pack she took out the damper Coralie had packed; she wondered if this was to be the sum total of their meal, and her stomach gave a low growl of hunger as she remembered the pork and vegetables of the previous night.

Lachlan had fixed a canvas shelter under the outcrop, weighted down with stones in protection against the winds gusting erratically over the saddle. The manuka tea was only just drinkable when the rain started again and put the struggling fire out altogether. He refrained from passing comment, but she felt guilty anyway—this was perhaps the worst place they could have chosen to bivouac, and she knew that he would never have set up camp here had she not slowed him up.

They crawled under the canvas to sip their tea and share the damper, and even though they used their packs to block out the wind at the end of the shelter, it was bitterly cold. She was shivering uncontrollably despite her warm clothing, and even wrapping her blankets tightly round her did not seem to help. But she was still surprised when Lachlan reached over in the dark and turned her towards him so that her face nestled under his chin and their bodies were pressed closely together. Far too closely. She stiffened, and tried to pull away.

In answer, he pulled her back against him, gently but firmly, this time putting his arm under her head and round her shoulders so that further movement was impossible. 'Why not stay as you are? It's better than being cold.'

She did have to agree that it was much warmer this way. They lay still for a very long time, listening to the heavy splashing of the rain on the rocks, his heart beating steadily under her fingers where they lay on his shirt, their legs comfortably entwined. But she found it impossible to sleep with him near. She was too acutely aware of the feel of his hard arms round her, of his skin smelling slightly of manuka smoke and that special clean male scent she had come to associate with him. The hair on his chest tickled her face, his stubbled chin caught strands of her hair, and there was no way that she could find any rest. She lay as still as she could until at last his soft, regular breathing assured her that he had fallen asleep. And, when she was quite sure, she dared to do what she had been longing to do for a very long time. She gently pressed her lips to the base of his throat, just inches away, but was mortified when he moved his head away slightly, as if to look at her in the darkness.

'That's not a good idea, Melissa.'

She glowered at him resentfully, ashamed at being found out in her tiny act of tenderness, and angry at his reaction. 'It was just a little kiss!'

'Well, stop it!' Defiantly she raised herself on one elbow and bent to cover his face with a dozen small, darting kisses. He pushed her over on her back and held her there with one hand, not quite gently. 'I told you to stop it!' He was half-way between laughter and anger, and she realised that she might have gone too far. 'If you can't keep your hands to yourself, you can damned well sleep outside.'

'You wouldn't!'

'Oh, but I would, lass. I'd do anything for a good night's sleep, and if that means throwing you out to fend for yourself, I'll do just that, believe me!'

She doubted it, but still hesitated to defy him further. He turned over abruptly and settled himself with his back to her. She immediately missed the warmth of his body. 'I'm cold!'

'Snuggle in behind me, then. But for God's sake stay still.'

She lay quietly for a long time before asking in a small voice, 'Is it my scars, Lachlan? Am I so ugly now?'

'Shut up and go to sleep,' he said roughly.

And, at some stage during the night, she did.

*   *   *

It was still raining heavily when they awoke. Lachlan opened the end of the canvas lean-to and peered out with a frown. 'This rain must be causing havoc back at the camp; I hope they're all right.'

'But now it's winter, shouldn't it be raining?'

'Not this much, no. Matt was taking his animals to higher ground yesterday—he said this much rain isn't normal here. And I remember, last winter when we came here, there was scarcely more than an occasional light shower. With the camp being set on the river-bed the way it is... well, I'm just a bit concerned, that's all.'

'But they'd go to higher ground if there was a flood, surely?'

'Ay, sure they would. It's just me being cautious,' he assured her with a grin, but she knew that he was still worried.

About mid-morning the rain eased, then ceased, and a murkily pallid sun struggled through the heavy clouds. They took down the heavy wet canvas shelter and then started on their way, sharing the apples from Melissa's pack as they went. They walked down the other side of the saddle, circling Coronet Peak and heading towards the Shotover River.

We must make an odd couple, she thought wryly, as she almost lost her footing for the umpteenth time on the loose shingles of the saddle. He, so big and sure-footed, striding out confidently with the bulky pack on his back, and she, barely to his shoulder, dressed like a man in her rolled-up, baggy clothes, teetering alongside. As they came lower, they could hear a deep roaring in the distance.

'It's Skippers,' Lachlan told her. 'We'll go and have a look. It sounds a bit different today—probably from all that rain we've been having.'

They stopped at the top of a mighty cliff towering over a vast canyon, its yellow walls as steep and fluted as those of a medieval cathedral. Far below ran the cold grey Shotover River, swirling and billowing over the rocks in a myriad of white-bubbled formations and falls. The sound that it made was like a living thing, humming vibrantly in the air around. Her fear of heights overwhelmed her, and she cowered back from the edge of the precipice against the invisible hand at her back pushing her forward.

Lachlan appeared not to notice, staring intently down at the rushing waters. 'Hell,' he said reverently. 'There's been one almighty flood down that river. I wonder how much there is left of Arrowtown?' He turned and saw her tight face, and understood immediately. 'I'm sorry, lass, I should have remembered how you feel about these long drops. Let's go on, shall we?'

'How much further is your claim?' she asked, when they were a safe enough distance from the dull roar of Skippers and were beginning to climb again over the wide hills of tussock and rock.

'Further upstream, the Shotover opens out, and my claim is on one of the tributaries there. We should make it by evening.'

He had not mentioned resting, and he had not mentioned food, she thought regretfully, following him obediently up the hillside. The dinner of damper the previous night and the apples she had had that morning now seemed like feasts from long ago, and to add to her misery she had blisters which were rubbing raw in her hard boots. Lachlan, on the other hand, seemed to be completely in his element out here, thriving on the fresh air alone, and she envied him the obvious pleasure he took in his surroundings. It was almost impossible now to picture him back behind the bar of the Regency.

Soon they came to where the Shotover spread out below them, just as he had said it would, cradled in a deep, glacial valley. As they descended to the water, she could see across on the far bank to the small irregular shapes of several tents; the first sign of other miners that they had seen since Arrowtown. There were no tents on the narrow river that he led her up, however; just the blank walls of a gully, and fast-moving, shallow water. He took her pack and they walked along a precariously narrow shelf down to a small shingled bank where they removed their boots and socks.

The water was like ice, but Melissa felt perversely grateful for its numbing coldness as it at least gave her some respite from the throbbing pain of her raw blisters. The river came only to her knees, but it flowed so swiftly

that she had to cling to Lachlan's hand as they made
their way upstream and round the bluff to another small
shingled inlet at the foot of a high, unscaleable cliff.

'This is it,' he announced, as they stood shivering on
the bank.

Her heart sank as she looked around. On all sides
towered sheer rock-faces that would allow only a couple
of hours of sunlight a day on the inlet she now stood
on. Without a doubt, it was the wettest, coldest, most
inhospitable site anyone could have picked. It took every
last bit of her self-control not to demand of Lachlan
whether he had lost his reason.

He directed her attention to the bank behind them
where, about a dozen feet above water-level, she could
see a large open cave. 'And that's home.' She looked at
him suspiciously, sure that this was another of his jokes,
but he met her gaze levelly. 'Second thoughts, lass?'

She put her chin up. 'Not yet. Can you help me up?
I'd like to have a look at my new "home".'

He cupped his hands to allow her to jump up to the
cave, and then unstrapped his pick-axe to cut some steps
into the rock-face. At her scream of sheer terror,
however, he dropped the pick to the ground and was at
her side in an instant.

'Melissa! What is it?' With a shaking hand, she
pointed to the far corner of the cave. He had to look
hard before he found the reason for her terror. 'Is this
it?' he asked disgustedly, holding up a large *weta* that
had been trying to hide behind a rock.

She stared in horrid fascination at the huge insect with
its horse's head and long, spiked legs. 'Take it away!
Kill it!'

'Och, you great bully! What's it done to you?' He
leaned outside the cave and carefully put it in the scrub
to one side.

'It'll come back in!' she quavered.

'Then we'll have to put it out again, won't we?' he
said patiently. 'It'll bite you only if it has to—and it's
just a wee nip. Now pull yourself together and help me
to get our gear up here.'

After he had checked that there were no other insects
sharing their new residence, they fixed a canvas partly

over the entrance to afford some shelter from the elements. Then Lachlan took his rifle and waded back upstream in pursuit of dinner, while she unpacked the bedrolls and then perched alone on the rocky shelf, feeling decidedly sorry for herself. Her stomach was so empty that it hurt, her feet were swollen and bleeding, and she was freezing to death. And, what was worst of all, was that the immediate future did not promise any change in her circumstances.

She also had to admit to herself that she was now terrified of what she had got herself into. Lachlan was being kind enough at the moment, but she was no longer sure if she could trust him as she once had. If he got tired of her, or if they had yet another of their fights, might he not leave her? And then what? She had never been by herself in the wilderness before, and the panic she had felt when she had thought herself lost in the mountains the previous night was still clearly in her memory. What was she doing in this place, with a man who clearly did not want her? Should she admit defeat and ask him to take her back to civilisation? And, if she did, would he? Not knowing any of the answers, she took refuge under her blankets in a deep and almost immediate sleep.

When Lachlan returned later in the evening, she was still asleep, snuggled so deeply in the blankets that all he could see of her was one rather grubby hand and her tangled hair as it lay on the dirt floor. He moved about quietly, laying a small fire with the wood he had collected on his way back, quickly plucking and jointing the red-nosed *pukako* he had shot, and putting it in the billy to cook.

He had noticed her limping that afternoon and, carefully so as not to wake her, he raised the blanket over her feet to examine the big raw blisters. She had said nothing about them today, but no doubt she would let him know all about them soon, he thought ruefully. Whatever had possessed her to follow him like that? By the time he had noticed her and slowed down to let her catch up, it had been much too late in the day to take her back to the Arrow. Unfortunately, he had left the money for her coach-fare with David in Arrowtown, so she would have to stay with him until he found enough

gold to pay for the fare again. If this claim was anything
like as good as he hoped, that should not be more than
a couple of days—and by then she would be begging to
go. The life of a miner was far too harsh for any woman
to survive, especially in this kind of terrain. Until then,
it was a matter of keeping her at arm's length and surviving her tantrums—he knew her well enough to recognise that one was not far off. She was literally crying
out for his tenderness and affection—and God knew she
deserved something!—but making love to her was completely out of the question. His own strong sense of guilt,
and the knowledge that then he would never get her to
leave him, made that a fact.

He took her boots down to the river and wetted them
thoroughly. Then, by the light of the fire, he worked out
the stiff leather where it had rubbed against her feet,
pressing it outwards with his fingers before stuffing the
boots firmly with grass and leaving them to dry by the
fire.

True to form, she woke up just as he was dishing up
the stew, and she demolished several platefuls in no time
at all. Then she fell asleep again, cuddled against him,
waking briefly, colder in the night, to notice in drowsy
surprise that he had moved away to the far side of the
cave. She wriggled over in her blankets and snuggled up
against his warm back, falling asleep immediately with
a sigh of contentment.

In the early morning she pretended to be asleep when
he stealthily climbed over her and went down to the river
bank to wash. She watched him covertly from behind
the canvas cover, marvelling at the smooth-muscled
power of his body as he plunged into the grey water.
She peered miserably down the front of her shirt. The
welts on her breasts and belly had by now faded to thin
ridges of raised skin, only slightly discoloured and tender,
but still perfectly visible. She wondered in despair if
Coralie had been right, and if they would never disappear. No wonder they had so repelled Lachlan—and
probably still would. Her self-pity had progressed to irritation by the time he climbed back up to the cave, still
damply glowing from his swim.

'Ready to start work?' He grinned at her, and she was sure that he was deliberately ignoring her woebegone face. He picked up his pick and shovel and handed her a pan. 'The sooner we start, the sooner we'll know what we're sitting on.'

She eased on her socks and boots before sliding down to join him on the bank. 'What makes you think you'll find gold here instead of somewhere else? There's no sign of any other mining up this stream.'

'Which is one reason to give it a try. And another is the type of rock just along here—I've seen gold come out of this kind of ground before. And . . . I suppose you can only call it a hunch. This place feels right.'

He showed her how to pan correctly, swirling the gravel from the river-bed around in the pan, being careful to keep the water flowing in one direction while looking for the tell-tale glint of gold. She squatted on the damp bank, dutifully panning, while he walked out into the water downstream and started to pick into the river bank; chipping away a bit here, and a bit there, looking for some signs of a seam. After an hour, he came to squat beside her.

'How is it going?'

She motioned towards the billy-can at her side, where a few small flakes glistened. 'Just that. Do you want me to continue doing this?' She spoke sharply, but he did not appear to notice.

'You might as well, lass. I know panning is slow work, but it's steady, and if one of us finds enough, we can build a sluice, and it'll go much faster then. But at the moment it's a matter of just going carefully.' Even from where she knelt, she could feel the heat emanating from his body. He stood up to take off his shirt, which was damp with sweat, and then held out his hands for her inspection. 'Look at these blisters, will you? I can't believe I got so soft in that bar. It feels so good to be working again, I tell you!'

She sat and glared at him as he waded back to the bank, pick in hand. He worked steadily for a while, his back and arm muscles straining as he heaved the pick, only slightly favouring his scarred shoulder. He seemed

so happy, so much at home here, that her discontent
suddenly boiled up into outright anger at him.

'You're actually enjoying all this aren't you?' she demanded bitterly.

He looked slightly taken aback. 'Of course I am.
Aren't you?'

Her stomach growled emptily, and before she could
stop herself, she burst out, 'No, I'm not! I hate it—and
I'm hungry!' She wanted a reaction, any reaction, but
after a long inscrutable stare, he turned back to the bank,
saying nothing. His refusal to rise to her bait drove her
recklessly on. 'Did you hear me, Lachlan?'

'I heard you,' he replied evenly, with a slight increase
in the speed of his digging to betray his annoyance.

His imperturbability infuriated her beyond measure.
With a scream of frustration, she threw down her pan.
It began to float swiftly downstream, where he deftly
retrieved it with the point of his pick and threw it back
at her feet.

His eyes now when they looked at her were ice cold.
'Carry on like that, lady, and you're going to be very
sorry.'

'Why? What can you possibly do that could make
things worse for me? I'm cold and hungry and
tired...and you couldn't care less, could you? I hate
you! I hate this place! I...'

She ran out of words. Her eyes fell on his pack sitting
at the foot of the cliff, and without thinking, she picked
it up and threw it into the river. It sank slowly beneath
the water, and she stood there watching it in savage satisfaction. Let him manage with wet clothes, and see how
he liked it now! She looked up at him across the water
and was amazed to see that, far from being furious, he
was grinning broadly.

'So you think that's funny?' she hissed. Spinning
round, she shimmied up to the cave and brought down
his bed-roll, which she added to the sunken pack below.
Now Lachlan burst out laughing. 'Stop it!' she screamed
over his laughter. 'What's so funny?'

He shook his head helplessly at her. 'You are, lass!
You're your own worst enemy. That pack had all the
food supplies I'd brought with me—flour mostly for

damper. There's precious little you can make with wet flour!'

She felt the hot tears start to her eyes. 'You're a heartless bastard!'

'You're the one who ruined the food supplies,' he pointed out reasonably enough. 'And wet your bed-roll to boot.'

'It's *your* bed-roll!'

'Not now it isn't.' He turned his back on her and returned to the rock-face, swinging his pick with complete unconcern.

Shaking with rage, she scrambled back up to the cave, and this time collected David's rifle. She checked that it was loaded, and then slid down to make her way towards the Shotover, keeping one hand on the bank to ensure that she did not slip over, holding the rifle high with the other.

As she approached Lachlan, he looked up, and she saw a sudden look of alarm on his face. 'Don't you think that's going a bit far?'

'It's not for you—I wouldn't waste a bullet on trying to puncture your thick hide!' she snarled at him.

He made a grab for the rifle as she passed, but she stepped back into mid-stream, evading him, and he let her go. He called her back, a conciliatory note in his voice now, but she ignored him. By the time she got to the top of the bluff, her progress hampered by the heavy wet boots she had neglected to remove, Lachlan was still nowhere in sight. If he could not leave his precious mining for even a minute to follow her, she thought, it was obvious that her safety meant less to him than the gold. She was going to have to learn to fend for herself.

She hobbled up into the hills, where scrubby thickets grew at the foot of sheer cliffs, and the sharp wind off the mountains cut her to the bone. She walked cautiously through the tussock, trying to move as soundlessly as possible, unsure as to what exactly she was planning to shoot. She jumped sharply at a small movement at her feet and spun round, holding the rifle at the ready. Then she relaxed—it was only a *kea*, one of the brilliant green mountain parrots, very large and extremely cheeky. It put its head on one side and looked piercingly at her with bright, knowing eyes.

'It's all right, you stupid thing—I'm not going to shoot you,' she assured it crossly. In fact, she had never shot a living thing in her life, and it was beginning to dawn on her that it might be a great deal harder than she had previously thought. She supposed it depended upon how hungry she was going to get. As she continued up to the thicket, the *kea* bobbed along behind her, cawing incessantly.

'Be quiet, you! You'll frighten away everything else and I'll *have* to cook you for dinner!' But the cacophony went on until her frazzled nerves could stand it no longer. 'Oh, go away, you horrible bird!' she screamed at it, stamping her foot. It retreated a few feet, and then rushed up to peck at the metal eyelets on her boots. She feigned a kick at her tormentor, but it only hopped around her, shrieking in excitement, sparring like a prize-fighter in a ring.

Over the racket of the bird's teasing, she was sure that she heard something moving in the thicket. All at once the *kea* turned and fluttered down the hill, stopping some way off to watch her again in silence, poised for further flight. Had something scared it off? She listened intently, and then she was sure—there was definitely something big rustling in the bushes.

'Who—Who's there? Please come out,' she called warily. There was a long silence as the movement ceased. Reluctantly she raised her rifle in the direction of the thicket, cocked it, and waited. Everything was suddenly very still, and all she could hear was her uneven breathing and the heavy thud of her heart as it seemed to turn painfully in her chest. Steady, she told herself. Steady.

As she continued to look unflinchingly down the length of the barrel, the bushes parted, and she saw what it was: the small white tusks glinting evilly, the malevolent eyes, the rough hair and that distinctive stench. It was a tusker—a wild boar. They stared at each other, motionless. Melissa felt her fingers freeze on the trigger, and knew if she delayed a second too long, she would be lost. Then, with a snarling grunt, the beast charged as if it were on springs, leaping over the ground between them, lunging straight at her. Her finger jerked on the trigger and she was flung back with the recoil. She rolled to one side as she stumbled, holding the rifle over her in what she knew would be a futile gesture of defence. She could hear screaming as the boar kept coming, and was barely aware that it was herself. Already she could feel the pig's tusks in her side, could feel herself trampled under those sharp feet, being gored to death...

A scant yard from where she lay, the boar slowed, stood stock still for a long moment, and then fell heavily across her legs, its knees buckling beneath it. Sickened, she pulled her legs out from underneath its massive head. It had seemed to take for ever, but as she knelt beside the beast she had just killed, struggling for her breath, she could hear the echo of her rifle-shot rebounding off the valley walls. It must have lasted only a couple of seconds, and yet she felt as if she had just lived an entire life and death on that hillside. The dead boar was twitching slightly, its eyes glazing as blood seeped slowly from the wound in the centre of its forehead. She suddenly felt profoundly sorry for the life she had just taken.

'Melissa!' Lachlan flung himself down beside her, frantically running his hands up and down her arms to reassure himself that she was still intact. He embraced her wordlessly, and she found he was shaking slightly—with shock, she supposed dully. She felt quite limp and drained.

'I'm all right,' she said quietly, when she could speak again.

He looked unconvinced as he helped her to her feet. 'When I heard that shot, I thought... Oh, God knows what I thought! I can't believe you're unscathed. Those tuskers can kill a man!'

His anxious face began to swim before her eyes, and he caught her as she started to sag at the knees. The next thing she knew, she was seated on the ground with her head being firmly pressed down between her knees. 'I'm going to be sick!'

'No, you're not—there's not enough in your stomach. You just fainted for a moment, is all. As soon as you feel able, we'll take what we can of this pig back to the claim and you can have a decent meal.'

'I couldn't eat that!'

'I think you'll find you can, once it's cooked. Now shut up for a bit, will you, and take a few deep breaths,' he admonished her gently. After a minute, the faintness and nausea passed and she raised her head to smile weakly at him. He stroked her hair, a rueful expression on his face. 'I'm sorry, lass.'

'It was my fault. I'm an utter shrew, and I don't deserve you,' she said abjectly.

'That's true. But I could have made it easier for you—and I should also have remembered that an empty belly never improves your temper.'

'It wasn't food I needed, Lachlan,' she said impulsively, and she could see in his eyes that he knew exactly what she meant.

But he only sat back on his heels, and looked over towards the dead boar. 'Ay... Well. I'll get to work. This shouldn't take long.'

He left her side to start skinning the tusker with the knife that he always carried in a sheath at his belt. His considerateness did not make her feel any happier, although her anger had long since been frightened out of her. He was so damned *nice*, she thought helplessly, watching him throw some unspeakable titbit to the irrepressible *kea* at his elbow. Despite what he claimed, he *had* tried to make life bearable for her in this godforsaken place. He had fed her, protected her, sheltered her... he had been a perfect friend, in other words. If she had wanted him as a friend, she would have been very happy—but she did not, and she was not.

She closed her eyes as a wave of self-pity swept over her. She fought it down, and, when she opened her eyes again, it was to the sight of an entire army of eager *keas* hopping up the mountainside towards her. A sharp oath from behind made her look over her shoulder to the object of their attentions. Having made the mistake of feeding one bird, Lachlan was now fending off dozens and receiving a few nasty pecks in return. She had to burst out laughing as he at last had to admit defeat and grab what he could to run down to join her. The gleeful shrieking and squabbling from below reached a crescendo, as the *keas* realised that it was now a free-for-all, and even more of their number appeared from all directions. Lachlan and Melissa watched in horrified fascination as the birds covered the huge carcass, leaving it only when they had some gory morsel clamped firmly in their sharp beaks. So absorbed were they, that they did not hear the horseman riding up towards them from the river.

He sat and watched them bemusedly for a while, both of them bloodied and soaked to the skin, Melissa clutching a rifle and Lachlan a dripping knife. They spun round at the sound of his voice.

'What civilised pastimes you two enjoy!'

'David!' Melissa flung herself at him as he tried to dismount.

When he had succeeded, he hugged and kissed her resoundingly, and then turned to Lachlan. 'I'm not shaking your hand while you're holding that knife and that piece of pork! It is pork, isn't it?'

'Ay, Melissa's been hunting. It's good to see you, lad—but what's amiss?' He had noticed what Melissa had not—the tense set of David's jaw and his pallor beneath his tan.

'Has anything happened at the camp?' she asked anxiously. For David did indeed look a decade older than when she had last seen him not three days before.

'The camp?' He slumped wearily against his horse. 'The camp no longer exists, Melissa.'

'Oh, hell,' Lachlan said softly. 'The floods...'

'Yes, the floods. It was like a nightmare! The night after you left, around midnight, the water came, like a huge, black wall. I'd moved our belongings on to higher ground, but most of the miners were still down on the river bank. The level of the Arrow hadn't gone up that much, you see... We thought it would be all right. Then there was this almighty roaring noise... I've never heard anything like it in my life...' He broke off abruptly, unable to continue for a moment, and Melissa put her arms round him in comfort. He took a deep breath, and went on. 'Thank God, most of us made it, but some poor devils...'

'Who?'

'Splints was one; two of the girls from the Bendigo Hotel; dozens of others... maybe no one will ever know how many.'

They stared at him, stunned. 'Not...Coralie?' Melissa managed to say at last.

'She's safe—she was with me, on higher ground. Most of the survivors are elsewhere now, although they might rebuild the camp. But you'd never know where the Regency used to stand—everything was washed away. I got Coralie on a mule-train to Dunedin, where at least she'll be safe and warm. And...she did a bit of straight talking about why you'd left, Mack. And why she'd sent Melissa after you.'

'Did she, now?' Lachlan raised an enquiring eyebrow at Melissa, but fortunately let David's statement go. 'I take it you no longer want to brain me for leaving, then?'

David shook his head. 'You should have told me, Mack. I'd have understood.'

'But would you still have come after me?'

David thought, and then nodded. 'Yes.'

Lachlan gave a laugh of exasperation. 'It looks like I just can't get away from your family, doesn't it? Are you going to stay here now?'

'There's nothing left on the Arrow for me to go back to. I exchanged the liquor for food, extra blankets, materials for a sluice... Have you started digging yet?'

Lachlan caught Melissa's eye. 'I'm afraid we got sidetracked into a spot of hunting instead. But, to tell you the truth, it doesn't look too good. I'm mighty glad to see you, Davey, but I wonder if we haven't all had a wasted journey.'

David shrugged philosophically. 'There are always other claims. And it beats running a bar, doesn't it?'

Lachlan fervently agreed, but Melissa found herself biting her tongue to stop from contradicting them both. David had brought both Maggie and Maud with him, and they walked the horses back down to tether them by the river bank, the two men talking enthusiastically all the while about sluices and diggings and rock formations. She could not recall Lachlan showing such animation since they had left the Arrow, and she was faced with the fact that he was heartily relieved at not being alone with her any more. David had always been an effective buffer between them, and now she knew that she and Lachlan would rarely be alone again.

Back at the claim, they roasted a leg of the wild pork and, supplemented with some of David's provisions, Melissa found that it was far from being inedible. After they had eaten, the men hammered together a sluice—a device only just beginning to be used widely in Otago. It was a long trough with ridges in the base, through which rock from the banks or gravel from the river bed was put. Water was repeatedly run over it, and the smallest and heaviest fragments, which were the ones likely to contain gold, were washed to the lowest level. It was a Californian invention that Lachlan had used there, but which was new to David, coming as he did from Ballarat, where the mining was dry.

The next morning, the real work began. For hour after hour Melissa hauled buckets of water up from the river to tip into the sluice, while the men, stripped to the waist and sweating heavily, dug shovelsful of gravel and carried it in buckets to the top of the sluice.

The weather improved, and with the cessation of the rain, the level of the rivers dropped to a safe level for the first time. Melissa worked as best she could alongside the men, her shoulders constantly aching with the weight of the full buckets, her hands quickly becoming callused and cracked, her nails broken and bleeding. Twice a day it was her job to go down the river to collect firewood, although this was not so much a chore as a treat. She would wander for an hour or more along the banks of the Shotover, staying clear of the thickets.

The pale winter rays of the sun on her face were the only warmth she knew these days, and she dreaded going back to the dank gully where every surface felt as cold as death. But eventually guilt would get the better of her, and she would make her way back to where the men still laboured on, their bodies slick with sweat and their breath misty on the icy air. They would always greet her cheerfully, and never said a word about the long periods she spent away from the claim, which—although she knew she had no reason to—made her feel even more guilty.

She envied the men their comradeship, developed from more than a year of doing just this sort of back-breaking work in Australia. They worked so well together, with no need for words save for an easy banter, each knowing as if intuitively what the other was doing or was about to do. She felt isolated and excluded, and strongly suspected that that was Lachlan's intention, if not David's as well; had she only said the word, they would have immediately and happily escorted her to the hotel at nearby Maori Point and booked her a passage on the first stage-coach out. It was only her stubbornness that kept her staying there—that, and the awful certainty that if she left Lachlan, she would likely never see him again.

Sometimes, in her long perambulations on the banks of the Shotover, she would wonder where her sense of pride had gone. Living in a hole in a bank in the wilderness with a man who did not want her around and whose affection for her was not a fraction of hers for him...but then she had only to go back to the claim and see that wide, white, cheerful grin of welcome, and she could steel herself for another day on the river, pride or no pride.

At the end of that first week, despite all their hard work, there was barely an ounce of the tiny, glittering fragments collected in a small can—an appallingly small amount, by Otago standards. On the eighth morning, David sat on the river bank, looking glumly into the can.

'That's worth about five pounds,' he announced. 'That'll buy four dozen eggs, or the handle of a shovel, or... Dammit—I feel like throwing all this back where it came from!'

Lachlan threw his pick-axe down, and came to sit heavily beside his friend, muttering something under his breath.

'What's that, Mack? Some Gaelic obscenity?'

'There's no such thing—that's why we bother to learn English,' Lachlan retorted. 'No. I'm just wondering if there's some kind of a jinx on me. This has to be the poorest stretch of river on the Shotover—they'd do better than this anywhere on the Arrow! And I was so damned sure...'

'It's odd, because I've never known you wrong in picking a claim before,' David said slowly. 'Ah, well...' The two men stared morosely at the water rushing past their feet, silently struggling with the fact that they had just wasted a week of some of the hardest work they had ever done in their lives. 'Want a drink, Mack?' And there was such a long hesitation before Lachlan declined, that Melissa knew his resolve was weakening.

'I'm going upstream to wash,' she said, but neither of them gave any sign of having heard her. She was in no doubt, however, that the moment she was out of sight, the whisky bottle would appear. She knew Lachlan had sworn off the drink a month ago, and he had held to that resolution, but at a time like this...

She picked up a blanket and a bucket of warm water from beside the fire, and walked around the rocks upstream to where she would be out of sight. This was the portion of the claim the men had announced to be completely unworkable, consisting as it did of deep, swirling waterholes. She stripped off, shivering, on a large, flat rock, and soaped and rinsed herself as quickly as possible. After towelling herself dry on the rough blanket, she was struggling with her shirt over her still-damp shoulders when her fingers accidentally caught in the leather strap round her neck. Helplessly she watched as her greenstone pendant spun through the air and fell with a tiny splash into the water, several feet from where she stood.

Flinging herself on to her stomach on the rock, she peered down into the depths, trying to make out the pendant through the swirling water. With the grey river stones and the distorting effect of the fast-running water, it was virtually impossible to distinguish a small green stone. She thought briefly about going and getting one of the men to help, but she was sure they would not think it worth it—the pendant had little value to anyone but her. She was about to give up in despair, when her eye was caught by a glimpse of green a little further away from the river bank than she had thought it would be. She stared at it hard for a moment until she was quite sure that it really was her pendant, and then rolled up the sleeve of her shirt. It was difficult to tell how deep this water was—the water was so clear and fast-moving that it acted like an optical illusion sometimes, and two feet could be closer to five feet deep. But she had at least to try! She leaned forward and reached out as far as she could, but her fingers closed on nothing but water. She withdrew her hand and shook it violently in an effort to get some feeling back into the fingers—it was so cold! She tried again, shifting her weight on the rock to give her arm more reach, and this time her fingers closed triumphantly over the small stone she sought, but then she overbalanced. It was as though the water caught at her arm and then pulled her in, and in just one horrifying second, she was under the river. Even if she had been able to swim, the numbing ice of the water would have prevented her from effectively fighting the swirling eddies she was caught in. She struggled to the surface, and had time to expel her breath in one sharp scream before she was sucked under again.

Further down the river, Lachlan had at last decided against a drink and was trying to hand the bottle back to David.

'Go on, Mack—you need it! We both do!'

'Sure I'd *like* it, but it isn't going to make things any better afterwards. No, take it back, lad.'

David reluctantly pushed the bottle back into his pack and gave a loud sigh. 'You and Melissa—you're like a couple of wet blankets. You don't drink, you don't smoke, and I feel damnably guilty if I do either!'

'You should have brought Coralie with you, so the two of you could have wallowed in vice together.'

'Hell, we need to do *something* to cheer us up! So…do we find another claim to work? Or is that a rhetorical question?'

'It is. I guess we move across the Shotover to where everyone else has had the good sense to mine—at least we'll make a living that way. But there's something else we have to do first.'

'Melissa?' Lachlan nodded. 'I've been worrying about her,' David said slowly. 'She's not going to last much longer, is she?'

'It's no place for a woman here—or for anyone in their right mind. I thought she'd have given up days ago, but it seems I've underestimated her.'

'Not for the first time,' David commented. 'I'd have thought you'd have known her better by now. She's not going to give up on you, you know.'

Lachlan ran his hand through his hair distractedly. 'I don't know what to do with her, Davey! I've tried being cruel, I've tried being kind. I've appealed to her reason and to her emotions...but nothing seems to work! I mean—look at her now. She's exhausted, she's cold, she believes I've got no further interest in her...and still she won't leave me.'

'There's a simple explanation for that,' David said briefly.

Lachlan looked away. 'Ay, I know.'

'And you? Do you still feel the same way about her?'

'I do. I love that lady more than my life's worth. Which just about sums up the entire dilemma.'

They sat in silence for a while before Lachlan raised his head, listening intently. 'Did you hear a noise? Like a splash?'

'What sort of splash?'

'A Melissa-sized splash.' He would have started up the river, but David jumped to his feet and restrained him.

'She's bathing, Mack. You can't barge in on a lady when she's...' He broke off as a shrill scream came to their ears, Without hesitation, the two men leaped over the boulders upstream to where they knew Melissa would have been washing. Thre was no sign of her.

'There she is!' David pointed to where a flailing hand broke the surface of the water. Having the longer reach, Lachlan threw himself on to the rock and managed to grab the hand the next time it appeared. As he pulled her towards the bank, her head collided with the underside of the rock he was lying on. 'Don't brain her instead of drowning her!' David shouted, and struggled to catch her other arm to pull her out of the water. She was deathly white and shaking uncontrollably, and her breath was coming in great sobbing gasps, but she was still very much alive.

Lachlan wrapped her in blankets, and then roughly rubbed her arms and legs to restore her circulation. 'How the hell did you manage to fall in?' he demanded, but she was shivering too much to answer.

David, meanwhile, was peering hard into her hair, slicked as it was to her head. Then he put out a finger and ran it across her crown. 'Mack—look at this.' On his finger, dozens of small flecks glinted in the pale sunlight. 'Is this what I think it is?'

Lachlan looked once, and then mercifully stopped rubbing Melissa's arms as he looked twice. 'Hell! From under the rock, do you think? Where she hit her head?'

Melissa was sufficiently recovered by now to be able to crane her neck to see what they were talking about. 'What is it? Oh . . . just a bit of gold.'

'Just a bit?' David looked at her incredulously. 'If this much rubbed off on your head from just that one rock . . . there must be a whole lot more down there.'

'I don't care,' she said wearily. 'At least I've got my pendant back.' She opened her hand to show them the stone she had hung on to grimly throughout the entire ordeal. There, on her palm, twice the size of her thumb, a gold nugget gleamed warmly. 'Oh no!' she said disappointedly. 'I thought . . .'

They never did find out what she thought. The shout of pure delight from the men completely drowned her sad explanation. It took some time before they could convince her that the nugget she held in her hand was worth every penny of two hundred pounds, at least. After they had ensured that Melissa was warm and dry again, they made a celebratory billy of tea and came back upstream to study the deep, swirling waters one more time.

'So this is where we have to mine,' David announced resolutely.

'I thought you two said that this part was unmineable?' she said in surprise.

'Ah, but that was before you discovered gold here,' Lachlan explained with a grin. 'Nothing's unmineable to a digger, Melissa—as you'll find out if you stay.'

She sighed resignedly. 'I don't see much point in walking off the claim, now that we've discovered gold. I'll stay.'

The next four weeks passed in a blur, the days and nights running one into another as they struggled to mine as much gold as they could while the weather held. They dammed alternate parts of the river to enable them to dredge thoroughly, which meant each of the men taking turns to work in the freezing waters, stacking logs and rocks with numbed, chilblained hands. They tried to spare Melissa the hardest work, and she ended by making constant billy-cans of hot tea and taking her turn at the sluicing, but she still spent her days in a mindless haze of weariness, staggering to her bed-roll at night to fall asleep with her boots still on. She slept deep, dreamless sleeps and would wake up in the cold clear dawns, stiff and unrefreshed, to face yet another unrelenting day.

The men freely admitted that it was the very worst site anyone could ever have worked, especially during the winter months, but it was an extraordinary lucrative claim. They never found Melissa's lost greenstone pendant, nor did a nugget the size of the first one ever turn up again, but every shovelful of gravel brought up at least one small nugget, and in parts of the bank, under the ferns, the gold shone like stardust in the soft black slate.

It seemed to Melissa, in the few moments she had for reflection, that they were all slightly crazy then. They must have been, to have worked so maniacally. Perhaps, she thought, that was how 'gold fever' manifested itself. It could only have been a fever that drove them ever onwards to work to the very edge of collapse day after day and never stop to ask themselves why. All that gold... They mined so much of it that the men had to leave every third day, armed with both rifles, to take it to the Bank of New Zealand Gold Office at Maori Point. From there, the gold was escorted weekly into Dunedin by the gold escort.

It began to snow, and still they worked on, breaking the ice over the water in the mornings to get to the river bottom. The exhilaration of those early finds had faded under the relentless pressure of the work schedule they had set themselves, and sometimes it seemed to them that it might as well have been coal they were mining, so easily did it appear in their shovels and pans.

One night, David got fed up with her complaining yet again that they had failed to find her greenstone pendant, and he bored a hole through the first nugget she had found to hang around her neck instead. When she had then complained of his extravagance, he had taken the gold-dust bored from the nugget and laughingly blown it over her. Much later it amazed her to think how casual they had all been about the wealth that lay around them. It had amused them, none the less, that a small fortune hung about her neck on a simple leather strap beneath the warm but ragged clothes she wore.

The snowfalls persisted, becoming heavier and more frequent. The horses had long since been sent to the livery stables at Maori Point, and the men sometimes found that it took hours to walk through the snowdrifts to carry the gold they had mined to the bank. She was awaiting their return one day, sitting in the cave by a small fire, looking out at the falling snow. If she listened hard, she could hear the faint sound of the water running under the ice in the river, but there was no other sound at all. She found herself fancying that she was the only person left alive in the world, and the memories she held of the Regency and its crowded heat and noise seemed to belong to another age.

She supposed she should be feeling happy, despite the cold, the constant exhaustion, and the isolation. She was wealthy now, wealthier than she could possibly ever have imagined, although none of them knew exactly how much money was waiting for them in the bank in Dunedin, just as none of them had been able to spare any thought as to what lay ahead when this was all over. So why was she not happy? Why did she have this tight coil of misery in her chest that was always there whether she was awake or asleep? Why was she so sure that no amount of gold was worth this? Too tired to weep, too tired to think. Her mind slowly became as blank as the snowdrifts outside, and she slept.

CHAPTER SEVEN

'MELISSA!' She was being shaken awake so hard that her teeth were rattling and she thrust Lachlan away in irritation. Behind him she could see David, his face alarmed in the reflected white light of the snow.

'What's the matter?' she managed to ask, her slurred voice surprising her. Her arms and legs felt like lead, and she wished the others would go away and let her sleep in peace.

'Get up!' Lachlan pulled her to her feet, and, when her knees gave way, he slung her over his shoulder and slid down to the river bank, where he began to frog-march her up and down.

She seemed to have lost contact with her feet somehow, and her legs would not do what she wanted them to do, but mostly she was angry at Lachlan's unreasonable insistence that she keep moving. Could he not see how tired she was? 'Leave me alone,' she mumbled, trying to break free, but Lachlan's arms were like a vice round her shoulders. David was up in the cave, lighting the fire again—she could not remember its going out. Exhaustedly she let her legs drag behind her as Lachlan pulled her along.

'Move your legs, Melissa. Come on!'

'You can go to hell!'

'Move your legs, or I'll slap you until you do.'

'You wouldn't . . .' He raised his hand, and she saw from his expression that he certainly would. She sullenly brought one leg forward, then the other, although it felt as if she was dragging them through heavy snow, or up a deep river. Up and down the river edge she walked, with Lachlan alternately threatening and cajoling her, the snow turning to mush under their feet.

At last he pushed her up to David waiting in the cave. They wrapped her in blankets, and slowly, and with the utmost care, removed her boots. 'Thank God!' David muttered, as he examined her feet.

She peered down to see. They were a funny colour, but that was all . . . She gave a small scream as the feeling started to return.

'You'll keep your toes,' Lachlan said unsympathetically. 'Not that you deserve to, letting the fire go out like that. What were you thinking of?'

'Mack, cut it out! We've driven her like a damned slave these past weeks, and she's exhausted. Can't you see? It was only a matter of time before something like this happened to one of us.' David had wrapped her feet up warmly again and placed a mug of tea in her hands. At least *he* cares about me, she thought miserably.

Now he fumbled in his shirt pocket and thrust a handful of receipts under her nose. 'It's official, coz! Guess how much we're all worth now!'

'I don't know.' Neither did she care any more.

David's face fell. 'Over six thousand pounds!'

She tried to imagine that much money, and failed— it simply did not mean a thing. All it seemed to add up to was the small pieces of paper David held so tightly and proudly in his hand.

'It hasn't been worth it, has it, lass?' Lachlan's eyes met hers in a look of such sympathy that she was taken completely by surprise.

David looked indignant. 'Of course it's been worth it! However else could we have got this much money in such a short time? We're all rich now! We can go anywhere we please, do whatever we want . . .'

'Do you mean . . . we can leave here?' she ventured. 'Go back to civilisation?'

David nodded. 'Why not? Mack and I were talking on the way back, and we think we've stuck it out for long enough. Certainly there's plenty of gold left in the river for any other miner who's prepared to put up with what we have. But we've made enough now, and with all the talk about the gold this claim is bringing in at the bank, it's more than likely we'll have a lot of company when spring comes. Coming back today and finding you like this makes me even more sure that it's the right thing to do. What do *you* think, coz? Like the idea of a roof over your head again?'

'A roof,' she said longingly. 'And a hot bath and warm dry clothes again. Just to wear a *dress* again would be heaven!'

'A hot bath and a huge steak for me,' Lachlan said wistfully.

'A hot bath, and a steak, and a cigar, and a magnum of champagne,' David contributed. 'All at the same time, if I can manage it.' They sat silent for a moment, lost in their dreams.

Then Melissa shook herself free of wishful thoughts and faced the reality of their frozen winter cave. 'How soon can we go? As soon as the snow starts to thaw?'

David grinned. 'Then we can travel to Queenstown and catch the steamer. We'd be in Dunedin within a couple of days, that way.'

'What will you do then?' she asked curiously.

'Have a bloody marvellous time! After that, I don't know. Travel a bit, maybe. All I know for sure is that I'll never swing another pick in my life.'

She laughed, and turned to Lachlan. He was not smiling, and she had a suddenly ominous feeling about what he was going to say. 'Well, Lachlan?' she prompted. 'What are *your* plans?'

There was silence in reply to her question, and the men exchanged a glance that told her a great deal. What new scheme had they hatched up between them now? Once again she had the frustrating sense of being excluded from their comradeship, peripheral to their decision-making. She fought down her anger, concentrating instead on staring at David, whom she knew to be the easier one to wear down. But it was Lachlan who at last replied.

'As soon as we're in Dunedin, I'll be looking for a passage out. Brazil or Argentina, I thought.'

'South America?' She felt a cold wave of apprehension wash over her. 'By yourself?'

'Ay.'

'Don't—Don't your plans for the future include us, Lachlan?'

He looked at her squarely, his face harder than his eyes. 'No. Not at all.'

Why, she wondered, had she thought it would be different now? After all this time together, working and suffering together, she had grown used to him being there beside her every morning when she woke up, every night when she went to sleep. His physical presence now was such a fact of life for her that the very thought of him not being there was like a bereavement. The fierce attraction she had always felt for him had long since been submerged under the more immediate pressures of work and sheer survival, but somewhere deep inside she had kept that spark alive. For weeks she had consoled herself that once they were back in civilisation, once she had pretty clothes to wear, and they had warm shelter and enough food to eat and time alone without David... perhaps, then, Lachlan might see her through different eyes. But it would seem that nothing had changed since that night at the Regency when he had announced that he was leaving to go mining.

She became aware that David was touching her arm. 'Lissy—I think we ought to talk.'

'About what?' she snapped. 'Tell me, David—what *have* you two decided to do with me? I'm sure you've had a good talk about the best way to dispose of me!'

He flushed at her anger. Lachlan had meanwhile been intently studying the scuff-marks on his boots, but now he got to his feet.

'Ay, well... I think I'll stretch my legs for a bit.' He pulled up the collar of his jacket and jumped down.

She waited tensely until they could no longer hear the crunch of his boots on the snow. 'Well, David?'

'Aw, Lissy, don't get like that. It's just that I've been thinking...' He frowned, groping for the right words, discovering that there were none. 'I've been thinking that we ought to get married.'

'Married?' she almost shrieked. 'Why would you want to marry me?'

'Dammit, Melissa, I've never proposed marriage to a girl before in my life! Can't you at least show a bit of appreciation, or something?'

'Appreciation? Why should I appreciate your proposal when it is painfully obvious that Lachlan has set you up to it? How hard did he have to twist your arm to get you to do this?'

'Not too hard at all,' he assured her. 'In fact, I should have thought of it a long time ago.'

'But you didn't. And, besides, you've got Coralie.'

'Come off it, coz! Coralie's a nice girl, but... Look, the two of us are naturals together. We like and understand each other—and with your looks and our money, there's nothing we couldn't do! We'd have a wonderful life!'

She shook her head firmly. 'No. And, besides, I've got no intention of getting married to anyone.'

'But you've just spent five weeks holed up with two men in a cliff on the Shotover River. If you're ever to re-enter polite society, don't you think it best to be married to at least one of them?'

'It depends which one,' she replied, feeling sorry, at the sight of the crushed look on his face, for her earlier outburst. 'I'm sorry, David, but I just...don't feel about you...in the same way that I do about Lachlan.'

'Feelings can change, Melissa,' he pleaded. 'I've cared about you deeply ever since you were a little girl, and now that you're a grown woman, I still feel just as much—only different. I do love you, Melissa. And I want you, too. I think we could be very good together. I know I'm not Mack, but maybe in time you'd love me back the same way. Please, let us try?'

She did not know what to say in the face of his obvious sincerity. She had always known that he cared for her, had suspected that his outraged reaction to her going to Queenstown with Lachlan had been at least partly due to jealousy, but she had never expected a declaration of love from her cousin. She did not stop him when he slowly put an arm round her shoulders and tipped her face up to his. He kissed her cautiously, experimentally, and she found it not at all unpleasant. It felt so good to have someone's arms round her again, to feel attractive and desired again, and if she closed her eyes, perhaps she could even pretend... But then David's lips became more insistent, and when his hand dropped

from her shoulder to slide inside her jacket, she had no
hesitation at all in disengaging herself.

'I'm sorry,' he said, contrite. 'Was it what William
did to you?'

'No, it has nothing to do with that.'

He sat back on his heels, the desire in his eyes slowly
fading to sympathy. 'You're a one-man woman, aren't
you, coz?'

'It looks like it, David. You are the nicest man I know,
and I love you dearly, but you're far too much like a
brother to me. And you're not Lachlan.'

David sighed. 'He's going to leave us, though—and
you must accept that. And when he does, I want to look
after you. Maybe you'll never feel the same way about
me, but I'd like you to stay with me none the less. And
it is what Mack wants too—for your safety, Melissa. Will
you do that?'

She nodded, suffused with guilt and misery. How very
wrong everything seemed to have gone. Now she felt like
some parcel, bundled up and passed over to David by a
Lachlan no doubt desperate to be rid of her. She willed
herself not to think like that, and to believe that the two
men in her life had only her safety and welfare at heart
in all things. But when Lachlan returned and she saw
David shake his head slightly at him, the feeling of being
little more than a chattel intensified, and it hurt.

Having made the decision to leave, they did very little
work for the next two days while they waited for a break
in the weather. The unaccustomed inactivity irked
Lachlan, and he would go for long, solitary walks while
Melissa and David huddled by the fire practising their
poker skills on each other. When the three of them were
together, there was an awkwardness, a straining of the
atmosphere that had never been there before.

At last it stopped snowing. The snow was thawing in
the river, and they agreed that the day had come to leave,
although the sky still hung dark and heavy with the threat
of more snow to come. David elected to take the last
bag of gold to the gold office and to return with the
horses, while Melissa and Lachlan dismantled the camp.
On his return, they would travel to Queenstown to take
the ferry for Kingston, and from there on to Dunedin.

They saw David off, and then busied themselves with packing up the bed-rolls and provisions. They spoke only to agree upon leaving all the mining equipment for the incoming miners, and then sat in silence in the cave, waiting for David's whistle to let them know he was back.

After a time, Lachlan began to fidget, and then he went to stand on the river bank, his body rigid with tension as he stared in the direction they could expect David to come from. 'I'm going up to the bluff. Are you coming with me?' He began to gather up their packs without waiting for an answer.

'Is something wrong?'

'I don't know.' There was a small muscle working in his jaw, and he had become very pale. David was not yet overdue, and there was nothing that could have gone wrong with their arrangements—and yet she found herself catching Lachlan's anxiety.

When they climbed to the top of the bluff overlooking the Shotover, Lachlan swore softly. His horse Maggie was there, cropping on the tussock. She was saddled, but there was no sign of Maud—or of David. Maggie came up to Lachlan, whickering as she recognised her master.

'David's in trouble. Get up, Melissa.'

She obediently let him hoist her up into the saddle and strap the packs and his rifle behind her. He strode in silence alongside the mare as they followed the route that David would have taken to Maori Point, but there was no sign of him, and the melting snow held no tracks for them to follow. At the small settlement of Maori Point, they asked at the livery stables, and the ostler informed them that Mr Frampton had paid for and collected both horses, that he had been alone, and had looked well.

Lachlan went into the bank, while Melissa waited outside with Maggie. She pressed her face against the soft, damp neck of the horse and wondered when this long nightmare would finally end. For weeks she had had to live like an animal in a hole in a cliff, longing for dry warm clothes, for a hot bath, for a properly cooked meal. By now she should have been well on her way to Queenstown and civilisation. She felt so tired, as if she had been pushed to the very limit of her endurance—as indeed she had. David's disappearance now was threatening to push her over that limit. Where *was* he?

Lachlan came back out, his face grim. 'He's been in, but some time ago.'

'Did you ask if he'd taken the money out?'

'No. Why would he have done that?' Lachlan looked so surprised at her question that she found herself longing to slap his honest, trusting face.

'Because, if you'll remember, he was the only one of us who was really happy about the money! Don't you see what he's done? He's taken it all and left us! We've got one horse, a few supplies, and just what we have on our backs! That's all he's left us with, Lachlan!'

'You're not talking sense, lass. Davey'd never do that, and you know it.'

'But he has! *I'll* go in there and ask, if it's the only way to prove it to you!'

'We haven't got time now for your foolishness! That snow's getting closer all the time, and if Davey's in trouble, we have to find him before it gets really nasty.'

'He's not in any trouble, I tell you. He's headed for Queenstown this very minute with our money!'

'Look, shut up about the damned money for a minute, will you! It's not important! Now get back on Maggie and we'll go and look for him. He's in serious trouble, Melissa. I don't know why I'm so sure of that, but I am. Please trust me.'

Stunned by his complete lack of logic, she remounted, and watched as he stood stock-still for a moment by the mare, one hand on the pommel. It was starting to snow again, big soft feathery flakes that caught unmelted in his hair. Only his eyes moved, ranging over the mountain peaks before them, and she knew that he was listening to that small inner voice, that uncanny sixth sense that he sometimes had. Only this time he was completely wrong.

'If Davey was off the track,' he said slowly, 'then he was being pursued. Being David, he would have taken the opposite direction to the claim, to lead them away from us.' He swung round, taking in the winter terrain, the cold hills and white mountains, to face the north-west. 'He's over there.'

'You're wrong!' she could have screamed at him, but somehow she was able to bite her lip and follow as he began to lead the way up into the foothills in the reverse direction to the way *she* knew David had gone. The snow flurry ceased as they climbed higher into the hills, following the gully known as the Moonlight. As they left Maori Point far below, Lachlan took the rifle from the saddle and held it under his arm at the ready. She had no idea where they were going, but he seemed to know. An hour from Maori Point, on a cliff over the Moonlight tributary, Maggie suddenly gave a snort, and pricked her ears.

Lachlan gave a low whistle, answered immediately by a whinny from further down the hill. To Melissa's shock, Maud came trotting up to them, reins trailing, anxious for company. David's bed-roll and rifle were still strapped to her back.

'Oh, my God! What do you think . . .?' she began, but Lachlan was not listening. He was intently examining a maze of hoof-prints in the fallen snow, and then went over to look at other marks, on the edge of the cliff. A long way beneath his feet the water ran deep and swift over high, cruel rocks. When he turned back to her, his face under the broad brim of his hat was unreadable, and she quickly slipped off Maggie's back to run to him and clutch his arm. 'What is it? What has happened here?'

'Some kind of a fight, from the look of it. And someone's gone over the cliff.'

'David . . .' she said faintly.

'Maybe.' He took her hands in his, and she could now see that he was fighting to master his own emotions. Every muscle in his face was tight, the lines round his mouth deeply etched. 'Melissa, are you listening to me?' She nodded jerkily, her face white. 'Good girl,' he said encouragingly. 'Now, I want you to take the track we came up on back to Maori Point. Go quickly, and don't stop for anyone or anything. When you get there, I want you to book into the hotel. Do you understand? You're not to stay here. You'll be safe for a while at the hotel

as long as you stay indoors, but you must get back to
Dunedin as quickly as you can. Use the gold pendant,
if there's nothing at the bank. Right?' He gave her a
little push towards Maud. 'On your way, lass.'

'Where are you going?'

He hesitated for a second. 'I'm going downstream to
see if there's a body. I don't want you with me if I find
it—it won't be a pretty sight.'

'That's not the reason! It's William you're expecting
to find first, isn't it? He's waiting out there somewhere
to kill you! Please—come with me? Come back to
Dunedin with me!'

'Listen, Melissa,' he said urgently. 'You don't realise
how lucky you'll be to get out of this alive. If it is
William, you know too much now to be safe even in
Dunedin, but at least, if we separate now, you've got a
fighting chance of getting somewhere safer than here.'
He swung himself up on Maggie's back, and thrust the
rifle down into the pouch at the front of the saddle.

'What are your chances then?' she demanded
desperately.

He laughed shortly. 'Damn all! Take care, lass, and
good luck.' He was gone in seconds, riding like a fury
down the hillside in the direction they had come.

She stood in the white silence, and for a moment the
world seemed to spin before her eyes. David . . . and now
Lachlan as well. She might never see either of them
again.

A sharp bump from Maud's soft nose reminded her
of the nervous horse standing behind her, and she turned
to hug the mare as much for her own reassurance as
Maud's. 'What do you think, Maud?' she whispered.
'Do you think I should run to safety? Or should I follow
Lachlan in case he needs me? Somehow this seems like
the very worst time of all to desert him—don't you
agree?' Another nudge from the mare was all the answer
she needed.

Remounting, she set off in the same direction, towards
Maori Point, riding swiftly but carefully, in case she
should come up behind Lachlan too quickly and be discovered. The snow deadened any sounds that he made
as he travelled, but Maggie's hoof-marks were easy to

follow. Towards the top of Mason's Bluff, a steep hill, the path dropped sharply and became narrow and uneven. They had to pick their way carefully on the way up because of the loose shingle which had recently been dislodged over the track. As she remembered that, her emotions threatened to overwhelm her; no doubt it had been loosened by David riding his horse up at speed, trying to break away from his pursuers. Poor, poor David. How could she have suspected him for even one second?

She reined in at the sound of voices on the track just below, and turned Maud back into the brush and left her tied there while she made her way to the brow of the hill from where she could see the track. If only Maud, already jittery, did not give her away by calling for her again! Crawling crab-like over the rocks and snow, she was at last able to make out the figures of the men some fifty feet below.

Lachlan was there, facing three other riders. She gave an inaudible sigh of relief as she recognised the leading rider to be Sergeant Kemp of the Otago Constabulary. He was responsible for the Queenstown–Arrow district, and was much respected by the miners. He had often stopped for a drink in the Regency, and was not above an occasional game of cards, or asking Melissa to play one of his favourite songs now and again. He and Lachlan had always got on well—if anyone could help Lachlan now and make him see sense, it was this man. She strained to hear what he was saying.

'. . . can't understand why you won't answer a simple question, MacGregor. I'll ask you again. Where have you come from?'

'I don't see that it's any of your business,' Lachlan replied, and she was surprised at the wariness in his voice. His left hand was resting lightly on his thigh, only inches from his rifle. Surely he would not draw it on the police, she thought in alarm—he could not possibly be so desperate! He would be a wanted man then, and the whole story of his past would come out. And he must know that that would be exactly what William would want!

Sense counselled her to rush down the hill and break the terrible tension between the men. Instinct made her stay where she was, biting her hand in anxiety, scarcely able to draw breath in case she missed whatever would happen next. Watching as intently as she was, she saw Lachlan's fingers flex slightly, and guessed he was waiting for a chance to pull his rifle clear of its holster. There was a strained silence while the sergeant rubbed his chin thoughtfully, his florid face grim and watchful under his peaked hat. Then, before she even had time to realise what he was doing, he had reached under his coat and pulled out a revolver.

Lachlan froze, his rifle half-way out of the saddle-bag. 'Damn,' he said low and savagely. 'Damn you!'

There was a quiet laugh from one of the two men behind Kemp, and as the man lifted his head, Melissa saw for the first time why Lachlan had tried to draw his gun. William Price sat easily astride his mount below her on the track, looking relaxed and very pleased with himself. She screwed her eyes up for a second in anguish as she realised that William had finally tired of his cat-and-mouse games and had decided to bring in the law to arrest his half-brother. His timing was too impeccable to be accidental; David's death, the amount of gold they had deposited at the bank...they all had to be connected in some way with him!

'I'm arresting you for the murder of Edward Price, in Inverness, nine years ago,' Kemp was saying now. 'Come on, lad—you've had a long run of it, but your time's run out at last. Hand that rifle over carefully, and don't make this any harder for yourself than you have to.'

Lachlan did not move, his fingers remaining poised on his rifle, and Melissa was suddenly and sickeningly sure that he was not going to hand it over to the police sergeant. She could see that he was looking past the policeman's shoulder to William, and she knew as clearly as if she could read his mind that he was calculating how long he would have to put a bullet in William before the sergeant fired... She thought frantically. There was no time to go back to Maud for the other rifle, and if she stood up and spoke, she could put herself in dire danger and perhaps make things even worse for Lachlan. Desperate to do something, anything at all, she picked up

a large rock and hurled it with all her strength and no
aim at all down the hillside. The rock spun as it fell,
glancing off the loose gravel and creating a small land-
slide. As the shower of gravel fell, the horses in its path
skittered in panic and a startled Sergeant Kemp fired accidentally into the air as his horse reared back in fright.

Lachlan did not waste as much as a second to look
up and see what had caused the rock-slide, but spun
round the moment Sergeant Kemp's attention was diverted, spurring Maggie back up the track he had just
come down. Melissa was running for her horse as he
came to the top of the bluff, and he drew up just long
enough to grab her by the back of her jacket and bodily
throw her up on to Maud. The pommel in her midriff
momentarily winded her, and as she gasped for breath
and struggled to find the stirrups, he smacked the mare
viciously on the rump and Melissa had to cling to the
saddle for dear life as Maud shot forward. He drew ahead
and began to lead the way back up towards the
Moonlight. Melissa could not remember ever having gone
so fast on horseback before. She had almost lost her hat
over her eyes as she had landed in the saddle, and was
finding it hard to see, let alone cope with the tight, constricting pain of terror in her chest. It was all she could
do to concentrate on Lachlan riding only a half-length
ahead.

There came a sudden whirring sound by her head, immediately followed by a sharp crack from behind. She
had no idea what it was until Lachlan cursed sharply.

'That'll be William, blast him! Get in front of me,
and *go*!' He dropped behind her to cover her back as
he spoke, just as another bullet passed somewhere to
their right.

Horrified, she did not need his urging to drop lower
in the saddle, urging the sure-footed but lazy Maud on
as fast as she could possibly go up the narrow track
winding round the hills. There was no longer any time
to think—all her concentration was focused on staying
on the horse's back. She had no idea how long they rode,
but it was some time before Lachlan once again took
the lead. The terrain was higher and harsher now, and
she knew that he was taking them deeper into the Harris

Mountains, northwards to Mount Repulse. At last he reined in on a rocky bluff and looked down at the way they had come. There was no sign now of their pursuers, and she gave a great shuddering sigh of relief.

'We've lost them . . .'

'I'm not so sure. Kemp knows these mountains a fair bit better than I do, and he'll be a hard man to shake off.'

'They *shot* at us, Lachlan! I can hardly believe it!'

'You were safe enough—it was only Willy,' he assured her.

'You've said that before about William's shooting— and you came very close to dying that time!'

'A lucky shot.' His face sobered as he realised how terrified she was. 'Are you all right, lass?'

'If you could stop being so—so flippant about all this, I would be! Why were they shooting at us?'

He shook his head slowly. 'If William was shooting at us, it's either because Kemp can't control him, or because they've decided that it's unimportant whether they take me alive or dead. Either way, it's not good.'

'Do we have to go on like this for much longer?' she asked, dreading his answer.

His eyes were on the horizon. 'I'm afraid we do, lass.'

Far below, across the foothills, the three riders were easily following their tracks in the freshly fallen snow. She saw the blue policeman's cap on the man in front, and wondered what she had got herself into.

'Persistent bastards, aren't they?' Lachlan spun Maggie round again and led the way up the track, but soon he swerved abruptly, travelling downhill to the west. Then he began zig-zagging furiously, fording streams and changing direction erratically.

Melissa could only grip Maud tightly with her knees and keep her head down, following him blindly. The suspicion crossed her mind that he had done this sort of thing before. When they next drew in, snow had begun to fall lightly again, and they were much further north, in high country bordered on all sides by towering mountain peaks. This time, they were completely alone.

Lachlan took off his hat, and rubbed his forehead wearily. 'I think that will have got them well and truly lost.'

'But so are we!'

'Ay,' he agreed, 'but that's quite different. We *want* to be lost.'

'I don't,' she said in a small voice, ashamed even as she spoke to be showing weakness at such a time. 'Did we *have* to run away like that? I mean . . . I don't want to sound disloyal, but . . . did I *have* to come with you?'

'It was a matter of coming with me or going back with William,' he said apologetically. 'You know too much now for him to let you get back to civilisation, especially with David gone. Even though Kemp was there and might have tried to look after you, there are a thousand different ways out here of losing people, and I don't think you'd have got too far. They had no qualms about shooting at you, remember.'

She remembered only too vividly, and trembled at the memory. So this was what it felt like to be hunted and hounded like some wild animal! 'What about you? Were you going to give yourself up if I hadn't intervened?'

'No, I wasn't.' He spoke quietly, and with conviction. 'I'll *never* give myself up, Melissa—I hope you understand that. I decided a long time ago that I'd never give William the satisfaction of watching me hang. Any death is preferable to that.'

Strangely enough, she could understand that, even though it sounded like a death-knell to her ears. She took a deep breath to steady her nerves. 'And, in the meantime, do you have a plan? Do we keep running indefinitely from the law?'

'I shall. But I'll leave you at the first farmhouse or settlement we come to where you'd be safe. As far as anyone knows, I could have kidnapped you, and that's the story you'll have to stick to. Are you ready to push on now, lass?'

'Please. I'm so tired,' she pleaded. 'And the horses are exhausted. Can't we stop for just a little while, or even find a place to camp for the night?'

'I wish we could, but we've delayed long enough already. Look at that.' She turned to see the heavy blue-blackness rolling quickly across the southern sky, and realised that the light snowfall now was merely the preamble to a heavy storm about to break any minute about them. 'That's why Kemp and William would have turned back, as like as not,' he said tersely. 'We've got to find solid shelter fast, but God knows where. I'd hoped to find some kind of forestation here—even a hut—but we're too high. We can only try to get to the lower slopes and find shelter among some trees as soon as possible.'

To her surprise, he reached over and put an arm round her shoulders, drawing her hard against him as he buried his face in her hair. 'Oh, sweetheart,' she heard him say softly. 'Christ, I'm sorry it's turned out this way.' He pulled away before she could see his face, but the tremor in his voice told her that for the first time he was acknowledging his doubt that they would come through this alive. She put her hand over his and pressed it reassuringly, but he did not look back at her.

As though sensing the gathering danger behind them, the tired horses valiantly sped up for a time, but soon the full force of the storm overtook them. Then they could only struggle on slowly, heading ever northwards, while the wind from the south rose to scream in their ears and make every step a gargantuan effort. At times Melissa was too blinded by the snow whipping into her eyes to see where—if anywhere—they were going. Even through the layers of heavy clothing she wore, her bones felt like icicles.

A small, detached, part of her thought how odd it was that she was not panicking—it was as if all her energies were being used up in simply staying in the saddle, on not succumbing to the wild white fury lashing her from all sides. Every ounce of strength she had left was taken with keeping in her sight the big dark outline of Lachlan riding alongside. At times, even this became blurred and distorted in the swirling snow, and once she thought she had lost him altogether. Then she did panic, screaming his name repeatedly, the storm snatching the words from her mouth. Then the blessed relief when she felt his gloved hand firm on her wrist, letting her know that he was still here beside her, that he would not let her go.

She wondered what it would be like to die out here in the snow. She had heard that it was not a hard death; one simply fell quietly asleep and never woke up again. If she could fall asleep with Lachlan's arms round her, she did not think she would mind so very much. She only hoped that the horses would not suffer.

Time had long since lost any meaning for her; it might have been half an hour or it might have been ten hours before she realised that the horses had stopped and Lachlan was standing beside her, pulling her off the saddle. The stirrups were tangled round her nerveless feet, and she could not help him as he struggled to free her. Then he pushed her roughly into a place that was very dark and still.

'Don't move!' she heard him shout quite unnecessarily over the screaming wind, and then came the sound of a door shutting behind her.

She pulled her gloves off with her teeth to feel cautiously about her, and her fingers touched a hard wooden wall. It was so strangely silent here, but her ears still rang with the memory of the shrieking storm outside. She said a silent prayer of thanksgiving as she sank to the ground, her back to the wall, shaking uncontrollably. After a time, the door opened again to the snow and wind, and then shut.

'Melissa?'

'Yes. I'm over here,' she managed to mumble through numbed lips. She heard him taking off his gloves and fumbling for his matches. He had some difficulty in striking one, but when at last he did, she took in a great sobbing gasp of relief. 'Where are we? What is this place?'

'It must be a musterers' hut, thank God!' Lachlan replied fervently. 'I'd started off following what looked like a sheep-trail, but I lost it as soon as the storm came up. There can't be another building for miles around. It's nothing short of miraculous that we practically rode straight into this.' He lifted an oil-lamp down from a shelf as he spoke, and lit the taper. In the strong warm light they could see the small, one-roomed hut clearly. Apart from a few shelves of tools and farming equipment it was completely bare, but it was soundly built, and in

a corner stood the unthinkable luxury of a stove. 'And
there's a good stable alongside with plenty of hay,' he
informed her, almost disbelievingly. 'We'll be able to
weather this storm in a lot of comfort—for however long
it takes.'

She lit a fire in the stove while he settled the horses
and brought in armfuls of wood from the pile outside.
It was only a short time before the little hut was sump-
tuously warm and they were eating freshly-made damper
washed down with hot tea, their boots and outer clothing
steaming away beside the stove.

'I think I've died and gone to heaven,' Melissa said
at last, around a mouthful of damper.

'I think I agree,' Lachlan murmured drowsily,
stretching himself out on the blankets they had laid on
the floor. 'Come over here, lass.'

She snuggled down under his arm, her head resting
on his shoulder. Why, she wondered, did his arms feel
the most natural and normal place on earth to be? She
finished her damper thoughtfully. Perhaps it was because
now their lives were permanently changed, and things
would never be the same again. With David dead, they
were on their own now, in every sense of the word. Now
there was only one person in a hostile world who was
completely on her side, who understood, and who cared
what happened to her. Despite everything, she felt a great
slow surge of contentment. Except for one thing. She
moved away from him to sit up.

'What is it?' he asked, nearly asleep.

'Is there any more damper?'

'You've just eaten the last of it. Do you want me to
make some more?' he asked reluctantly.

She shook her head, although she was still hungry.
After all the weeks of hard work and deprivation on the
Shotover, it seemed that her stomach would never feel
full again. Lachlan closed his eyes, absently rubbing her
back as she sat beside him.

'Lachlan?'

'Mmm?'

'What would you have done if you hadn't found this
place? What would have happened?'

He shrugged. 'At the last, we could have dug out a snow-cave and got into that. But that would have meant letting the horses go in that blizzard. And if this weather had kept up, we could have survived for only a very little time.'

She shivered at the thought. 'We were so lucky.'

'We were, indeed.'

She lay down beside him again, hearing his heart beat steadily under her head. How wonderful it was to have survived! To be alive! 'I wonder,' she said slowly, 'if we were allowed to live for a reason. David's dead, and we should have died out there tonight, too—and when you think of how unlikely it was that we should find this place…doesn't it make you wonder if there is a purpose to it all? Lachlan?'

But he had gone to sleep, deaf to her philosophising. She watched him for a while before, with a small sigh of satisfaction, she followed his example.

Later, Melissa was never sure which of them had woken first, but as she came back to consciousness, the first sensation she was aware of was his arms round her holding her closely against him. It felt so warm and comforting and familiar; only now there was a slowly waking need in her for something more than even this.

She raised her head, and their lips met in a tender, infinitely gentle kiss that was quite unlike any they had exchanged before. It was a completely undemanding kiss of affection and affirmation, but as Lachlan raised his head, there was a question in his clear grey eyes. She answered it in the most natural way she could. Reaching up, she pulled his face back down to hers and kissed him again, but this time it was with all the hunger and need and love that was threatening to explode inside her. He ran his hands slowly over her body, unbuttoning her shirt, tugging at the belt of her breeches. She struggled to help him, unwilling to take her lips from his, eager to become as close to him as she possibly could.

In the golden, flickering light of the stove, Lachlan leaned back to look at her lying beside him on the blanket. 'How lovely you are,' he whispered, a catch in his voice. 'How very lovely.'

She knew that she was too thin, that the scars on her body still remained, but none of that was important now: he was speaking the truth. She had never felt so beautiful as when she saw herself reflected in Lachlan's eyes.

He made love to her carefully and slowly, every touch of his hands and his lips on her body making her gasp with impatience and desire. When at last he entered her, she was grateful for his self-possession and control—her sharp cry of pain took them both by surprise. But it was almost immediately forgotten in the wonder and delight of both giving and taking so much pleasure; of belonging to each other so completely. She lay afterwards cradling his head between her breasts, running her fingers lightly through his damp, fair hair and down over the hard-muscled arms encircling her. The warmth from the stove and the silence around them enveloped them like a soft blanket.

She was thinking with amazement of how one single event could change a life so completely. Just a few hours ago, she was sure she had reached the limits of her physical and mental endurance. She had even been sure that she was going to die. Now she was suddenly warm and cherished, and more alive than she had ever been in her life. How strong and wise and new she felt! She wondered if she looked different. 'Do I?' she asked of the man in her arms.

'Mmm? Do you what?'

'Do I look different?'

He leaned back on one elbow and regarded her solemnly, his eyes dancing. 'Not a bit. You've still got one nose, and two eyes, and lots and lots of teeth, and...'

She giggled, and pushed away his hand. 'Lachlan, be serious for once! That wasn't what I meant, and you know it!'

'I know it wasn't, lass.' He sobered. 'Yes, you do look different—you're growing lovelier and lovelier every second that I keep looking at you.' He kissed her very softly, and she saw everything that she had ever wanted to see shining in his eyes. 'I love you, Melissa. I should have told you that a very long time ago.'

She lost her voice for a moment from sheer happiness. When she found it again, she said rather unevenly, 'Why

didn't you? All this time, when you were trying to get
rid of me, when you got David to ask me to marry
him...you *could* have told me. It would have helped
sometimes, when I was so sure that you didn't care a fig
for me!'

He looked rueful. 'You are the most perverse, irritating, stubborn, bad-tempered wench I've ever known!
Sometimes you drove me crazy with wanting you, and
sometimes I could have cheerfully wrung your neck. But
I've always cared. I began to care the moment I saw you
scared stiff on the back of the dray, ordering William
off with a shotgun. I've never met a woman as special
as you—but it took me a long time to admit to myself
that I loved you too much to let you go. And, by
then...you'd been through so much, all on account of
me, and I couldn't let you stay with me and be hurt any
more than you had been.' He ran the tip of one finger
down her nose, tracing the curve of her lips with a slight
frown. 'I—I had no idea that this was your first time,
sweetheart. I hope I didn't hurt you?'

'You don't regret what we've done, do you?' she asked
anxiously.

'Lord, no! I love you, and as you fortunately seem
to feel the same way about me, regret is the one emotion
I'm not feeling! No, it just came as a surprise to find
that you'd never been with a man before. Especially
after...' He broke off in embarrassment.

Realisation of what he meant dawned on her.

'William? You didn't think *William* had made love to
me, did you?' she said, horrified at the idea.

'Made *love* to you? I was sure he'd *raped* you, woman!
He didn't beat you like that for nothing. What did
happen that night?'

Briefly she told him, and she was vaguely surprised,
even as she spoke, to find that it all seemed now as if
it had happened to quite another person. She felt sorry
for the other woman—for that younger, vulnerable
Melissa—but it no longer mattered as it once had.
'...then after he whipped me,' she finished, 'I was such
a mess that I think he was rather put off the idea of
touching me. And I suppose he thought there would be
plenty of time before you returned.'

Lachlan was looking slightly sick. 'Why don't you hate me, Melissa? What I did to you... What I tried to do to you...'

She took his face in her hands, desperate to reassure him. 'I didn't hate you even then. Because...in a way, I understood.'

'You *understood*?' he said incredulously. 'There was nothing to understand! I had no reason to do what I did apart from my own stupid, blind, drunken jealousy, Melissa. To have thought even for one second that you'd willingly have gone to whore for William...'

'Not me—Phyllida,' she corrected him.

He stared at her, stunned. 'Phyllida? What do you know about her?' he demanded.

'Nothing—apart from the fact that you called me by her name that night. It was her you were trying to hurt then, wasn't it? Please, Lachlan, won't you tell me about her?'

He shook his head adamantly. 'No. She's over and done with. She belongs to a part of my life that has nothing to do with us.'

'I don't think that's true,' she persisted. 'If you remember her so vividly—if you react like that just at the mention of her name—then she still matters to you. I know you love me, and that she is in your past now, but I do need to know about her—what she did to you. Please, Lachlan?'

'No!' He began to move out of her arms, but she clung to him tightly.

'If you don't tell me, then I'll only think the worst. Is that what you want?' It was blatant blackmail, but it worked.

'Very well,' he said resignedly. 'If you really have to know...she was a woman I met over a year ago, in a gambling-house in Melbourne. She was very beautiful to look at, and for a short time I thought that I meant something to her. I was...wrong. And that's all there is to it.'

'No, it isn't!' she said fiercely, almost angry with him now. 'There's much more to it than that, I can tell! William's involved somewhere, isn't he? Please don't lie to me now—tell me the truth!'

'For God's sake, Melissa!' he groaned, and buried his face in her shoulder. But she lay hard and unrelenting beneath him, determined to know what he was hiding. Finally, hesitatingly and not meeting her eyes, he told her. 'I knew what she was, I knew how she lived—but I thought I was different. I thought I loved her, and she swore that she loved me. It was like a madness, the way she made me feel... We were...together, one night. When I looked round, William was standing at the foot of the bed, laughing. It was only then that I understood. It happened to be my birthday, you see, and that day tends to be something of an anniversary for both William and me. He'd set the whole thing up as some kind of sick practical joke. I should have known...but I'd been so eager to believe that Phyllida was all that she presented herself to be that I let myself become too careless. And then William tried to use you in very much the same way, except that this time he was serious. He's learned after all these years exactly how to stick the knife in and how far he has to twist it before he gets the reaction he wants from me.'

'It *wasn't* you who killed your father, was it?' she asked him softly.

He shook his head. 'No. It wasn't me. And even with all the evidence against me, William knows that. I'm not sure myself who did it, or just how—but I've got a fair idea. And William knows that, too. It's one of the reasons he's hounded and tried to intimidate me for years without ever actually going to the police with what he knows.'

'Until now.'

'Ay—until now. And I don't know why he's chosen now to do it. It's probably got everything to do with his mother's death; while she was alive, he seemed quite happy simply to torment me. I was never able to hold down a job, or stay for long in any one place. He always had me followed, and years might pass, but he or one of his men would eventually turn up, wherever I was. I had to stay on the move, keep away from him, never knowing when he'd carry out his threat to turn me in. It was that power over my life that he enjoyed, and after a while I stopped trying to change my identity and find quiet hiding-places. I guess I gambled that he wouldn't ever turn me in, and that one day he'd get fed up with his games and stay permanently in England. Things only got really serious after his mother died. I suspect that she was the reason he couldn't stay in England.'

Melissa looked at him sharply. 'Are you saying...that you think William is the one who murdered your father?'

He nodded. 'But I've no evidence, understand. Not one bit. And he's got more than enough to convict me in any court in the world. Hell, I thought I *had* done it at first—I virtually said as much in front of a dozen witnesses when I saw my father's body. It was only later that I realised that I couldn't have, ever... The only reason I can think of why William has suddenly brought in the police after all these years is because of you and David. He's...disposed of David, and now...'

'And now I'm next,' she finished for him. 'Oh, Lachlan—what will we do?'

'I don't know, lass. Somehow I've got to get you to safety, somewhere where William can't touch you. We've got time to think about it now.'

'Poor David...' Her voice broke.

'I know, I know,' he soothed her. 'He was more than a good friend to both of us. After I'd made such a fool of myself in Melbourne, he was the one who picked me up out of the gutter, sobered me up and booked a passage for the two of us to see his old Uncle Toby in Otago. I owe him a great deal.'

She managed a smile. 'He always said the same about you. He said you were as close as a brother to him—and he was like a brother to me. William has *so much* to answer for! David...and nine years of your life, wasted...'

'Not wasted, lass. There's you.'

There was such sincerity and love in his eyes that she could say no more. Lachlan was here beside her, and he loved her as she loved him. Here in this place and at this time, no one else—no shadow from the past—should be allowed to come between them. She moved into the warm shelter of his arms and held him closely, promising herself that she would never, could never, let him go.

They stayed in the musterers' hut for three days while the blizzard raged outside and the threat of pursuit could safely be ignored for a time. Lost in their own world, they scarcely noticed the days and nights passing by outside as they strove to make every minute precious and memorable for each other. While they knew that each time together could be their last, still they did not talk about the future that lay outside the little hut. For once, time was on their side.

But they woke one morning to hear the icicles falling off the roof of the hut, and they knew that their time of peace together was over. When Lachlan opened the door, clear golden sunshine flooded the room, and in the distance they could hear the *keas* calling to each other. She came to stand beside him, wrapping a blanket round her, and looked out to the mountains glistening ice-hard and pure in the early morning.

'The light in this country is so beautiful, so new,' she said wonderingly. 'I used to think there could never be anything lovelier than Otago in the summer, and yet now... I don't know if I could be happy living anywhere else but in these mountains. Can you imagine how wonderful it would be to build a house in a place just like this, with big windows all about so that you could always see them? And maybe even a rocking-chair, so that when the day's work was done you could quietly sit and rock and watch the sun go down over the mountains.' She laughed at her fantasy. 'Listen to me... I sound like an old woman...!'

Her smile died at the bleak look on Lachlan's face, and she could have bitten her tongue off. She had broken their cardinal rule of never speaking to each other of their hopes for the future—a future in which they knew that very little was hopeful. 'I'm sorry...' she began, but he smiled gently at her.

'Have your dreams, sweetheart. Sometimes they can be all that makes life worth living.'

They made coffee, and Lachlan went to stand by the door again, looking out assessingly at the wide, deserted terrain. 'From the looks of it, we've got fine weather for the day, at least. Assuming they're going to mount a full-scale search for us from Maori Point, we'd better move on today. But where the hell do we go?'

'We could go to the North Island,' she suggested. 'If they're watching the ships across the Strait, we'll have to disguise ourselves, and change our names, too.'

'It costs money to get across Cook Strait—and all we've got is that nugget round your neck. We'll have to sell it somewhere without raising anyone's suspicions.'

'But we've got plenty of money! There's near enough to seven thousand pounds in the bank in Dunedin, and...' She stopped as the realisation of their true situation sank in. 'The bank account... We can't touch any of the money in there, can we?'

'Not unless we want to get ourselves arrested, no.' He leaned back against the door-jamb, looking at her thoughtfully over the rim of his mug. 'But it's not too late for you, though.'

'You mean if I go back to... well, the Dunstan, for instance. If I can convince them that you kidnapped me, eventually I'd be able to take the money out of the account and travel to Christchurch. If you met me there, we could go on to Auckland, Australia, or...even South America! Of course that's what we'll do! Oh, it's all going to be so easy!'

'No,' he said emphatically. 'You've forgotten William. As soon as he hears that you've reappeared, he'll be tracking you wherever you go. If you were to go north by yourself and keep quiet about what you know, he might leave you alone. But you'd be followed every inch of the way. If you were to help me—if you have anything at all to do with me—then we're both dead. As it is, he could make things very difficult indeed for you with the police, especially if they saw you start the rock-slide. Whatever you do from now on is going to be dangerous, and if you stay with me...it's not worth the risk, sweetheart.'

'You're worth *any* amount of risk! What else can we do, then?'

'I don't know,' he said helplessly. 'I don't know. I want you to be with me, but even more than that I want you to stay alive. The only way out that I can see is if

I go into hiding for a while—six months or a year, maybe. Until things have died down.'

'A year without you!' It was an eternity. 'There has to be another way, Lachlan. Some way in which we can stay together.'

In the end they compromised, deciding to head for the north-west, over the Southern Alps, to the West Coast. Habitations there were even rarer, and they had a good chance of remaining safe from detection. They could not agree on what was to happen after that. She knew Lachlan was still hoping to persuade her to return to civilisation without him, but she was utterly determined to stay with him, whatever the cost.

Melissa felt sad at leaving the little hut, where her life had so suddenly taken a new direction and meaning, and it felt strange to be out in the brilliant sunshine again after the soft firelit twilights of the past few days. As Lachlan checked the saddles on the horses, she stretched luxuriously like a cat, enjoying the lusciously ripe feel of her body. Every inch of her felt well-loved and desirable. 'I must look a sight,' she yawned happily, her fingers tangling in the knots of her hair.

'But a delicious sight, minx,' he replied, laughing at her. Her stomach lurched with desire as she looked at him—so big, so handsome, so completely hers! He put his hands on her waist to help her on to her horse, and she mischievously slipped her hands under his jacket, running them over the solid muscle covering his ribs. 'Melissa! Stop that!' he groaned against her hair, and she chuckled, feeling his unmistakable response to her touch, loving the power she had over him now.

'Do we *have* to go on today?' she asked ingenuously, pressing herself against him.

'Och, woman, have you no shame?' He drew himself up and broadened his Scots accent in mock disapproval. 'Get on your horse, ye wee baggage, before I take my whup to you!' He started to lift her into the saddle, but she forestalled him by winding her arms round his neck, a plea in her eyes.

'Please, my darling? Just a little longer?'

'We can't, Melissa! We've got to get going soon—
we've no idea how close a pursuit party is behind us.
Tonight, sweetheart, please.'

She clung to him fiercely. 'Promise me something,
Lachlan? Promise me you'll never love another woman
like you love me?'

'Jesus, woman, I'd never have the strength!' His grin
faded as he realised that she was in deadly earnest. 'I
could never love another woman, sweetheart. Believe
that, no matter what happens now. There will never be
anyone else for me.'

She melted joyfully into his arms and he took the opportunity of putting her up into the saddle. Once she
was there, however, he stood gazing at her with a look
that frightened her suddenly.

'Darling, you look as if you've seen a ghost!' She
laughed nervously.

He shook himself, strangely pale, and forced a smile.
'No, it's all right. I just had a feeling that...you shouldn't
be on that horse.'

'Maud? But she's lovely. Aren't you, girl?' She patted
the mare's neck affectionately. What a perfect day it was!

She followed him as he chose a track leading down to
the foothills, more familiar ground to her with its red
barren rocks and the golden tussock flourishing everywhere. Tarns glinted sapphire-blue in the tenuous new
sunshine. It was odd to think that it was almost spring.
The seasons in this country were so undefined, one
running almost imperceptibly into another, but they were
always enchantingly beautiful.

Shall I ever be as happy again as I am at this moment?
she wondered, reining in Maud for a moment on the
edge of a bluff in order to drink in all the glorious view
below her. Lachlan, seeing her stop, indulgently turned
round to wait for her and she smiled across at him,
knowing that he always understood—and fully shared—
the irresistible pull of this wild country.

A small bird, perhaps startled by her horse's hooves
so close to its nest on the ground, suddenly scurried out
from between some rocks. Taken by surprise, the normally placid Maud reared up, back from the edge of the
bluff. Melissa grabbed at the saddle, missed, and with

a shrill scream rolled over and over down the cliff-face, banging her head on the rocks, the world spinning crazily as she fell. She had lost consciousness before she stopped falling, and when she came to, it was to see Lachlan's face, tight with agonised concern as he bent over her.

'Don't move, Melissa! Please!' he said urgently, as she tried to reach up to her head, where the pain was greatest.

She watched as if from a great distance as he carefully felt her arms and legs to check that nothing was broken. His hands, she noticed, were wet and sticky with blood, and she wondered vaguely where it had all come from. He had brought the horses down with him, and now he tore up one of his shirts to wind round her head. But when he tried to lift her up, she screamed with the agonising pain, and he gently laid her down.

She must have lost consciousness again, because the next thing she saw when she opened her eyes was a canvas over her head. He must have set up camp around her, and she felt herself securely wrapped in blankets. Her vision was badly blurred, but she could make him out beside her, quietly holding her hand, his eyes never leaving her face. She continued to drift in and out of consciousness, with just a few moments of clarity—like diamonds in the dark sea of her mind. Her most enduring memory was of riding, held up against Lachlan's chest, one of his arms firm across her shoulders to keep her upright. She had tried to say his name, but he did not seem to hear her, his face stark in the moonlight...or was it sunlight? She could not tell.

There was a carriage then, rocking steadily from side to side, and Lachlan's face no longer came into her field of vision. Then came a long time of white sheets and pain, and hushed voices and sickroom smells. She heard herself screaming and calling out Lachlan's name as she thrashed about, but he never came, and at last she would lie still and silent beneath a halo of concerned, soothing faces. He would not come. He had deserted her to these strangers, and she wanted to die.

One day, she woke up and knew that she had come back. She was lying in a white-sheeted bed in a stone-walled room with a wooden floor. There was a window with red curtains, and a vase of daffodils stood on a table beside the bed. Daffodils? It was too early for daffodils... She struggled to sit up, and instantly a woman came to her side: a nun, in a black robe and spotlessly white wimple.

'Ah, my dear, you are with us again!' Her smile was sweet and sincere, and Melissa longed to push her aside to go to where Lachlan would surely be waiting for her. 'No, my dear, don't get up. Let me call Dr Campbell to see you—he's been working very hard to bring you back to us, I must tell you.' She hurried out of the room in a rustle of starch, and returned a minute later with a small, kindly-looking man.

'Miss Edwards—welcome back! How are you feeling now?'

'Where's Lachlan?'

Dr Campbell looked puzzled. The nun whispered something to him, and his expression changed to one of sympathy. 'The young man who brought you to the Dunstan isn't able to visit you here, I'm afraid. Now, we have to concentrate on getting you back to full health; you have been very ill...'

'No! He can't have left me here! He can't!' She began to scream. She would have thrown the bedclothes back, but her limbs felt like iron weights.

The nun hurried to shut the door, while the doctor took a bottle from a cabinet and shook it into a cloth. 'Now, my dear, just breathe deeply, and you'll feel much better...'

She bit the hand holding the chloroform over her mouth, and the doctor recoiled with an oath. 'Oh, the little savage!' she heard the nun say indignantly. Then they were holding her down, and at last she had to take a breath, had to breathe the nauseous stuff and sink back into black oblivion...

CHAPTER EIGHT

WILLIAM PRICE hummed a little song to himself as he waited in the office of the Dunedin police station to be escorted to his brother's cell. He had, as usual, taken care to dress for the occasion, in a new suit by one of the colony's best tailors. It was in a sombre shade of grey, as befitted a still grieving son. He had worn it that morning at the brief hearing in the Magistrate's Court when he had given evidence against his half-brother in exactly the right tones of moral outrage and regret. MacGregor, blast him, had stood in the dock staring off into the middle distance throughout the entire proceedings, coming to life only when they had tried to implicate Melissa Edwards in his escape and in Frampton's murder. The Frampton murder charge had been dismissed, unfortunately, because as yet there had been no body recovered, and with Miss Edwards at death's door in the infirmary, it was decided not to proceed with investigations into her part in MacGregor's escape.

MacGregor, predictably enough, had sworn blind that he had kidnapped her, and there was no evidence to the contrary, except for William's affirmation that she had started that rock-slide. Not to worry, he consoled himself—MacGregor could swing for one murder as much as for two, and if that little Edwards bitch recovered and gave him any trouble, he could convince any court in the land that she was as guilty as hell. She could wait.

His half-brother was due to be shipped north to Auckland the next day for trial in the High Court. Depending on how conclusive the evidence was that William had produced, he would hang either there or back in Scotland. William rather hoped it would be in Scotland; until Miss Edwards was taken care of, he was reluctant to leave Dunedin, and an Auckland hanging might bring the date forward too much.

'Your lordship? This way please, sir.'

William followed the constable down the row of cells, noting with some disappointment that they were newly constructed and therefore in much better condition than the cells he had had occasion to visit in London. He had rather relished the notion of his brother languishing in some noisome pit, with rats running over his feet.

Lachlan was stretched out on the narrow bed, his hands behind his head, staring up at the window. He turned his head to look impassively at them.

'I wondered when you'd turn up, Willy.'

'Can I go into his cell to talk to him?' William asked the constable. 'I really would appreciate some time to speak privately with my brother—I'm sure you can understand that this is a very—er—difficult matter.'

The constable gnawed his lip anxiously. 'He's regarded as being a very dangerous criminal, my lord. I couldn't really...'

'Please, constable, I want to make my peace with my brother. This will be the last time we ever speak together.'

There was a quiet chuckle from Lachlan on the bed at the deep sincerity throbbing in William's voice and the manfully compassionate look on his face, but the constable was obviously more sentimental than he cared to admit.

'Over here, MacGregor,' he ordered curtly. When he had fastened a pair of handcuffs over Lachlan's wrists, he opened the cell door to admit William and then left them alone, assuring them both that he would be just down the corridor, listening for the slightest hint of trouble.

Lachlan resumed his position on the bed. 'So it's "my lord" now, is it?'

'The title has been mine for the past nine years, as you well know, MacGregor, and it does open doors, even out here. You, of course, can have no idea how useful it can be.'

'I can imagine. I can't understand why you never used it before it came out at the hearing this morning.'

'Can't you? Intelligence never was your strong point though, was it, MacGregor? I needed money, you see— no one could survive on the miserly pittance my dear mother ensured was all I received. That's where all my little investments came in handy. But it simply wouldn't have done to have it known that a peer of the realm was the owner of a dozen scruffy little bars and gambling-halls in the Otago goldfields, would it?'

'I suppose not,' Lachlan allowed him. 'And now that your dear mother has gone . . .'

'I have no financial constrictions at all. I'm looking forward to going home, MacGregor.'

'I'm sure you are.' Lachlan turned away to look back up at the window.

William, feeling oddly ill at ease, perched on the small cabinet that was the only article of furniture in the cell beside the bed. There was a long silence before he said heartily, 'Well, you look to be very comfortable here. Better than a cave, at any rate, eh, MacGregor?' Lachlan still said nothing. William tried again. 'It was a shame about Frampton dying like that, wasn't it?'

'Ay. Did you shoot him, or was it one of your men?'

'One of the men winged him, and he fell into the Moonlight. Unfortunately, they didn't find the body in time for today's hearing. Damned disappointing.'

'Life can be pretty unfair that way, Willy.'

'Still, there's always Father's murder to hang you for, isn't there?'

'There is that,' Lachlan agreed.

He turned to look at William, and there was a look in his eyes that William had never seen there before. He had come expecting—hoping for—some defiance, anger and certainly bitterness from his half-brother. But his highly-developed senses could detect none of that in the man sitting opposite him, staring at him so dispassionately.

'I've worked out how you did it,' Lachlan said. 'How you killed Father.'

'Really?' William said politely. He could not help but dart a nervous look up the corridor to check that no one was listening.

'It's all right, Willy—it's just you and me. But before you go, I want you to tell me how you did it.'

'You said you'd worked it out,' William hedged.

'I have. Do you remember Cathy?'

'Cathy?' William pretended to dredge his memory. 'Why, yes, I believe I do. Wasn't she that simpering little village bit you were engaged to years ago, back in Inverness?'

'The one I found you with just weeks before our wedding.'

William raised his shoulders in an elegant gesture of indifference. 'So we are talking about the same girl. What of her?'

Lachlan looked faintly surprised. 'Did she really mean so little to you? You ruined her life, man!'

William gave a snort of derision. 'I prefer to think that I gave her a couple of the happiest hours of her life, MacGregor. She seemed to enjoy it rather more than your hand-holding and chaste promises!'

'Perhaps she did,' Lachlan conceded, quite unruffled, 'but her happiness wasn't exactly your primary aim, was it? You'd gone to some lengths to ensure that I'd come across you and her that particular day. And you knew I'd go to Father about it, too.'

William gave a brief, humourless laugh. 'It was a fair bet that you'd go running off to the old man with your latest complaint about me, yes. Not, of course, that I think that I can be blamed if you can't hold your women. Your trouble, MacGregor, is that big tender heart of yours; you were always vulnerable while you persisted in fancying yourself in love with a woman. You can buy any woman in the world, if you've got the money.'

'Is that so? What currency did you use on Melissa, then?'

'Oh, her,' William said dismissively. 'She's as simple as you are. You deserve each other. At any rate . . . what do our divergent views on women have to do with this remarkable theory you have regarding Father's murder?'

'They concern it in that you were trying to drive me off the estate. You damned near succeeded with Cathy. Of course I went to see Father—to tell him that I was leaving.'

'And a jolly good thing too. Except that you went in to see him when you were drunk. Not a sensible thing to do. But then, you always did drink rather more than was good for you; your breeding showing, I suppose.'

'I didn't drink so much in those days. Like Father, I enjoyed a dram now and again, but that was all.'

'But all the shouting everyone heard all over the house?'

'That would have been me telling Father what I thought of you. What did you put in the whisky, William?' William did not answer but simply stared at him, frowning. 'You took a chance on that, didn't you? But then, I guess, you knew Father and me well enough to be aware that we always shared a drink in the evenings when we were going over the estate accounts—it was just a matter of biding your time. It didn't strike me as odd, until much later, that there wasn't the usual decanter on the sideboard in his study; he had to summon one of the servants to bring it in. That's the only time I can think of when you'd have the opportunity to doctor it unseen. Whatever you used, it worked well. I don't remember anything until the servants woke me with their screaming about a murder. And Father lying there in all that blood... How could you have done it, William?'

'I never said I did,' William said coolly. He felt in his breast pocket and pulled out a small silver cigar-case. 'Would you care for a cigar?' Lachlan shook his head, and William lit one for himself. His hands, Lachlan noticed, were trembling very slightly. 'So,' William said at last, drawing deeply on his cigar, 'you think I drugged you both, went in, stabbed the old man and put the knife in your hands. After which, I locked the door and went off to let the rest of the household discover you... Is that your considered conclusion?'

'In a word—yes.'

'In a word, MacGregor, you're insane! You killed my father in a drunken rage after locking the door upon the two of you...'

'Then where was the key?'

'What?'

'The key I used to lock the door. Where was it? It wasn't anywhere in the room, and it wasn't on me. I remember your mother, of all people, asking why it couldn't be found.'

'Don't you dare bring my mother into it!' William said furiously. 'She was too shocked to accept what you'd done—killing her husband like that. Your own father!'

'Because I didn't have any reason to kill him, did I?' Lachlan said quietly.

'You had plenty of reason! You were never satisfied with what he gave you, were you? You might have been the bastard son of some whore who claimed my father as yours, but you thought you were entitled to that estate—*my* estate. Just because you ran it, you still had no right to any of it! And the old man was going to give it to you, wasn't he? Because he was sentimental enough to think "it would be in safe hands", as he put it. Certainly there were other properties, but that Inverness estate was *mine*! You had him twisted round your little finger, didn't you? You were *always* his favourite! He was...' William broke off abruptly, realising that he had just stepped into Lachlan's trap.

'Thank you, William,' Lachlan said softly. 'I wouldn't have wanted to go to the gallows without knowing what had happened that day, and why.'

'You've no proof!' William blustered.

'No, not a shred. Which is fortunate for you and very bad for me.' He lay back on the narrow bed and stared up at the window again, as if to terminate the conversation.

William threw his half-finished cigar on the cell floor, and ground it into dust with the toe of his boot. He had not expected to leave this interview without destroying his brother, but things had taken a different turn, and for once he felt quite shaken. There was, however, just one chink he was sure of in his brother's armour. 'I went to see that little friend of yours today, MacGregor. The one in the infirmary.' He was rewarded by Lachlan's immediate and complete attention. 'She's not at all well, is she? In fact, I understand she's not been given very good odds on surviving.'

'She'll live,' Lachlan said briefly. 'She's tougher than she looks.'

'Let's hope so, shall we? Especially since you gave up your life and liberty to take her all the way to the Dunstan. Very noble of you, I must say. She'd actually regained consciousness just before I arrived at the infirmary, but they'd had to sedate her because she became uncontrollable. I suppose, with such massive head-injuries, there's bound to be some brain damage. Such a pity, too—she might have been a little light in the thinking department, but she always struck me as a woman of great character.' He stood to go. Lachlan was sitting rigidly on the bed, staring at the floor, his fists clenched tightly in the handcuffs. William was pleased that he had struck home at last. 'If, by some miracle, she should recover, you can rest assured that I shall keep a careful and concerned eye on her. You can trust me, dear brother, when I say I shall look after her. I always take care of...loose ends.'

'Don't you ever touch her, William!' The words were ground out between gritted teeth as Lachlan slowly rose to his feet, his face white. 'Don't you dare to lay so much as one finger on her!'

'There's not much you're going to be able to do about that, where you're going,' William was unable to resist saying, as he went over to the bars and signalled to the waiting guard at the end of the corridor. Suddenly he was swung around and his throat gripped between two iron hands. He lashed out with his arms and feet, but the steady throttling pressure on his windpipe did not slacken for an instant. Through blood-glazed, popping eyes, he saw his brother's face set in a murderous mask and the cell slowly becoming black. Then, unbelievably, the pressure stopped, and he dropped retching and gasping to the ground at MacGregor's feet.

'Christ, man—you're not even worth killing,' he heard Lachlan say disgustedly.

The constable's hands were under his arms, helping him to his feet, and he somehow managed to stagger out into the corridor. With the cell door safely locked behind him, he turned for one last look at his brother, but could force no words from his injured throat. Even if he had been able to, Lachlan was looking at him no longer—

his eyes were back on the small square of barred window, with the blue sky beyond.

The maître d'hôtel at the Clarendon Hotel peered superciliously over his pince-nez at the young American woman waiting patiently for admittance to his dining-room. He had at first ignored her, and then politely informed her that the dining-room was full. But she had just as politely maintained that she had a luncheon engagement with Miss Edwards, and he had kept her waiting as long as he possibly could. With an audible sigh, he caught her eye and began to lead her to that lady's table. He kept a watchful eye on her as he escorted her across the dining-room, taking care to ensure that the young person did not accost, or give offence to, any of the hotel's patrons. The dining-room was particularly full that day as there was a large livestock auction in progress in the city, and many of the rural gentry visiting Dunedin had come to refresh themselves with the Clarendon's fine food and its tasteful surroundings.

To his relief, there were no incidents as he led her to the quiet corner where the thin pale woman with fair hair was sitting by herself, gazing out of the large draped window on to the street. He drew the line at seating the young person, however, and gave a small sniff of disapproval as he left.

'Melissa, honey, don't you look goddamned awful!'

Heads turned, and the maître d'hôtel flinched, but Melissa stood to embrace her friend warmly. 'Hello, Coralie. How good it is to see you again.'

She still does not look well, Coralie thought anxiously to herself, as she took her seat. The watered silk dress of soft green with its fichu of creamy lace was slap up to the minute, and the diamond earrings she wore looked quite genuine to Coralie's experienced eye. But none of the expensive trappings did anything but highlight her thin, tense face and haunted eyes. The hand Melissa extended was scarred with old calluses, the nails bitten to the quick.

'Well, at least you look better than when I saw you at the infirmary. Do you remember me coming in? And why did they have to cut off that gorgeous hair of yours?'

Melissa put her hand to her head, self-consciously touching the cropped hair. 'They had to cut it off to get to the wounds. And, no, I don't remember your coming in, I'm sorry. I don't remember anything very much of those two months. Things are still coming back only very slowly. Even though it's been three days since they let me out, I still find it difficult to ... cope.' She broke off as the waiter appeared to take their order. Remembering that Coralie could not read, she said tactfully, 'I was just going to have some soup, Coralie. Would you like some fish as well? And the steak, perhaps?' She gave their orders and sat back, regarding her friend somewhat apprehensively. 'I wanted to see you ... to talk about David.'

'If you're worried about convincing me that Mack didn't kill him, don't be. I know well enough who really sent him over the Moonlight, despite all that carry-on in the courtroom last month.'

'Good. I'm pleased you know.' Melissa was busy fiddling with her napkin, and Coralie studied her curiously.

'I saw Mack before they took him up to the High Court trial in Auckland,' she volunteered. There was still no response from Melissa. 'Don't you want to know how he was, honey?'

'No.'

'But why ever not? You and he were so...'

'I know we were, but that's all over now, isn't it?' She spoke jerkily, her voice harsh. 'Lachlan made sure of that when he chose to give himself up. It wasn't enough to leave me at any farmhouse—he had to take me straight to the Dunstan, straight into the arms of the police...'

'But from the Dunstan they could take you to Dunedin, to where there were doctors and a place where you could be looked after properly!' Coralie interjected. 'It must have taken a helluva lot of courage to do that.'

'Courage? Or stupidity! He never could get anything right. We could have had a life together, but he threw his away quite needlessly. I don't want to talk about him ever again, Coralie.'

'How can you be so hard on him?' Coralie wondered.

'Hard on a man who ruined my life? It's easy, believe me,' Melissa said bitterly. 'Can we talk about something else now, please?'

The soup was placed before them, and Melissa arranged the napkin in her lap with precision and picked up her spoon, her face rigidly composed. She took one sniff of the soup and put her spoon down with a sigh. 'It smells ghastly. Oily.'

'No, it's really very good...' Coralie paused, spoon half-way to her mouth, a sudden suspicion in her eyes.

Melissa saw it. 'Yes, I'm pregnant. Dammit,' she said quietly.

Coralie was caught off guard. 'Whose is it? I mean...it's Mack's, isn't it?'

'Of course it is! Whose else would it be? William's?' she snapped. Then, as Coralie's tense look remained, the penny dropped. 'Oh Lord, Coralie, did you think it was David's?'

There had been very few times when she had seen Coralie Jones flustered, but this was one of them. Instantly contrite, she touched Coralie's arm in a gesture of understanding. 'You poor thing, you really cared for him, didn't you? I'm so sorry—you must be grieving, too.'

Coralie smiled wanly. 'Yeah, I miss him, even though he was a bit of a bastard sometimes. I don't know why I even thought, there, for a moment, that... Well, it was always you he wanted, only he didn't want to break up with Mack over you. That was the main reason why I went back to Dunedin, if you want to know the truth. I'll get over him soon enough. But you... When are you due, honey?'

'Early June, I think. I think I've worked out the date correctly. The nuns at the infirmary were scandalised that I wouldn't tell them I'd been raped by the murderer who'd kidnapped me, so they were rather uncommunicative on the subject. It does take nine months, doesn't it?'

'More or less.' Coralie smiled sadly, and shook her head at her friend. 'You're still such an innocent, aren't you? All that time in the goldfields, and none of it really rubbed off on you. I think that's what Mack treasured about you...'

'Stop it, Coralie! I don't want to talk about him, I said!'

'But the baby...'

'Is a baby. *My* baby. I don't want it, but I'm stuck with it, so I'll just have to do the best I can under the circumstances. Ah—here's your fish.'

Coralie ate her fish in an awkward silence, while Melissa proceeded to fiddle with a glass of water. At last she could stand it no longer. 'So what are you going to do now, with a baby on the way? Do you have enough money to take care of it?'

Melissa almost smiled at her typical bluntness. 'If I'm careful, yes, I can manage. I thought I'd stay here and have it, and then think about what I'm going to do.'

'Hell, what do you want to stay here for? All these staid fuddy-duddies talking about you behind your back, and the gossip there'll be when you produce a baby! There'll be no doubt in *their* minds who the father is! It'll be awful for you here, honey. Look...' She leaned forward conspiratorially. 'I'm going to Sydney next week. I've had it with this place—it's all full of puritanical Scots and churches on every block. And it's as cold as hell here in the winter; it might suit all those hardy types from Scotland, but I'm from California, and I like to see the sun occasionally. Why don't you come with me? I kind of like the idea of being an aunt. How about it?'

Melissa sat trying to think of objections, but failing to come up with even one. 'I'd like to think about it,' she said at last, cautiously.

'All right then, honey, you know where to contact me. And, before I forget...' she pulled out a piece of paper from her reticule, 'here's something for you. It's a receipt from McCulloch's Stables for Mack's horses. I know how fond he was of those animals, and I didn't think it was my responsibility to sell them to some stranger. So they're your responsibility, now.'

They spent the rest of their lunch talking of inconsequential things, with Coralie trying valiantly to cheer Melissa up. When at last she left, Melissa felt tired and

wrung out by the strain of trying to converse politely
and to remain coherent. Perhaps it was the result of her
injury, perhaps it was her pregnancy, or simply the fact
that she had had a hard and trying day.

She had finally plucked up the courage to go into the
Bank of New Zealand that morning. She had asked the
manager to verify the amount of money that was in the
joint account she had held with David and Lachlan. It
was a considerable sum, the manager had politely commented, as he handed her a note with the amount written
on it. It was exactly two thousand, two hundred and
fifty pounds.

'There should be three times that amount in the account!' she had said, horrified.

The manager had hurried off to check, and came back
to affirm that there had indeed been six thousand, seven
hundred and fifty pounds in the account at one stage.
Exactly two-thirds of that had since been withdrawn.
The signature on the withdrawal form he showed her
was David's, and the date was the day he had died in
the Moonlight.

'You damn fool, David!' she had sworn aloud,
standing on the steps outside the bank. Why on earth
had he withdrawn that very amount? The more she
thought about it, the more convinced she was that he
had withdrawn his share and hers at Maori Point, so
that the two of them could travel separately from
Lachlan, and would not have to wait for the bank in
Dunedin to be notified to allow them to withdraw the
money there. If he had, as she had first thought, tried
to abscond with the money, he would surely have taken
everything. But why had he not asked permission first
to withdraw her third of the money? Now it was all no
doubt rotting somewhere in the waterways of Central
Otago, along with David's body. And she had a baby to
prepare for!

She did not regard her anger as being particularly
callous—her anger at David, at William, at Lachlan, was
all that she had to fuel her now. Once she stopped being
angry, she knew she would no longer be able to cope.
And she needed to cope, because, despite her very real
resentment at her pregnancy, she found that the tiny

being growing inside her was daily becoming more important.

She had compensated for the unpleasantness of the visit to the bank with a small shopping-spree afterwards. Although she knew she must be careful with her money, she could not resist buying some new dresses and a pair of diamond earrings; she had lived like a pauper in ragged men's clothes for quite long enough, she told herself. Coralie had brought in her old clothes to the infirmary for her to wear, but the familiar dresses hung on her unflatteringly, and she was reminded too much of her previous life. It did feel wonderful to be back in feminine underthings and silk dresses again, to feel soft fabric against her skin and light slippers on her feet instead of heavy leather boots. But she avoided looking into mirrors. She did not like the new, hardened face that looked back at her.

Now she felt very tired, and the smell of cooked food in the hotel dining-room nauseated her. It was time to compose herself to walk the length of the room, past all the other diners with their animated conversations that would slow as she passed, their knowing eyes that would drop before they met hers. She had taken a room at the Clarendon and found herself longing for its peace and privacy. She needed time, too, to make some plans for the future and to think seriously about Coralie's proposal.

Taking a deep breath, she went to push back her chair and rise, when her eye was caught by a man sitting directly across the room, who had been watching her steadily ever since he had come in. It was William, as elegant and as handsome as ever, lounging idly at a table by the door. She was not going to be able to leave the room without passing right by him. As a hot flush run over her, she sat down quickly to let it pass.

Seeing her distress, the corners of his mouth went up and he raised his glass of wine in a silent toast. The woman sitting next to him looked up at his movement, and Melissa caught her breath. She had never seen a woman before who looked like *that*! Thick black hair framed a perfect oval face, each feature exquisite and even. Her huge green eyes were reflected in the simple

but obviously expensive emeralds she wore at her ears
and throat, and her quietly stylish clothes displayed her
beautiful figure to perfection. Every other woman in the
room was suddenly plain and drab.

It had to be Phyllida! There was no one else it could
possibly have been. No wonder Lachlan had been so
nearly destroyed by her; no wonder he had never forgotten her—no man surely could. Melissa's own beauty
had always been much admired, but it was like com-
paring a candle with the sun. Even before she had become
ill, how could he ever have looked at her after knowing
a beauty like Phyllida?

She gripped the edge of the table, willing her legs to
hold her steady, and then forced herself to stand and
make her way directly to the door, her eyes fixed straight
ahead. Somehow—she never knew quite how—she
managed to walk past the couple at the table and out
into the hotel foyer. She had one foot on the stairs before
she felt William's hand on her arm.

'Miss Edwards—how nice to see you up and about
again. Won't you join us at our table for a moment?'

Her flesh seemed to crawl where his hand lay, and she
drew back with as much dignity as she could muster.
'We have nothing to say to each other.' She looked
straight into his eyes, and immediately regretted it. They
were Lachlan's eyes, after all—compelling, amused and
intent upon ruining her. That much at least the brothers
had in common. She looked away again.

'But I have someone I'd like you to meet,' he coaxed.
He spoke softly, so as not to be overheard by the few
other people in the foyer, but his voice now had a slight
huskiness to it, as if he had a bad cold. The effect was
subtly menacing, even in the innocuous surroundings of
the Clarendon Hotel.

'I have no wish to meet her. It *is* Phyllida, isn't it?'
Even as she spoke, she could hear the sullenness in her
voice.

William gave a delighted chuckle. 'It is, indeed. So
MacGregor felt compelled to tell you all about her, did
he? Well, I'm not surprised; she is quite a beauty, isn't
she? Once upon a time he was completely smitten with
her, and made an utter fool of himself, as well.' He smiled

at the memory, before adding cheerfully, 'He'll be standing trial in Auckland any day now, you know. Then off to Scotland and the gallows. I wonder... which one of you lovely ladies do you think he'll be missing the most right now?'

'You're sick, William!' she hissed at him, and tried to back away up the stairs.

His hand darted out and caught her wrist, twisting it back sharply against her arm, and she gave a small, involuntary gasp of pain. His body blocked anyone else from seeing what he was doing. She thought for a second of calling for help, but the physical fear he had ingrained in her months before made her powerless to do even that. Like a mouse in a cat's paws, she stood rigidly waiting for what he would do next.

'Now don't rush off like that!' he said soothingly. 'I just want to make quite sure that we both understand where we stand. You're not going to do anything stupid, are you? Because if I thought for one moment you were...'

'I'm going to Sydney,' she interrupted him. He would find that out sooner or later, and she could not see that it would do any harm to tell him that much now. 'Next week, with Coralie. I'm in no position to make trouble for you. I just want to be left alone to get on with my life. To put... all this behind me.'

He stared down at her for a long moment, his face inscrutable, and then at last he smiled and let her go. 'Sensible girl. That's what I wanted to hear. I'll keep an eye on you until you've left the country, of course, but I'm sure you know what's best for your health. And once you're on your way, I'll be free to go and watch the entertainment in Auckland—and then to go home to England. I've got rather a lot to look forward to there. So don't delay, will you... Miss Edwards?'

She turned and slowly mounted the stairs, nursing her aching hand, her legs feeling like iron weights. On the first landing, she stopped and glanced down. He was still watching her.

As he raised his head, his high collar was pulled back slightly, and her eyes were drawn to the livid bruises on his neck. They were black, fading to deep raspberry red, as if someone had tried to throttle him...

He saw her eyes widen, and knew that she knew. His face tight, he turned on his heel and walked stiffly back to the dining-room, leaving her to grip the hand-rail as a spasm of irrational laughter welled up inside her.

So Lachlan had at long last managed to get his hands on William! He had finally had his chance, somewhere, sometime, to avenge her beating and David's murder. How typical of Lachlan that he had not been able to do even that properly! Justice was on the side of the wealthy and cunning, not the poor and simple—that was what William would have said, at any rate. And William was always right.

Somehow, she got to her room, and she collapsed on the bed, shaking uncontrollably. The anger and resentment and bitterness inside her was making her physically ill, she realised. She *had* to get away! The nuns at the infirmary might have healed her body, but the scars on her mind were so hideous that she was genuinely frightened at what she was becoming. And in seven months she would have the responsibility of a baby as well to protect from William. What sort of mother would she be if she stayed here? Working like an automaton, she began to pack the few personal items she possessed, forcing herself to organise her mind into making plans for her immediate future.

She would close the account at the bank. She would make arrangements for Lachlan's horses by note and bank draft. That should tie up any loose ends and ensure that no one here would need to—or would be able to—find her again. There was no point in making it too easy for William to track her down, should he ever change his mind. For now, she would go away and stay with Coralie at her lodgings until the ship left for Sydney. In Australia, there would be no William Price to haunt her, and nothing to remind her of Lachlan. She would make it her business to forget completely the brothers who, between them, had put an end to her health, her happiness and her life.

She savagely slammed shut the lid of her portmanteau, picked up her jacket and hurried to the door to summon a porter. She had no regrets about leaving New Zealand now. None at all.

CHAPTER NINE

IT WAS mid-February, and the hills and mountains cupping the opal-blue gem of Lake Wakatipu were scorched a dusty gold from the relentless late summer sun. Melissa, in a well-cut travelling-gown which did much to disguise the evidence of her six-month pregnancy, stood at the railing of the lake ferry. It had been nearly a year since she had last set eyes on the white-painted settlement of Queenstown, nestled into the bend of the lake that was now directly ahead. The lake ferry was an ex-whaling ship, used by the miners to transport the gold out of the Otago fields, and by the district's traders and farmers to bring in supplies and livestock. The mournful lowing of several dozen bullocks could be heard below decks, all destined for new farms somewhere in the high country of Central Otago. As ever before, she was left breathless with delight at the extravagant wild beauty of the lake and its clear, mirror-like reflections of the awesome peaks above. Her very last doubts about her sanity in insisting on coming back to New Zealand vanished.

Coralie, with whom she had shared a rented house on the outskirts of Sydney, had tried hard to dissuade her from returning, and it had taken weeks before she had been able to accept that Melissa was unshakeable in her resolution. They lived a quiet life in Sydney—there was a huge garden in which Melissa had spent many contented hours working, and Coralie was excellent company. But it was a different Coralie, these days. She had found an admirer worthy of her at last; an older man with his own business and honourable intentions. He was as different from David as chalk from cheese, but he adored Coralie, and it was clear to Melissa that she would accept his suit very soon.

It had been on one fine morning, just after Christmas, that Melissa had finished working in the garden and come to sit in the wicker chair on the veranda next to Coralie. They had spent some of their leisure hours teaching Coralie to read, and now she was squinting painfully over a book of verse, determined never to let her Mr Watson know that his intended had been illiterate for the first twenty-five years of her life. Melissa watched her fondly for a while. Was this buxom young woman with the smear of flour on her cheek from the morning's bread-making really the hard-faced young bargirl she had met on her first night at the Regency? The mouth now silently spelling out the words from her book had not held a cigar, drunk an alcoholic drink or uttered a swear-word for months! 'Preparation for being an aunt,' Coralie had called it, but that was not the only reason.

'Is your Mr Whatsit worth all this, Coralie?' she had asked curiously.

Coralie put her finger on the word she was spelling out, and looked up at her crossly. 'It's Mr Watson, and yes, he is!' She went back to her book, managed a couple of words, and then gave up with a sigh. 'What's the matter, honey? Something's been worrying you for days now.'

Melissa looked out at the garden she had made to look beautiful. She loved it here—the peacefulness and green lushness of it. The birds congregated in the big eucalyptus tree beside the house for the bread she threw them every morning; it had taken her a little time to adjust to this luxury, so used was she to seeing every sizeable bird as a prospective meal. Yes, it was lovely here ... but it wasn't home.

'I want to go back to Otago.'

Coralie did not look as surprised as she had expected. 'I've guessed you might be feeling that way. You've never really settled here, have you? Well, as soon as the baby's old enough to travel ...'

'No. I want to go back to Otago before then. In fact, I want to have the baby there—in Dunedin, at any rate.'

Now Coralie looked horrified. 'You're crazy! Here you've got this nice house and me to take care of

you ... and what's over there for you? A lot of gossipy
old tongues wagging, a whole heap of bad memories,
maybe William Price sticking his nose in ...'

'William said he was returning to England, and he
had every reason to, now that Lachlan's ... gone. I've
nothing to fear from him. And ... it's hard to explain,
but ... I just feel I've got to go home to have this baby—
and this isn't home. I don't know if it ever could be. Do
you understand?'

Coralie shook her head. 'No, I don't. *I* don't want to
go back!'

'And I'm not asking you to!' Melissa took her hand
warmly. 'You've been the dearest friend I could ever have
wished for, but it's time I stopped relying on you so
much. I'll have this baby in a few months, and you'll
have your Mr Whatsit ...'

'*Watson!* And what's he got to do with it? If Frederick
Watson wants to marry me, he'll just have to take on
this entire family! And that's what I've come to think
of us as, honey—a family. Please don't leave because of
him, or at some crazy notion that you don't belong anywhere but in Otago. Just think of your baby!'

It had been almost impossible sometimes to withstand
Coralie's pleadings, but eventually Melissa had had her
way and booked her passage to New Zealand. Mr
'Whatsit' had not been entirely unhappy to see her leave,
despite Coralie's insistence to the contrary, and Melissa
was sure that she was doing the right thing in leaving
Coralie to her new life alone.

The ferry bumped into Queenstown wharf with a thud,
and the child inside her turned over restlessly. She smiled
at the still-new feeling of sharing her body with someone
else.

She had denied the growing child and the loss of
Lachlan for months, and little by little the high wall she
had built round her heart had started to crumble in the
serenity of the new life she had made for herself in
Australia. Eventually she had found that she could think
of Lachlan with some forgiveness, even with a degree
of bitter-sweet pleasure as she recalled his tenderness,
his courage, and the way he had always been able to
make her laugh. The sharp irrational anger that had

served to protect her in those early days had all but gone now, and she felt free at last to make her peace with her memories.

And the baby... Every day the changes in her body brought home to her the realisation that something positive, healthy and even miraculous had come from all that she had been through, and she was now looking forward to holding her child in her arms. She carried well but large. Sometimes she wondered if she were carrying twins, but, as Coralie had so inelegantly put it, 'You don't get mice from horses,' and she supposed that any child of Lachlan's would be bound to be rather larger than average.

For her time in Queenstown, she planned to rest and take long walks around the lake and the hills. She freely acknowledged to herself that it was a test—a test of her strength and commitment to the future as she faced the past here. The gang-plank was affixed, and the handful of passengers disembarked. Now that the hectic peak of the gold-rush had passed, they were mostly farmers, businessmen, and even tourists these days. The floods and great snows of the past year had driven many miners off the fields, and it was the West Coast's turn now to boom as gold was discovered there. No doubt many of the thriving gold towns in Otago would become sad and abandoned as the gold ran out, but at least Queenstown was likely to survive; it had grown even since she was last there, and had a prosperity and purposefulness she had only glimpsed before. A number of new shops and offices lined Ballarat Street, as she walked up it from the wharf, and there were no signs of the infamous grog-shanties that were the hallmark of all mining camps— she suspected that any that still survived would now be discreetly on the edge of the town. She turned round to watch the cattle being unloaded from the bowels of the ferry and driven to the cattle-pens to await collection. They were big, lively beasts, and for a moment it seemed that several of them were intent upon a flight down the street towards her, but they were quickly urged back by the drovers into the holding pens on the lake-front.

She chose the Lake Hotel to stay at, and was made welcome by Mrs Kennedy, the cheerful Irish proprietress. 'I hope you'll be most comfortable here,' she said, after showing Melissa her clean, airy room. 'Would a cup of tea be welcome after all your travellings, Mrs . . . er?'

'Mrs Brown. Thank you, yes it would.'

Mrs Kennedy looked a little disappointed—she had no doubt sought to link her with some benighted husband in the district. Melissa wore a wedding ring all the time now, and allowed it to be generally assumed that she was a widow. But, wherever possible, she avoided explanations, preferring to leave people ignorant than lie about her situation. Soon she was ensconced in the hotel lounge with a pot of tea and a plate of fresh-baked scones, looking out of the bay window on to Ballarat Street. She appeared to be the only guest, and was able to sit undisturbed for some time watching the mid-morning passers-by as they went about their business. What a sedate place Queenstown is now, she decided, when only a year ago it flung off the name of Canvastown! She wondered what the rebuilt Arrowtown was like, although the hair-raising trip there was not one she intended to make.

There was an increasing commotion from down by the wharf, and the bullocks from the holding-pens began to thunder up the street and past her window, carefully guarded by a number of men on horses and a bevy of watchful dogs, keeping any bullock of an independent turn of mind from darting to freedom down an alley. The cattle passing by the shop-fronts was a thrilling scene, and she was intrigued to see how expertly the unruly cattle were herded by the stock-riders and their whips as they proceeded through the town.

One rider, in particular, caught her eye. It was something about the breadth of his shoulders under the dusty, sweat-streaked shirt, the sleeves rolled back over strong forearms, the easy way he had of sitting in the saddle, the familiar way he wore his hat pulled forward over his face. And that horse . . . ! She jumped to her feet and ran to the door, but by then he was already well up the street and disappearing in a great cloud of dust. In a few seconds, there was nothing but the settling dust and the distant lowing of the cattle as they began to wind their way up into the hills towards their new home. Weakly she slumped back against the doorway. Had she made a dreadful mistake in coming back? If she were going to see his ghost everywhere she turned in this town, it would be more than she could bear.

For now, she could no longer stand the confines of the hotel, and retrieved her bonnet from her bedroom and set off for a soothing walk round the lake. Almost unconsciously her feet led her along the shore to the promontory where she and Lachlan had sat on that festive, starlit night a year ago. She had not intended testing her courage, confronting her past, quite so soon, but the stock-rider in Ballarat Street had unsettled her far too much to delay the moment. Now she felt compelled to go to where her memory of Lachlan was strongest, no matter what it cost.

She came to the same large, flat rock that they had sat on that night, so long ago, and she lowered herself awkwardly on to it. The dark blue water, as clear as the ice-caps it came from, lapped inches from her feet. Although she knew she should not, she took off her bonnet and sat with it in her hands, fanning herself slightly in the still mid-day heat. Gradually the motion of her hands slowed, and then ceased altogether, as she let herself slip gently back into the past, easing herself into all the old, good memories that this place held for her. The memories hurt, but they were healing her as well. A single tear trickled down her cheek and she did not feel it to wipe it away.

A small sound behind her made her turn abruptly, startled and embarrassed that someone should intrude on her private grief out here. She looked straight into Lachlan's grey eyes, alight with love and relief and...laughter? It was impossible! Unbelieving, she thrust out a hand to touch him, and felt the wiry hairs on his forearm. She withdrew her hand as if she had been stung. He was really there! He had filled out a little since the lean days in the mountains, and was as deeply tanned as he had been the first time she had seen him. He held his hat in his hands as he squatted beside her, and his hair shone sun-washed white again. If it were not for the new lines round his eyes and mouth, she

would have sworn that he had not changed at all in that
year.

'Hello, sweetheart. What took you so long?'

Her shock turned suddenly to anger. 'You're supposed to be dead! I ... thought you were dead! And now
look at you! You're—You're filthy!'

He looked down at his stained, sweat-soaked shirt,
and the corners of his mouth quirked down in the familiar expression of amused apology that had always pulled
at her heart. 'I'm sorry! We were well on our way home,
when one of the lads remembered to tell me that a woman
fitting your description had come across the lake this
morning with the bullocks. I wasn't very popular when
I turned round and came back, but I couldn't wait.'

'You've waited all these months!' she almost screamed
at him. 'I believed you dead, and all this time you've ...'
Her voice broke, and she burst into helpless tears. As
his hand touched hers, she flinched in anger and confusion. She was wiping the tears away with her sleeve,
when he handed her a handkerchief—that, at least, appeared to be reasonably clean. She dried her eyes and
tried to hand him back the handkerchief, but he took
her hand, and held it until she looked at him again. This
time, his eyes were serious.

'For a while, I wasn't sure if you'd survived, either.
When I got to Dunedin, I found the horses, but no sign
of you or Coralie. You'd apparently covered your tracks
very well. I left messages everywhere I could think of,
and I've had private detectives looking for you all over
the country. I knew, if you were still alive, you'd come
back. All I could do was wait—and hope.'

'I went to Sydney with Coralie. I—I suppose we could
have been hard to find,' she admitted. 'I didn't want
William to know where I was.' She withdrew her hand
from his. 'And what happened to you?'

He settled down beside her on the rock. 'Not very
much, as it turned out. I was awaiting trial in Auckland
when the authorities were notified of two sworn affi-
davits from former servants of William's mother. It
seems they'd seen William leave my father's study and
lock the door behind him at the very time that I'd been
supposed to be murdering the old man. William's mother

apparently knew, too, which was why he was never welcome home while his mother was alive. Once she had died, her servants decided to clear the slate and went to the police. When William heard that the police were coming to interview him, he took a gun and blew his brains out, which seemed to satisfy everyone as an admission of guilt.' He spoke lightly, but the pain behind the words could not be disguised.

'I'm glad he's dead,' she said fiercely. 'I'm glad he'll never be able to hurt anyone ever again!' When Lachlan did not reply, she looked at him sharply. 'Aren't you?'

'I always thought I would be,' he said slowly. 'And then I realised that I knew exactly how he felt the second before he pulled the trigger.'

It took a moment for his words to sink in, and when they did, she turned her head away and fumbled with the ribbons on her bonnet so that he could not read her expression. Suddenly she felt rather small-minded and bitter beside him, and it was not a comfortable feeling.

'Saint Lachlan!' she muttered.

She could hear the amusement back in his voice. 'No, I'll never be that. But I've learned not to waste time regretting the past. It's the present and the future that are so very much more important.'

'How pompous . . . and how boring!' she said coldly.

He threw back his head and laughed out loud. 'Oh, Melissa!' He shook his head helplessly at her. 'Why did I ever worry that you might have changed? You're just the same lass—except for that lovely hair. Did they cut it off at the infirmary?'

'It's growing back,' she snapped, brushing his hand off her hair. She started as his hand twisted round to seize hers, the left hand which wore the fake wedding ring.

'What's this?'

'What does it look like?' She struggled unsuccessfully for repossession of her hand. 'Lachlan—let me go!'

'Who gave you this?'

'That's none of your business!'

'*Who*, Melissa?' His eyes had gone black, and his mouth was white in a face suddenly pale. 'You . . . *stupid* woman! What the hell have you gone and done?'

She recoiled from him, shocked. 'It's nothing to do with you!'

'It has everything to do with me! You were going to be *my* wife!'

'I never said I would, and you never asked me! We never made any plans...'

'Because we didn't think we'd ever have a future together!' He shook his head in angry frustration. 'Now we have. Now I've a farm, a house, a whole lifetime to offer you. You can't tell me *now* that you've gone and married some Australian dunce!'

'And why shouldn't I marry whom I choose?' she retorted. 'I thought you were *dead*, Lachlan. It took me a long time, but I've finally adjusted to living without you, and I'm perfectly happy, thank you! I don't need you to come sailing back into my life, as if nothing had ever happened, and expect me to give up the life I've worked so hard to make for myself. I'm pleased that you're a free man and doing well...but I can't be part of your new life, and I don't want to be.'

She might as well have struck him. She had to lower her eyes because she could not bear to see the look on his face, and she was ashamed of her own weakness. This was the man who had destroyed her life! How could she possibly soften now? Besides—Phyllida would be free now, and no doubt ready and available to fall into the arms of a new protector. The thought of Phyllida helped to harden her heart immeasurably.

After a long time, he sighed, and got slowly to his feet. 'It's hot, lass. I'll take you back to your hotel.' He extended his hand to help her up.

She stared at it in confusion. She had not intended getting up—her pregnancy could show then, and she did not want *that*—but she was aware that she could not stay sitting on the rock all day until he decided to leave. Very reluctantly, she took his hand and stood up as smoothly as she could manage, stooping slightly to hide what the cleverly cut dress could not.

'You're pregnant,' he said, the instant she was on her feet. *'You're pregnant!'* The last two words were a shout of pure joy.

'For goodness' sake!' she tried to silence him desperately. 'I don't want the whole of Otago to know!'

'I do!' He went to put his arms round her, but she backed away.

'Stop this, Lachlan! You don't even know that it's yours...'

He looked at her blankly. 'I'm not so stupid that I can't count, lass! You're six months' gone, I'd say. And it's been exactly six months since...'

'No! Stop it!' She was losing control of the situation, and he was gaining it, wearing the assured grin that she knew so well. But this time she would be damned before she let him walk all over her again! 'It is not yours, I tell you!'

'Then what's his name?' he shot at her, so unexpectedly that she stared at him in surprise.

'His name? He's...um...'

'He's not a memorable character, at any rate,' Lachlan observed, and, before she could think to stop him, he had pulled the gold ring off her finger and flung it far out into the lake. 'There—now you're divorced. And you're coming home with me.' He took her firmly by the hand and propelled her back towards the township.

Too hot and tired to argue for the moment, she followed him, dragging her feet sulkily. She had learned a long time ago that it was impossible to withstand Lachlan when he was set on something; the only time she had ever been able to make him do something *she* wanted him to do was when they were in the mountains together, drunk with lovemaking. No doubt the proficient Phyllida was a great deal better than her at *that*—and would have had more sense than to get herself pregnant as well. Why was this domineering, arrogant, selfish, womanising bully not pursuing Phyllida instead? Why could he not leave *her* alone?

Mrs Kennedy was flushed and excited, fluttering over them in a ferment of sentimentality. 'I *knew* it was you, Mrs MacGregor,' she assured Melissa as she handed her her still unpacked bag. 'There's not been a week in which he hasn't come in to ask if I've seen you. And you're just as pretty as he said, too!' She sighed, moist-eyed.

'But you were a naughty wee thing having me on like that—telling me your name was Brown, indeed!'

'Brown, is it?' Lachlan murmured. 'Now that *is* a hard name to remember.' Melissa glowered at him. 'And thank you for taking such good care of her, Mrs Kennedy,' Lachlan said, planting a kiss on the woman's cheek. She gazed up at him so besottedly that Melissa was sure that she was going to be ill.

'Mrs MacGregor!' she mimicked as soon as they were outside and walking up the street together. 'How dare you let her think I'm your wife!'

Lachlan merely grinned unrepentantly, and looked up towards the end of the street. Maggie and Maud, together with a third horse, stood tied up outside a public bar. She heard Lachlan say something sharp under his breath, and then he bounded up on the hotel's veranda and turned to her with an apologetic look. 'I'll just be a minute.'

'You...!' She put her hands on her hips, and glared at him. 'Are you expecting me to wait out here in this heat while you go in there and have a drink? You can go to hell, MacGregor!'

He raised an admonitory finger. 'All right, sweetheart—just as long as you're still waiting when I get back.' He disappeared inside.

Shoulders slumped with weariness, she went over to the horses and remade her acquaintance with the two mares. Maud, in particular, remembered her, and thrust her head affectionately at her, as if begging forgiveness for what had happened so long ago. Melissa kissed her nose and whispered her absolution in the mare's soft ears. It did seem a *very* long time ago.

She turned with a scowl at the sound of heavy boots on the veranda, and then her jaw dropped in amazement. Mug of beer in hand, blinking owlishly at the sudden change in light, David was being bodily hauled out of the bar by Lachlan. They stared at each other before she turned to Lachlan. He was grinning broadly, and nodded in confirmation. Yes—it really was him!

She flung herself into her cousin's arms, laughing and crying with relief. It was minutes before she could say anything, and when she did, he began to speak at the same time, making them laugh again. It was, she thought later, the first time she had laughed—really laughed—since her accident.

'I can't believe this!' she managed at last through her laughter and her tears. 'Two resurrections in one day! How can it be?'

'Hasn't Mack told you? Then let's head home and I'll tell you on the way.' He led her over to Maud. 'Do you feel up to riding Maud again?'

'Of course I do! Poor Maud couldn't help what happened last time!'

David went to swing Melissa on to Maud's back in the way he always had, and found himself grunting with the effort. 'Hell, coz, you've been piling on the weight! All that infirmary food, was it?'

At Lachlan's muffled chuckle, and Melissa's baleful glare at the sound, he comprehended the situation in an instant. 'Oh,' he managed to say. There was an awkward silence, while he blushed a deep rose red under his tan. She had never seem him do that before and found it rather touching, just as she found Lachlan's barely restrained mirth at it contemptible.

Lachlan swung up into Maggie's saddle. 'I'd better get a move on and catch up with the herd. Davey, can you take tender care of Melissa for me? I'll come back for you if you're not at the homestead in three hours.'

'Shouldn't you . . .?' David began, and then looked worriedly at them both.

'Ride carefully.' Lachlan raised his hand in a salute of farewell, before urging Maggie on up the track leading out of the township. Soon he was out of sight, and they began to plod sedately after him.

'I can't believe it!' Melissa said for the hundredth time. 'It's like a miracle!'

'Miracle? It didn't seem like it at the time! After I'd gone to Maori Point that day with the gold to deposit, William's men hounded me up into the hills. One of them shot at me—it just clipped me, but it was enough to make me come off my horse. Then I could either stay around to get killed or jump into the Moonlight. I took my chance, and jumped.'

'Thank goodness you did!' Melissa said fervently. 'But we didn't think anyone could have survived that drop—how did you do it?'

'I had a bit of a rough ride downriver, but managed to make it to Maori Point eventually. When I found out that you two had been there, I put two and two together and decided to lie low for a bit. I took out most of the money in the account, bought a horse and some dry clothing, and got out. I never expected to be listed as a missing person, but it suited me—I didn't want Price on my tail again.'

'What did you want with all that money?' she asked, trying to keep the accusation out of her voice.

'For ready cash, in case the police were watching the bank for Lachlan, or if he'd been able to get passage out on a ship... anything like that. I was just playing it very safe, for once. In the event, I followed him up to Auckland, planning to pay for the best defence we could possibly get for him. Thank God, it all worked out as it did, and he didn't have to go through all that. It was the last thing he needed, with you at death's door in Dunedin.'

She rode silently, her throat tight, remembering all the horrible things she had ever said and thought about David, and of how staunchly Lachlan had defended his friend. At last she said miserably, 'I should have thought of doing that—of defending him. But everything seemed so hopeless at the time. I just... gave up.'

'You were so ill, coz, you couldn't have done anything else. I'm only sorry that you were alone then and not knowing what was going on. I wish I'd been able to tell you, but you were still unconscious when I left Dunedin, and you'd gone when I got back. It was one hell of a situation to be in—for all of us. Mack was the only one who was sure everything would turn out all right.'

'Was he?' she said in surprise.

'Hell, yes! He always knew you'd come back.' He threw her a grin of pure delight. 'But it's good to see you again, coz! Tell me—how's Coralie?'

'About to get married to a very nice Mr Whatsit in Sydney. She is very happy—and very respectable too, these days.'

'Coralie respectable? Never!' David was thoughtful for a moment. 'I really miss that girl. No one's called me "honey" for a long time now. Look, I'm setting up a station alongside Mack's as soon as we get his on its feet. Do you think she'd...'

'No, David,' she said sternly. 'Leave the poor girl alone. She's happy now.'

'What's her Mr Whatsit like? Short and stout and balding? I'll bet he runs something like a hardware store or a newsagent's.' She stared at him speechlessly—he had summed up Mr Watson with uncanny accuracy. He nodded in satisfaction. 'Thought so! The exact opposite of me. She's on the rebound, you see, coz—so I'm duty bound to go and rescue her from Mr Whatsit, aren't I?'

'I suppose so, David,' she said slowly, still stunned by his smug and simple logic. 'But don't make it too hard on her... and you'd better be quick. They were planning a May wedding when I left.'

'I guess yours will have to be a little sooner than that,' David said carefully.

She shook her head. 'There's not going to be a wedding.'

He reined in abruptly, and stared at her incredulously. 'You're joking!'

'No, I'm not at all. I'm not marrying him.'

'Why not?'

'Because... he's domineering and arrogant.'

'He's always been like that! He's also the finest man I've ever known. And there was a time when all he'd have had to do was snap his fingers at you and you'd have married him like a shot.'

'Hardly! At any rate... that was a long time ago. I've grown up since then...'

'And out too, coz. And if that offends your delicate ears, I'm sorry, but you can't ignore that baby you're carrying. It needs a father. Mack was born illegitimate, and there's been hardly a day in his life when he hasn't had to face that fact one way or another. Is that what you want for your baby? Because it's sure as hell not what Mack wants for his. Do you want more reasons, Melissa?'

'David, I...'

He ignored her white face and pleading eyes. 'We're on MacGregor's Station now. Mack's got fifty thousand acres to work here. It's tussock country, hard and demanding. We started off with a couple of hundred sheep, and that was his first shipment of cattle you saw come in today. Do you know what it's like to break in new country? To work until your back is breaking and your hands are bleeding and you're so tired you're staggering like a drunkard? Sure, you do—we worked like that at the claim, and we all swore we'd never work like that again. But Mack's been doing just that for months; twenty hours a day, fencing and building. And why do you think he's done that?'

'He's always wanted a farm here!' she retaliated. 'I'm pleased he's got it at last, but it doesn't mean...'

'Melissa, you're not listening to me! He's done six months' work in less than three! He thought this was what you would want, you see... He's even built you a house, mostly working at night when the rest of us were sleeping. None of us is allowed inside, because it's *your* house. He's done it all for *you*!'

'I never asked him to! I never expected him to do all that for *me*! I don't even know if it's what I want!' She felt hot and guilty, and very close to tears. She had thought that she was coming home when she came back to Central Otago, and instead she had never felt so torn and confused. Too much had happened, too fast. She needed time to think!

'Then you'd better tell Mack that,' David said tersely. 'He could have had anything he wanted from that family of his in Scotland, after what they put him through. But he chose this, because he was so sure you'd be back and it was what you'd want. You'd better tell him he's wrong.'

'I've already told him,' she said quietly, suffused with misery. They rode in silence the rest of the way.

They had long since risen to the foothills, and all around the mountains towered, silent and serene. At last home-loving Maud whickered and sped up. 'We're almost there,' David said unnecessarily.

A few minutes later, she saw the first of the newly-built fences and gates. Beyond them, on a ridge, was a long, low stone building with a tussock roof. And beyond that, on the top of a small hill, stood a lone house made of wood. They rode up to the stone building, outside which half a dozen weary-looking and very dirty men were gathered round a camp-fire, drinking mugs of tea from the huge steaming billy. She recognised them as the drovers she had seen in Queenstown that morning. They raised a tired, sardonic cheer as David jumped down from his saddle.

'Had a pleasant ride, laddie?'

'Decided to turn up at last to do some work, did you, Dave?'

He grinned at their cheerful ribbing, and turned to help Melissa from the saddle. The men slowly got to their feet. 'This is Mack's lady and my cousin, Melissa Edwards. Melissa, meet Angus Findlay, Thomas Watene...' He introduced each of the six men; she shook six grimy, roughened hands, and was in turn scrutinised closely by six pairs of eyes. She accepted a scaldingly hot mug of tea so strong it caught in her throat, but she attempted to drink it rather than give offence.

'Where's Mack?' David asked briskly.

'At the pens,' one of the men said. 'Putting out the feed. Shouldn't be long now.'

'Do you want to go and see him there, Melissa?'

'If you don't mind ... I'd like to go and see the house. By myself.' She saw the unhappy look on his face, and smiled suddenly. 'It's all right, David.'

She left him standing with the men. Behind her she heard one of them pronounce, 'Not bad. Worth waitin' for, I reckon.'

Another man guffawed. 'Doesn't look like Mack waited, if you ask me!'

There was a burst of good-natured laughter at this remark, and she could hear a mortified David trying to hush them. Dearest David! She smiled to herself. Across the valley from the homestead, she could see Lachlan filling the water-troughs for the thirsty cattle, his dogs flopped around him, tongues lolling in the heat. She watched him for a little while, but he was oblivious of her, and so she continued to walk up to the little house on the hill.

As she approached, she realised that it had been su-
perbly sited. While enjoying full sun, it was sheltered
and had obviously been built with a wide drive and extensive gardens in mind. She paused for a moment,
imagining it when flower-beds had been set around it,
and trees behind... She stepped up to the wide, shel-
tering veranda, and tentatively tried the front door. It
swung open to reveal four small but perfectly propor-
tioned rooms within, all with wide windows giving out
on to the mountain views. A stove had been installed,
but there was only one, rather incongruous, piece of
furniture in the house. She went slowly to the big bay
window in the front room. In front of it stood a wooden
rocking-chair, beautiful in its carved simplicity, waiting
for her. Putting out an unsteady hand, she pushed it
forward slightly, making it rock. She could hardly
breathe for the lump in her chest. He had not forgotten
her dream—so how could she have forgotten it herself?
She eased herself into the chair, and rocked a little, experimentally. It felt wonderfully soothing, and after a
moment the baby inside her shifted itself sleepily and
lay quietly.

She heard Lachlan removing his boots on the veranda, and then the door opened. Rocking quietly, she
waited for him, her eyes fixed steadily on the mountains, fire-tipped in the evening sun. He came to kneel
beside her, his eyes on her face. She turned to smile at
him. 'You still haven't taken off that filthy shirt.'

'Och, you...' He shook his head at her. 'You're an
impossible woman! Thank the Lord I'm used to you—
no other poor beggar would put up with the way you
carry on.'

'It rather looks as though I've got to stay here, then,
doesn't it?' she said softly. He gathered her to him with
a groan of relief, and she held him tightly, letting herself
love him unreservedly as the last traces of bitterness and
suspicion left her heart for ever. 'Lachlan, I've been
beastly to you!' she managed to mutter at last into his
filthy shoulder.

'Ay—well, you always are. I've got used to it after all
this time. At least you're consistent,' he teased her.

'Not any more,' she promised recklessly. 'I'm going to be a perfect wife and mother, and I love this house and—and how soon can we get married?'

'As soon as I can get the minister over here from Earnscleugh to perform the ceremony. So, lass, if you want to travel back to Queenstown tomorrow and stay there until I can get everything ready...'

'Go back to Queenstown? Why?'

'Because the furniture I ordered for the house hasn't arrived yet! There's no table and chairs, no bed...'

'I've slept on a blanket on the floor in front of a stove before now,' she reminded him archly.

'Ay—but you weren't expecting, then. I've got to take much better care of you... both of you... than I did then. You're not sleeping on any floor and catching a chill!'

She wound her arms round his neck. 'I won't catch any chills with you to keep me warm, my love!'

He opened his mouth to argue some more, and so she kissed him to silence him. He pulled her to him hungrily, only to release her suddenly when he received a disgruntled kick in the chest. 'Oof!' he complained. 'Your baby's got a temper just like its mother's!'

'And hob-nailed boots like its father's!' She looked at him anxiously. 'Do you mind very much? I mean...am I still attractive to you?'

'Melissa!' He looked quite aghast, and drew her up against him, pressing his lips to her hair. 'I love you, lass, and never more than now. You're beautiful, and you always will be to me. And as for this...' he gently prodded her stomach, '...I'll have to get used to this. If you're going to get pregnant every time I so much as wink at you, it's likely to be a permanent condition.'

'Oh, no!' She stared down at herself in dismay, trying to imagine it. 'I suppose you're right. What can we do?'

'Build on to the house every time we have another bairn, I guess,' he said thoughtfully. 'What would you say to a twelve-bedroomed mansion?'

'I'd say you'd better start building right away, then,' she replied with equal composure, promptly lost when he began kissing her again.

He let her go only when David put his head round the door to see how things were progressing. One look at them was enough to make him grin in delight and quickly shut the door again.

'Perhaps,' Lachlan suggested, 'a lock on the front door before I start work on all those extra rooms?'

THE COMPELLING AND UNFORGETTABLE SAGA OF THE CALVERT FAMILY

April	August	November
£2.95	£3.50	£3.50

From the American Civil War to the outbreak of World War I, this sweeping historical romance trilogy depicts three generations of the formidable and captivating Calvert women – Sarah, Elizabeth and Catherine.

The ravages of war, the continued divide of North and South, success and failure, drive them all to discover an inner strength which proves they are true Calverts.

Top author Maura Seger weaves passion, pride, ambition and love into each story, to create a set of magnificent and unforgettable novels.

W●RLDWIDE

AROUND THE WORLD WORDSEARCH
COMPETITION!

How would you like a years supply of Mills & Boon Romances ABSOLUTELY FREE? Well, you can win them! All you have to do is complete the word puzzle below and send it in to us by October 31st. 1989. The first 5 correct entries picked out of the bag after that date will win **a years supply of Mills & Boon Romances** (*ten books every month - worth around £150*) What could be easier?

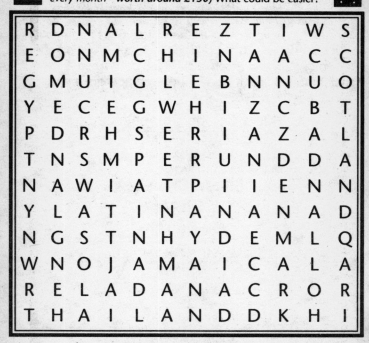

```
R D N A L R E Z T I W S
E O N M C H I N A A C C
G M U I G L E B N N U O
Y E C E G W H I Z C B T
P D R H S E R I A Z L L
T N S M P E R U N D D A
N A W I A T P I I E N N
Y L A T I N A N A N A D
N G S T N H Y D E M L Q
W N O J A M A I C A L A
R E L A D A N A C R O R
T H A I L A N D D K H I
```

ITALY	THAILAND	SCOTLAND	SWITZERLAND
GERMANY	IRAQ	JAMAICA	
HOLLAND	ZAIRE	TANZANIA	**PLEASE TURN**
BELGIUM	TAIWAN	PERU	**OVER FOR**
EGYPT	CANADA	SPAIN	**DETAILS**
CHINA	INDIA	DENMARK	**ON HOW**
NIGERIA	ENGLAND	CUBA	**TO ENTER**

HOW TO ENTER

All the words listed overleaf, below the word puzzle, are hidden in the grid. You can find them by reading the letters forward, backwards, up or down, or diagonally. When you find a word, circle it or put a line through it, the remaining letters (which you can read from left to right, from the top of the puzzle through to the bottom) will spell a secret message.

After you have filled in all the words, don't forget to fill in your name and address in the space provided and pop this page in an envelope (you don't need a stamp) and post it today. Hurry - competition ends October 31st. 1989.

**Mills & Boon Competition,
FREEPOST,**
P.O. Box 236,
Croydon,
Surrey. CR9 9EL

Only one entry per household

Secret Message _____

_____

Name _____

Address _____

_____

_____

_____ Postcode _____

You may be mailed as a result of entering this competition

COMP 6